THE ROMANTICS

THE
ROMANTICS

Galt Niederhoffer

ST. MARTIN'S PRESS

NEW YORK

THE ROMANTICS. Copyright © 2008 by Galt Niederhoffer. All rights reserved. Printed in the United States of America. For information, address St. Martin's Press, 175 Fifth Avenue, New York, N.Y. 10010.

www.stmartins.com

Library of Congress Cataloging-in-Publication Data

Niederhoffer, Galt.
   The romantics / Galt Niederhoffer. — 1st ed.
      p.   cm.
   ISBN-13: 978-0-312-37337-5
   ISBN-10: 0-312-37337-6
   1. Best friends—Fiction.   2. Jewish women—Fiction.   3. WASPs (Persons)—
Fiction.   4. Weddings—Fiction.   5. Triangles (Interpersonal relations)—Fiction.
6. Maine—Fiction.   7. Domestic fiction.   8. Chick lit.   I. Title.
   PS3614.I355R66   2008
   813'.6—dc22

                                                            2008012934

First Edition: July 2008

10 9 8 7 6 5 4 3 2 1

FOR JIM

ACKNOWLEDGMENTS

I would like to thank Elizabeth Beier for her genius mind, enormous heart, and killer vocabulary.

I would like to thank Joy Harris for her brilliant brain, endless patience, and gorgeous knitting.

THE ROMANTICS

ONE

Laura sat in her car at the foot of a dirt road, clutching her cell phone and map. The map was just an accessory. She knew exactly where she was. The name of the house was etched on a wooden plank tacked to one of the elms that flanked the drive. A wreath of peonies hung just below, woven with white ribbons. Using her thumb as a ruler, she measured the distance between Dark Harbor and New York, as though time had stopped as a favor to her, to allow her to catch her breath.

In fairness, Laura's hostess was a girl who expected a lot of her guests. Beauty, wealth, impeccable lineage, and intelligence joined forces in Lila Hayes. At times, the combination was lethal. In college, when the two girls first became friends, Lila had been demanding—but back then she had been more endearing. The day before midterms freshman year, she hopped a plane for Guatemala, informing her roommate and parents of the trip only when she deplaned in Quezaltenango. She returned with a suitcase of indigenous textiles and new political beliefs. In April, she founded Yale's Guatemalan Peace Corps. By May, she had the entire freshman class wearing sarongs.

Soon after that, Laura and Lila renewed their rooming vow, moving on from the misfits assigned by lottery to the greener pastures of a sophomore double. They lived together for the duration of college, first in a storied upper-class house where every bed nestled in a dormer window, and later in a swank off-campus apartment that they found in the *New Haven Gazette*. Since graduation six years ago, the friendship had wilted somewhat. But rivalry glued the girls together in a way that regular contact could not. When Lila called and asked Laura to be her maid of honor, Laura accepted with mixed delight and dread.

"Lo," said Lila, her voice simmering with excitement.

"Li," said Laura. "Is that you?"

Lila answered with a shriek of laughter that forced Laura to thrust the phone from her ear.

"The day has finally come," Lila declared with signature melodrama. "I can finally flush my degree down the toilet."

"You passed the bar?" Laura asked.

"No, stupid, I'm getting married."

"Li, that's wonderful," Laura replied, raising her voice to the appropriate giddy pitch.

"He did it in the most amazing way," she elaborated, rushing the plot points as one does after the third or fourth telling. "Completely perfectly perfect."

Lila, though beautiful, was not graced with the gift of beautiful verbiage.

"Anyway, I can't talk now," she went on. "We're driving to Maine to tell the family in person. But I wanted you to be the first to fireflies every night, as though they had been dispensed to herald evening cocktails.

The family history was well archived for anyone who cared to learn it. Polished picture frames planted throughout the house told a paradoxical story of abundance and humility. But if these pictures didn't conjure a sufficiently clear picture—capturing Mrs. Hayes at her wedding, svelte and mischievous as a cancan girl, Mr. Hayes on the squash court, the year he was captain of the Yale team, fathers and forefathers, secret society brothers and Seven Sisters alumnae, and countless snapshots of curly-haired blond athletes in various states of tennis dress—Mrs. Hayes would be the first to regale you with tales of the house's lineage, beginning with the estate's formidable array of ghosts. From the pride and glee of her description, you would think the number of spirits that wafted through a house was proof of its pedigree, incrementally increasing its value like hardwood floors, closets, or a finished attic.

Like all great estates, the Hayeses' Maine home had a name: Northern Gardens. But in Laura's opinion, it would have been more honest to call it "Eden." It was just as sheltered and more corrupt.

It had taken nearly nine hours for Laura to get there from New York, if you counted the time taken, after the car was packed, while she sat on the stoop of a Brooklyn brownstone and finished her fight with her boyfriend: forty-five minutes. She was further delayed by rush-hour traffic, a plight worsened by the aforementioned fight, and her failure to fill her rental car with gas. Luckily, the oversight caused only a minimal setback, resulting in a frantic unsignaled exit from the Hutchinson River Parkway and twenty misguided minutes in the town of Yonkers. By the time she left the state of New York, she was suitably flustered, still reeling from the mixed blessing of finding a gas station. She spent most of the state of Connecticut deciphering a scribble of directions. By the time she hit Massachusetts she was totally drained. It was only as she crossed the state line into Maine that she hazarded a guess at the highlights of the weekend ahead.

It would be a veritable seminar on the Wasp culture, a study in paradox. Impeccable planning would be paired with feigned nonchalance, excessive spending with a disdain for ostentation, good wine with mediocre food. And of course, the wedding would feature all the pompous, vapid Yale alums in the Hayes family, a group that provided ample proof on its own of the importance of affirmative action. The prospect of the weekend was not improved by Laura's troubled relationship with the bride, a ten-year rivalry—really, a protracted war—over borrowed clothes, bisected bedrooms, and battled-over boyfriends that had reached its most explosive point on the subject of the groom.

Luckily, Tom McDevon was a man worth fighting for. He was nothing short of legendary at Yale. Fondly known as Heaven McDevon among female company, he was coveted by women of Lila's caliber, and yet he still greeted lower lights with an earnest smile. That he was good-looking was simply a corollary to his identity. He had green eyes, brown hair, and shoulders built to comfort a weeping girl. On the basis of looks alone, he could have bedded an entire field hockey team. But his confidence—he was not oblivious to his power—was tempered with admirable qualities; sensitivity and smarts served as an antidote, or at least a foil, to his other blessings.

Tom was equally entranced by each of the following things: an August sunset, a woman's ankle, the clapboards of a Colonial house, and the shape of a soccer ball. His mind was rigged to receive those signals for proportion, shape, texture, and color that only artists receive. He was blessed with an encyclopedic memory of every beautiful thing he had ever encountered, whether the pitch of a mansard roof or the meter of a Shakespearean sonnet. This kind of sensitivity was in itself his most compelling trait perhaps because it was so atypical of a boy with his popularity. In this way, Tom was more like a hermit than a homecoming king, because he perceived not through the lens of his favor but rather the magnifying glass of an outsider. This sharp focus instilled a zeal for life that was quite unparalleled. It also made him highly vulnerable to beauty.

Tom's critics argued that he downplayed his intelligence. Like a politician, he spoke more simply than he thought, so much so that even very close friends often failed to grasp the depth of his ideas. It was hard to say whether his bride-to-be knew the contents and capacity of his mind, not to mention what fraction of it was at work when they were together. But to Laura, Tom's mind was the most beguiling thing about him, and the most unusual. It was almost female in its propensity to obsess.

Of course, it might be considered odd for a woman other than the bride to be thinking so clinically and constantly about a man scheduled to wed in twenty-four hours. But Laura's interest in Tom was beyond her control. They had dated for two years in college before Lila deemed Tom fair game. But even after Tom and Laura broke up, they had remained close friends, the kind that speak, e-mail, or exchange telepathic messages several times a day. They had maintained this correspondence throughout Tom and Lila's relationship in college and during the six years since, until Tom fell out of touch suddenly and without explanation. One month later he proposed to Lila.

A chorus of honks interrupted Laura's meditation. Startled, she raised her head from the dashboard to recognize a carful of friends.

Tripler, Pete, Weesie, and Jake had caravanned to the wedding together, a concise and painful reminder that Laura was attending alone.

"You lost," yelled Pete. For a moment, Laura struggled to discern whether this had been a statement or a question. A rugged twenty-eight-year-old with overgrown bangs, Pete brought his car to an abrupt stop. A mere inch separated the two cars.

"Completely," Laura admitted. "How do I get to New York?"

"Pete, don't move. I'm getting in," Tripler said.

"What," he said. "Where?"

Before she could respond, a long golden leg extended from the passenger window. A second one followed, and, several thrusts later, Tripler wriggled through Laura's window, over her lap, and into the passenger seat.

"Desperate situation," she announced. "I had to get out of there."

"Tripler." Laura smiled. The weekend would be saved by her friends.

Most of Laura's friends had held on to their college nicknames long into adulthood even though the names now seemed annoyingly precious. They were names that grew out of circumstance, because they carried easily across soccer fields, or referred to some hallowed drunken night, or, in the case of Tripler, was her family's alternative to Katherine III. Each name had unceremoniously graduated to permanent status, creating an individual and collective group identity. The names all rang with the same cheerful clang of a dinner bell summoning a family to a meal, signifying not only the gated intimacy of the group but the crest of its members.

Tripler grabbed Laura's bag from the floor of the car and rifled through it as though it were her own. "Pete is such a fascist," she said. "He won't let me smoke on the off chance that we conceived last week."

"You guys are trying?" Laura asked.

"*He* was trying," Tripler corrected. "*I* was trying to sleep."

"That's so exciting," Laura said.

"Oh, spare me," said Tripler. She found a cigarette, lit it, and propelled the smoke out the window. "You got anything else in here?" she asked, still rifling through Laura's bag. "I need something to get me through the rehearsal dinner. There's only so many times I can hear people toast that bitch."

Laura laughed and shook her head at her friend. She indulged in a jab even though she had vowed to abstain for the weekend. "I would like to congratulate the McDevons," she said, assuming the bloated tone of a wedding toast, "on getting one to the other side. I would like to offer the Hayeses my sympathy. There goes the bloodline."

With that, the two girls threw back their heads with the combined force of hilarity and hatred and, goaded by a honk, followed the other car up the driveway.

The drive was underscored by the whirl of wheels on dirt and the bumpy condition of the unpaved road. Cathedral elms formed a canopy overhead. A warm breeze carried the scent and the silvery light of the sea.

Tripler leaned back in her seat, making the most of the bouncy ride. "Where's Ben," she said.

"Wasn't invited." Laura swerved to avoid a pothole.

"That little bitch." Tripler exhaled at a passing tree.

"Oh yeah," said Laura. "Gussie's policy." She still could not believe she had been subjected to this affront. Members of the wedding party had been asked not to bring a date unless they were married or engaged, a gracious rule of etiquette designed to shame the lonely on a night that celebrated the loved.

"Oh, honey. I'm sorry. That sucks."

"That's nothing," Laura quipped. She directed her friend's gaze toward the dress that hung in the backseat, encased in plastic. "She wants us to look bad. Didn't even try to hide it."

"Is it gray?" Tripler asked, wincing. "Or pewter?"

"Tin," said Laura.

"Tin to match her ring?" Tripler quipped.

"Tin to match her heart."

Finally, the bouncing stopped as the car rolled onto smoother ground. The transition was marked by a change of tune. The raucous hum of wheels on dirt switched to the whirl of tires on gravel, a quiet rush that was not unlike the sound of the nearby surf.

The arrival of the two cars at once was a feat of geography and timing. It marked the simultaneous arrival of almost half the wedding party—the maid of honor, two bridesmaids, and two groomsmen—and the reunion of seven-ninths of a group that had not been together for over a year. Like all college cliques, these friends made frequent and zealous attempts to reunite. But their attempts were often thwarted by delayed flights, pressing deadlines, or last-minute catastrophes at work. Still, the effort was earnest and unanimous. They were as tight as friends can be ten years, two marriages, and several moves later. Of course, changes of job and heart had caused some wear and tear on the relationships. But with every inch they grew apart, they held more tightly to each other, as though maintaining the friendships might enable them to keep their grasp on youth itself.

Throughout college, they identified themselves as a pack in all the usual ways. By graduation, all but a few had slept with one another. Tom dated Laura before dating Lila; Oscar dated Weesie before dating Annie. Pete and Lila had shared more than one drunken night. And all the girls had kissed Jake. This amorous behavior earned the clique a nickname from their fellow students. They were dubbed "the Romantics" as a nod to their incessant intra-dating and their byzantine incestuous history. But gradually, eight of the nine lovebirds paired off into the inevitable groupings, drifting toward monogamy under the looming threat of their thirtieth birthdays.

The wedding party included every member of these original nine college friends, most of whom could be conveniently broken down into couples. The totem pole descended like this: Lila and Tom were the reigning Homecoming King and Queen; Lila's rank was built on beauty and class, Tom's built on charisma and talent. Tripler and Pete were Second-in-Command. They had fallen in love junior year at St. Paul's and enrolled together at Yale, keeping their relationship intact for all but a hairy period during freshman year. Confidence and athleticism honed on prep school fields made these two a formidable pair.

Weesie and Jake occupied the next rung on the ladder. They could go head-to-head with the others on the vital statistics— summer communities, yacht club memberships, and boarding schools. But Weesie's shyness and Jake's lack of direction kept them out of a more prestigious spot. Annie and Oscar often seemed like something of an afterthought. Their recent engagement was viewed by some as a response to peer pressure. And geography put them at a disadvantage; they lived in Boston while the others lived in New York, and so were often left out of spontaneous local plans.

Laura was the only Jew in the group. Once in a while, she shuddered at this fact. Did it make her a self-hating Jew? But rather than think of herself as an infiltrator or worse, a traitor, she preferred to think of herself as a chameleon. It was simply a function of circumstance, she told herself, that these people had ended up her best friends. They had chosen each other out of a crowd (at the Freshman Ice Cream Social, to be exact) in that mysterious way that friends choose one another, identifying attitudes, comportment, clothing—the indefinable flags of personality—as though shopping for groceries. They chose each other instinctively, ignorant of their own criteria, gleaning all they needed to know from the first meeting, starting with a sighting across the quad. Just like this, Laura had chosen her family, and it had chosen her, ensuring that she would always feel like its misshapen black sheep.

Northern Gardens was even more beautiful than Laura remembered. The house itself was the ultimate hostess, recently groomed and fussed over, manicured and perfumed. Traditional Victorian architecture furthered its feminine effect. Intricate dormer windows extended over the third and fourth floors. Elegant brackets courted the eye from the roof and gutters. The wraparound porch circled the house like a grand dancing skirt, its floor painted a warm chocolate brown and its roof painted the traditional robin's egg blue. The house rested on a newly mowed lawn

whose perimeter was lined with red and orange zinnias and perfectly haphazard clumps of marsh grass. These vibrant bursts of
color accented the lawn with the pleasing flourish of an impres-
sionist painting.

When one gazed out at the water, the tableau was complete. The
sand at Northern Gardens was grayish blue, a hue that seemed to
have been chosen expressly to complement the sky at dusk. But in
fact, this color was chosen during the continent's last ice age, when
an ocean of ice extended over what would become the coast of
Maine.

Laura pulled the car to a full stop in the gravel driveway. She and
Tripler sat motionless for a moment as though they expected the
house to issue its own greeting. Finally, a car door opened and noise
exploded from the other car. Jolted, Laura opened her door. The festivities began with a bloodcurdling scream.

"Finally!" Lila yelled. "What time did you leave? You nearly
missed the rehearsal. For the last two hours, I've been sitting here
trying to figure out who was going to replace you."

Laura turned her head and scanned the driveway to locate the
object of Lila's rage. It was a cursory gesture. She knew perfectly
well: She was the only person in the world Lila would speak to
that way.

Bags were dropped and hugs were exchanged as the group assembled in the driveway. The girls greeted each other in the customary way, assessing each other's clothes, accoutrements, and
weight fluctuation with rapid and indiscernible scans. The boys exchanged halting hugs and busied themselves with the girls' gear.
Squeals of joy resumed after these formalities.

But before the group could begin their long-awaited reacquaintance, they heeded tradition and commenced the token but true assessment of the bride's beauty. The typical bride is bent on entertaining the falsehood that she is the most beautiful bride in the history of the world. Lila's effortless radiance suddenly made it clear that every other bride before her had been horribly misled.

"Positively disgusting," Tripler exclaimed, shaking her head in a caricature of disbelief. It was customary, among this group, to turn the corner from superlative to pejorative in the service of extreme praise.

"Completely vile," Weesie agreed. "You've never looked worse in your life."

A moment passed while Lila waited for Laura's consensus.

"Wholly repugnant," Laura confirmed. "Every wretched inch."

Lila smiled with satisfaction while the girls surrounded her.

Laura stifled a secret thought. It felt way too good to insult Lila to her face.

Then, after the pleasantries, the mandatory questions, a decoy while the girls perused one another in greater detail.

"Was the traffic bad?"

"Terrible," said Tripler. "Pete had to stop at the office, so we got stranded in the middle of rush hour."

"It's true," said Pete. "I have this irksome little commitment Tripler finds terribly frivolous. It's called work."

"Oh Pete. Shut up," said Tripler.

"I torture my poor wife," he confessed, mock contrite. "I'm so sorry I have to work, darling." He laced his arms around her neck. "I only do it to put a wrench in your travel plans." He twisted her neck to face him and deposited a kiss on her lips.

"This is his new thing," Tripler said, turning to the group. "Apparently, what I do no longer qualifies as work. It's only called work when you go to an office every morning at eight, dressed like a shithead."

"No, no," said Pete. "It's work so long as you get there before noon."

"All right, you guys. Let's save this for couple's counseling," said Jake.

"Very funny," said Pete.

"Jake's right," Tripler said. "We're here to celebrate a happy couple. Let's keep the sorry states of our own marriages to ourselves."

Laughter swelled and subsided. But swipes like this were far from fatal. On the contrary, the disappointments of the group were a comfort to all.

A moment of silence passed as the friends settled into their new surroundings. Lila regained command quickly. She glanced at her watch, gasped, and beckoned to the group. Jake took this as his cue to hoist several monogrammed leather bags onto his shoulder. Pete followed Jake's example, shouldering several more overstuffed bags. The girls looked on, smirking slightly at this rare show of chivalry, then they wove their arms around shoulders and waists and dragged each other onto the sunny lawn.

"Let's hope this weather holds up," said Tripler.

"God, Trip," said Weesie. "Don't taunt her."

Lila tugged subtly on Laura's arm as Weesie and Tripler broke into their usual barbed banter. They, too, had roomed together in college and so toed the line, in all conversation, between jovial and strained. Laura took the cue and released her grasp, allowing

Tripler and Weesie to take the lead while she and Lila fell behind.

"So . . ." said Laura. She attempted, with the one-word question, to convey delicious excitement.

"So . . ." said Lila, matching Laura's tone but infusing it with a more personal demand.

Laura paused, suddenly aware she had absolutely nothing to say. She made a sweeping gesture at the activity on the lawn. "So how's it all going up here?"

"What? The wedding?" Her tone was defiant, her volume loud enough to seem angry. "I really don't get why people make such a big deal. I mean, it's just one day of your life." She shrugged as though baffled by a complex scientific fact, at once asserting her wonder and disdain.

It was this type of comment that made Laura seethe. Did Lila actually think she was comforted by her trivial generalizations, her denouncement of the wedding institution? On the contrary, it made Laura feel terrible that Lila thought she needed to be comforted. And it irritated her that Lila considered such a condescending statement comforting. It would have been less patronizing for Lila to pat her on the head and commend her for coming to the wedding on her own.

"Did you pick up your dress?" Lila demanded. "The store called me Tuesday and said it was still there."

"Yes, I got it," Laura said.

"Thank God." Lila sighed. "I've been totally panicked that the bridesmaids are going to look bad."

"How could we look bad," said Laura, "in such a flattering color?"

Lila paused, mistrusting Laura's tone. But thankfully, when it came to detecting sarcasm, Lila's "hearing" was slightly impaired. "Thank God Weesie's lost the weight," she whispered.

"You were worried?" Laura asked.

"Well, yeah. She insisted on ordering her dress a size too small to motivate herself. I'm just glad she came through. It's not her problem if she looks bad in my wedding pictures."

Laura sighed, conveying sympathy where, in fact, she felt disgust.

"But Annie, I'm a little worried about. Have you heard anything," Lila hissed.

"About what?"

"Oh forget it," said Lila. "Just last time I saw her she looked a little pudgy."

Laura nodded, conveying understanding when, in fact, she felt rage.

"I'm so glad you're here," Lila whispered. "It didn't feel real without you."

Laura paused for a moment, touched by the childlike sweetness of the sentiment. She tightened her grasp around Lila's shoulders. "I'm glad I'm here, too."

There was always this moment between the two friends when they reunited, this process of resistance and submission. First, Laura acknowledged the bile and bitterness she had harbored toward Lila since she'd seen her last. Then, Lila welcomed Laura back into her thrall with seeming obliviousness to Laura's treachery. Finally, Laura cursed herself for harboring such hateful feelings and, embarrassed by her quickness to yield, converted hatred into resentment.

It was not Lila's fault, Laura always decided, that she was so lucky. Her greatest crime was entitlement, her greatest curse, good luck. How was she to know the wisdom earned by yearning? And why should she be faulted for the circumstances that had precluded her having to yearn?

"I'm so sorry Ben couldn't be here," Lila whispered.

Comments like this threatened Laura's precarious composure. For every ten blundering, callous things Lila said, she said something eerily telepathic.

"I'm completely enraged with Gussie for holding me to it. I should have told her to fuck off at the time, but it was just easier to appease her. And now, you're stranded up here all alone with all your friends and their husbands. I would understand if you never spoke to me again." She gripped Laura's forearm.

Laura flinched on reflex.

"But I've done my best to make it up to you with the seating arrangement." She smiled devilishly.

"Oh God." Laura sighed. "I thought I would be at the wedding party table with you."

"You are," Lila said, batting her eyes.

"Next to who?" Laura asked.

"You'll see," Lila cooed.

"Who?" Laura demanded.

"Someone smart, gorgeous, and brilliant."

Laura stopped walking, forfeiting her only remaining leverage. "Tell me right now," she tried.

Lila kept walking but turned her head while she kept her pace. "Someone you haven't seen in a very long time," she said. "Someone you absolutely adore."

"Please tell me who it is," Laura begged. As she stood, hands on hips, in the middle of the lawn, she felt completely degraded, not unlike a defiant pet, refusing to enter the house.

Finally, Lila stopped and turned to face Laura. The setting sun struck her eyes and doubled their intensity. "Why, the groom. Who else?"

Just like that, Laura kicked herself for her self-recrimination. Lila deserved every bit of ill will she bore her. Breathing deeply, Laura picked up her pace and hurried to catch up with her friends, praying Lila's lucky streak would end with a rainy wedding day.

TWO

Augusta Hayes had spared nothing in her efforts to ensure beautiful weather on her daughter's wedding day. She had spent the last two weeks paying homage to that most pagan of Protestant deities: superstition. A bottle of Chivas Regal, her own drink of choice, rested in the crook of a majestic beech tree at the end of the property, hovering, like Augusta, in that delicate space between paganism and propriety.

Her expertise with the venue afforded her a certain amount of confidence. She had hosted innumerable picnics and parties at Northern Gardens over the years and had herself been married on the lawn far too many years ago. Seniority seemed as likely to help the cause as prayer. She hoped her efforts would not be looked upon as hubristic, but rather as a logical extension of her faith. Whether that faith was in God or the house was hard to know.

Historically, the strict observation of etiquette had served her well. Writing thank-you letters within three days of receiving a gift, thanking the hostess before leaving a party, stripping the bed after an overnight stay—all of these rules, when observed to the letter, had wrought not only order but loveliness. It seemed wholly plausible that for one day, one as important as her eldest child's wedding, strict observation of etiquette might suffice to impose order on the gods themselves.

Like many women of her generation, Augusta viewed matrimony as an achievement. The simple veil that Lila would wear might as well have been a crown of laurel leaves. For Augusta, the day was both a celebration and display of social triumph. The extent of that triumph was measured according to the same stringent criteria that applied to an engagement ring. Size, lineage, sheen, and pedigree were intrinsic to the assessment; extra marks could be earned for the relative quotient between price and pocket depth. Tom, in turn, was not unlike the emerald he placed on Lila's finger: impressive, but not flawless; robust, if unrefined. Augusta often wondered if something had been lost in the trade between size and quality. But his higher marks compensated for his lower ones, giving him an impressive dazzle despite his lackluster facets.

The wedding required that Augusta pull off a jeweler's greatest challenge: downplaying the defects of a jewel while flaunting its beauty. Luckily, she had spent a lifetime honing this skill. The fine art of bragging while trivializing was as natural to her as drinking iced tea on the porch, as automatic as playing doubles tennis on Sundays at the club. It was, in short, the modus operandi of her culture. Furthermore, Tom himself did much to help the cause, aspiring to membership in her club with the same intensity with which Augusta wished for his eligibility. Tom's critics would argue that he compromised himself in this effort. His enemies would argue that Lila herself was the compromise.

Even Tom's best friends would point out the ways he changed when he was around Mrs. Hayes. When he introduced himself, he lowered his voice and all but dropped the first two letters of his last name. His *a*'s lengthened in the Anglican way and his mouth tightened into an affected smile. The whole thing seemed like a bad impression of affability.

Regardless, Augusta would prevail over all such imperfections. She had orchestrated a wedding more lavish and lovely than any she had attended to date, and she relished the chance to watch her plans unfold. In the weeks leading up to the day, she had felt disproportionately anxious, like a sergeant planning for battle. She had quickly and quietly co-opted the occasion, imposing her taste, her guest list, and her rules, an imposition Lila allowed because of her aversion to details; she was far more interested in the fact of her wedding than the minutiae of the party itself.

Gleefully, Augusta took the reins, consulting Lila on aesthetic decisions as a mere formality. She selected the menu, lifting many of the dishes from her most successful dinner parties. She involved a caterer not as a chef, but in the capacity of a cook. She supervised the guest list, culling the one hundred fifty most deserving friends and family members from her network. One hundred additional spots were filled by the enormous McDevon family and the fifty-odd peers Tom and Lila insisted upon.

Augusta auditioned and hired the band—they had been a big hit at an engagement party she threw for her niece in the spring. She commissioned the flowers, integrating local blooms with the ubiquitous Maine spruce. She designed the palette, drawing on the dominant colors of Northern Gardens: the shimmering blue of the ocean, the welcoming white of the house and, as an accent, the lush green of the grass that separated the two.

It was divine inspiration, she felt, to weave these colors into the wedding tableau—grass green for the tablecloths and napkins, Maine coast blue for the ribbons and bunting, and the two colors joined together for the table centerpieces. Each centerpiece would be fashioned from a branch harvested on the property and adorned with sea glass collected from their beach. The large floral arrangements would draw upon the same color scheme while the wedding party's bouquets would consist exclusively of white: peonies and lilies of the valley. The menu was classic coastal with touches of urban sophistication. A raw bar would feed the guests during cocktails. Hors d'oeuvres would include a cornucopia of cheeses and savories. Dinner itself would be served in time with the setting sun. Guests would choose between broiled lobster and carved lamb, enjoying a decadent truffled pasta and cascades of colorful grilled vegetables. Drinks would flow throughout.

The weekend's schedule was as meticulously planned as the menu and décor. Festivities would begin on Friday afternoon as the wedding party and family arrived. The wedding rehearsal would begin at four, followed immediately by cocktails and dinner at the yacht club. The rehearsal dinner was called for six—early to allow for a long evening of toasts. In keeping with custom, the rehearsal dinner would involve copious drinking and gratuitous toasts, transforming the bride and groom into idols and guests into wild heathens. After dinner, the bride and groom would separate for the night, forbidden from exchanging a glance until they arrived at the altar. For the next eighteen hours, they would be sequestered with greater care and security than dangerous spies, a traditionally farcical attempt to replicate the feeling of virginity.

Saturday morning would be a time for precious parting words. It would begin with a gathering on the porch for family, during which gifts would be exchanged, croissants and strawberries nibbled. The groomsmen would simultaneously congregate on the back lawn, taking any measure—aspirin, orange juice, or more alcohol—to lessen their hangovers. Chatting and bear hugs would end just in time for a casual lunch buffet. The rest of the afternoon would be spent greeting arriving guests, reuniting with old acquaintances, playing tennis at the club, or simply working on an early buzz for the evening.

At this point, the real work began. Members of the wedding party were expected to report, ceremony-ready, to the main house at three. The groomsmen would uphold the difficult promise of distracting the groom while the bridesmaids devoted the remaining time before the ceremony to assisting the bride. A squadron of five was expected to complete the following tasks: the transportation of the wedding dress from closet to sitting room, the installation of Lila into the dress, the closure of the dress—a task that required securing eighty roped buttons—the achievement and maintenance of perfect hair and makeup, the pinning of the veil, and the fastening of the garter. Successful completion of these drills culminated in a ritual pose, with the bride fixed to the floor at one end of the room, the train of her dress extended and draped over an upholstered chair. It was unclear whether this was indeed a trick to ensure a long and billowing train or simply another chance for the bride to pose and preen.

The elaborate preparations would be rewarded in the hours to come when months of planning melted into one magical day. The wedding was scheduled for half past four so as to coincide with the most opulent afternoon light. Champagne would be uncorked and hors d'oeuvres passed immediately after, busying guests while the wedding party posed for photographs. Dinner would be served at seven just as sunset gave way to the lavender shades of evening. Two toasts would serve as a call to arms, bugles heralding the celebration, one from the best man and one from the bride's father. Drinking and dancing would proceed until the stroke of midnight, at which point the bride and groom would depart in a flurry of white rose petals and sparklers. Revelry would continue as the guests relocated for the after-party.

Augusta had planned and predicted every one of these pending moments. Prediction, she felt, was a necessary means of ensuring perfection and, of course, it was widely accepted in the family that she was something of a psychic. But now, as she peered out the back door at her daughter and her guests, she was pricked by a sense of foreboding. Was that a rain cloud overhead? As she stood, her expression matched and mimicked Lila's like an audience member watching a riveting play. She remained like this for a moment, allowing Lila's guests to catch up on recent parties and promotions, then, tapping the screen door officiously, she marched out the back door onto the porch, greeting the crowd with a perfect combination of charm and rigor.

"Greetings!" she said, scanning the crowd.

She looked terrifyingly tall to the guests standing below on the lawn.

"My goodness," Augusta went on. She projected the same volume and intensity as a street performer. "You have all grown impossibly old. Either that, or I'm getting younger."

Laura often wondered if Augusta understood her own performance. How could she not be aware of her method and effect? She used this saccharine anachronistic tone as a means of disconcerting her guests so that when she barked, and she inevitably did, they were wholly unprepared. But perhaps it was unfair, Laura considered, to make this critique. Mrs. Hayes was of a different generation, one that learned to speak from Mia Farrow, learned to dress from Doris Day. Checking herself, Laura mustered a cheerful smile. A failure to feign the expected thrill would only cost her more effort later on.

"Mrs. Hayes!" the girls exclaimed, their voices rising an octave.

"Please, girls. We're beyond surnames."

"Mummy," barked Lila. "No one wants to call you by your Bryn Mawr name. Gussie went out of fashion fifty years ago."

"Now Lila," said Pete, "don't be rude." He smiled flirtatiously at Augusta. "We have to call you Mrs. Hayes. Otherwise, we're liable to mistake you for a bridesmaid."

Augusta blushed and replied with a grateful smile.

Tripler eyed her husband with annoyance. His obsequiousness was more troubling than his flirtation.

"Tripler," said Augusta, "I saw your mother last week at the Colony Club. She seemed positively giddy."

"She gets that way," Tripler said, "whenever she redecorates. She asked me to send her love."

"And Weesie, I understand Kate has added another cherub to that gorgeous brood."

"Yes, she gave birth last Tuesday," Weesie said. "That was so very thoughtful of you to send a gift."

"Oh, it was my joy," said Augusta. Her golly-gosh demeanor gave way to the breathy largesse of royalty.

The exchange of greetings was, for Laura, the first in a series of painful moments. The ritual was ostensibly designed to be an update on vital life changes but, in truth, it was yet another opportunity to assert one's status, to mark territory with the same grace and compulsion as a urinating dog. The demarcation of shared memories, the plans for future ones—it all made Laura yearn to be back in her apartment, shades drawn, covers yanked above her head. What she would do to be deaf to all this nonsense.

"Laura, don't you look wonderful," said Augusta. She indulged in a shameless head-to-toe scan.

The subtlety of her grammar was not lost on Laura. The compliment was, of course, posed as a question.

But worse yet, the question was, in fact, code for something else. "Don't you look wonderful?" actually meant "Have you lost a little weight?" Hip to the lingo, Laura smiled back, an appropriate signal for thanks. She had always found Mrs. Hayes's awareness of her weight a bit disconcerting. And worse, the compliment begged a response about Mrs. Hayes's appearance, a comment whose intimacy made Laura cringe.

Then, the inevitable question. "Now how is your mother?"

It was expertly phrased to mimic the tone of her queries to the other girls, designed to simulate the affection of truly close friends. In fact, Mrs. Hayes barely knew Laura's mother, nor had she made any effort to get to know her during the years since Lila and Laura had met. While the other parents of the group had attended numerous dinners and parties at the Hayeses', Mrs. Rosen had never been invited to a single event.

"She's very well. Thank you for asking," Laura said. "Asked me to send her best." Somehow, this felt like a triumph. Saying "best" versus "love."

For a moment, Laura wondered if Mrs. Hayes had noticed the distinction. But she turned away, mercifully distracted by Annie and Oscar's late arrival. They hurried toward the group, hair mussed by the journey, eager to join the revelry. With the whole group finally together, everyone's spirits lifted. They breathed more slowly, as though impersonating the breeze as it skipped across the water.

Laura took the opportunity to disengage from conversation. She surveyed the group, studying her friends with the detachment of an anthropologist. Most of them had come at their Yale acceptance honestly—with impressive high-school transcripts, exceptional test scores, and a dizzying list of extracurricular accomplishments. But they were cursed by their good fortune, stunted by their abundant gifts. Beauty, Laura decided, was their greatest burden in life.

Early and consistent attention on Lila's looks had fostered an unhealthy preoccupation, causing her personality to form around the facets of her beauty like a setting around a diamond. It was almost a fluke that intelligence had flourished alongside such perfection. Sometimes, it seemed she had cultivated it—or at least, the appearance of it—as an added bonus for her admirers. Her decision to pursue a law degree had always seemed incidental, as though she had flipped through a leaflet on impressive careers, closed her eyes, and pointed to a random page. At best, it was a token nod to the nascent activism of her college years. At worst, it was a merciless bid to entrap a worthy husband.

But criticisms of Lila were always foiled by undeniable compliments. As Lila chatted and smiled, Laura couldn't help but note the quality of her teeth. They were as straight, shiny, and white as keys on a typewriter, as perfect at the age of twenty-eight as they had been when she was three. Annoyed, Laura scanned the group for someone with more flaws.

Tripler had come close enough to beauty to merit an obsession. Her desire to be an actress was, to Laura, a function of this shortcoming. Auditions occasionally offered a reprieve, but mostly they validated her fears. With reddish hair and a pointy nose, her looks were too odd and her body type too average to make her eligible for leads. Most often, she was cast as the quirky best friend or the unhinged jilted lover. But the insult of both was heightened by the infrequency with which she landed either role.

Before trying acting, Tripler had tried her hand at designing clothes. The business was entirely funded by her father, a fact that enabled her to avoid competing with market trends. Even her friends struggled to wear her clothes out of the house. Ample pocket money wrought its own havoc on Tripler's ambition, facilitating, depending on the time of year, a bad shopping or cocaine habit.

Weesie's plainer features left less up for debate. Light brown hair and murky blue eyes gave her a pleasant, if unmemorable look. Her family was of the same ilk as the others but hers had landed on the wrong side of Plymouth Rock. Her great-great-great-grand-parents had made money; her great-great-grandparents had saved money; her grandparents had hoarded money; and her parents had squandered it. In its absence, she was taught to act as though she had money.

She had concentrated in art history in school basically by default—how anyone could declare a major by sophomore spring was truly beyond her. But the classes were easy to sleep through, and there was something relaxing about being in a dark room, watching colorful slides flutter by. The choice turned out to be wise, positioning her perfectly for her job at Gagosian's gallery. She knew just enough to impress the clients, and too little to aspire to a museum job.

Annie was the least beautiful girl in the group and, as a result, had developed the most interesting personality. She was what admissions officers at Yale called a well-rounded applicant. As editor in chief of her high-school newspaper, valedictorian of her graduating class, captain of the squash team, and president of the French Club, she had been bound either for Yale admission or a nervous breakdown.

Her robust physique and her sense of humor gave her an endear-ing heartiness, making her somehow more equipped than the others to withstand the New Haven winters. A history major in college, she had become the de facto archivist of the group, memorializing their news and secrets with reportorial detail. She was perfectly suited for the job she'd secured at the *Boston Globe*, but her journalistic skills were sharpest when she was gossiping about her friends.

Pete was, almost as much as Lila, defined by his good looks. His popularity among freshman girls at Yale was legendary. Luckily, neither his looks nor his awareness of them curbed his sense of hu-mor. In the years since college, he had accepted and quit three dif-ferent jobs, and enrolled in two graduate programs—first law, then business. Of course, family money made Pete's choice of vocation less pressing than for most. But he still resented the compulsion to make a choice.

Jake, like Pete, had fashioned his identity in relation to his looks, but he had worked harder for the attention. His deep-set eyes and long eyelashes made him look brooding and sensitive, and he culti-vated the look by growing out his hair to an unkempt shag. These attributes—and his knack for writing—earned him a loyal female fan base at the *Yale Literary Magazine*. But after spending college in a uniform of tweed and corduroy, he quickly traded in his wardrobe—and his literary aspirations—for the blue gabardine suits of a banker.

Throughout college, Jake indulged a writer's appetite. He devel-oped a rare form of alcoholism whereby he drank himself into a comfortable stupor while simultaneously plying his date with a dizzying amount of liquor. Fortunately, none of these women held the "disease" against him. Or perhaps, like Jake, they simply forgot the experience by the next day.

Oscar, much like his bride-to-be, was unfettered by extreme beauty. He had gained acceptance to Yale the old-fashioned way, scoring a perfect 1600 on his SATs. Unlike most members of the group, he had actually pursued an education in college. It was only after graduating that he realized the benefit of being a geek. With a simple purchase—a pair of square-rimmed glasses—he earned a spot at a start-up dot-com, and, three years later, a share of its millions.

Now, as she appraised her friends, Laura indulged a guilty thought. They were painfully transparent, easier to crack than a combination lock. In school, they had seemed impenetrable. They had glowed with confidence, talent, promise. But what had they done since graduation? It was as though they had stopped trying as soon as they received their degrees—not even: as soon as they got to college. Their looks and personalities were still intact, but something had atrophied ever so slightly. Their faces bore the distinct wear of goals gone too long unfulfilled.

A clap of hands jarred Laura from her critical musings. She looked up to find Augusta focused on her and shuddered at the notion that she had somehow intuited her thoughts.

"I'm putting you all at the Gettys'," Augusta announced. "Right across this field. It's a sweet old house, a strange house, but a sweet house nonetheless." She waved majestically at a large expanse of lawn that extended several acres from the Hayeses' to the neighboring house. The Gettys' was a smaller, less formal version of Northern Gardens, likely built as a home for the daughter of the Hayes who built the house.

Mrs. Hayes spoke about houses and people in the exact same way, with a cryptic mixture of professed adoration and obvious condescension. When she described the house, she could just as easily have been talking about a dear friend's overweight child.

"I should warn you the house is a little rough around the edges." This was her way of saying the house was not as well kept as her own. "The Gettys keep threatening to do something about it, but they haven't been up since June. What I would do to tear down that porch." She stared wistfully at the house as though watching a loved one recede across the field. Then, in a final aside—as though to share the location of the linen closet—she covered her mouth, and whispered, "Like Northern Gardens, the house is haunted." She paused. "But the Gettys' ghosts aren't as friendly."

"A haunted house and a wedding," said Pete. "Sounds like the makings of an interesting night."

"Don't encourage her," Lila barked. "Or Gussie will make you come round the campfire and listen to her ghost stories."

"Oh boy. Do you have marshmallows?" Pete cried. His excitement was quickly deflated by another glare from his wife.

"Yes, do tell, Mrs. Hayes," said Weesie. "I love scary stories." Currying favor with Augusta was perhaps the only goal for which a member of this group would knowingly defy Lila.

Lila closed her eyes and sighed theatrically.

Only Laura knew Lila well enough to know this was not a performance of irritation.

"Her proof," said Lila, "is a couple of slamming doors and a few mysterious footsteps."

"That is false," said Augusta. She addressed Lila directly. "How about the time Joe was run out of the Gettys' when he was working on the attic." She paused for a moment, satisfied with this irrefutable proof. Then she offered the group an apologetic shrug as though it was selfish to deprive the others of such scintillating lore. "Joe was the contractor," she explained. "He was working on the house one cold December night when all of a sudden—"

"Mother, I think you've made your point—"

"When all of a sudden," Augusta continued, "he heard loud and furious footsteps. He took this as his cue that he had overstayed his welcome."

"Speaking of which . . ." Lila interrupted.

"Slamming doors, mysterious footsteps, overheard voices," Augusta continued. "The occasional apparition. And, of course there was the time your father saw your great-great-grandmother sitting on the roof."

"Mother," said Lila, "you have just single-handedly made a case for interracial marriage. This is what happens"—she turned to the group—"after generations of inbreeding."

"On the contrary," snapped Augusta. "You are evidence of the gene pool's formidable state."

Lila glared and dismissed her mother, asserting her dominance. "This is why my mother thinks she's psychic, and the rest of us think she's insane." She eyed Augusta with a maternal scold and nodded toward the Gettys' house.

"I don't think she's insane," Pete said. He winked mischievously at Mrs. Hayes.

"Me neither," Tripler agreed. "I think you're brave. I would have been on the first ferry back to Rockland."

"Oh, they don't bother family members," Mrs. Hayes clucked. "On the contrary, they protect us." She nodded instructively, as though addressing an errant toddler.

The wedding party stood in rapt silence, muted by the reprimand.

Finally, Pete broke the silence with a signature quip. "Honey," he said, turning to Tripler, "you sure you don't want to stay in that lovely bed-and-breakfast in town?"

"Can I come?" Laura chimed in.

Mrs. Hayes's playful smile froze as she turned to Laura. She paused, staring unabashedly. It was one thing for *her* to tease the family but another thing for an outsider. "You will all be fine," she said conclusively. "Because you're all family."

"Phew," said Pete.

"No kidding," said Tripler. "Last thing I need is an angry ghost mussing up my bridesmaid dress."

Laura mustered a polite smile as laughter swelled and abated.

Finally, Lila tired of negotiating with her mother. She asserted the power conferred by this weekend alone and shooed Augusta back into the house with a ferocious look. Assuaged somewhat, Lila refocused her energy on supervising the group. They had better hurry to the Gettys' right away and get settled. Tom would be returning momentarily from his tennis game. And the wedding party would need to be dressed for the evening in an hour so that they could leave for the yacht club immediately after the rehearsal.

A cheerful calm returned as the group followed Lila across the field. But even after the affable resolution of the ghost conversation—it had been hostility, had it not—Laura still felt the chill of Mrs. Hayes's gaze. Yes, in fact, she was completely certain it was hostility. And she was sure that when Augusta referred to family, she meant everyone except her.

Tom had never felt completely at home with the Hayes family. He had felt welcomed by them, included by them, but never accepted. In their presence, he felt much as he had as a freshman at Yale, as though he was discovering a new side of his personality. His college friends, he later realized, got to know Tom McDevon precisely when Tom did. He had found and formed his adult personality with them—because of them, he sometimes felt. Like most writers, he had borrowed and invented in equal part.

But what did it really mean "to feel at home" with someone? It was an overrated sentiment and a hackneyed cliché, Tom thought, a feeling that he was not even sure he wanted. He had never harbored particularly positive feelings about home, nor had he felt particularly "at home" in his own childhood. On the contrary, from a very early age, he was plagued by the feeling that he did not belong in the family in which he grew up. It was not that he didn't love his parents. They were adequate, to be sure. But there was no escaping the fact that they had produced a child with superior intelligence, and this fact engendered unavoidable tension in the house.

Tom's mother, Kathy McDevon, was the fifth of seven children, the only one in her generation to achieve a version of the American dream. She had emerged from a rough upbringing in Dorchester, Massachusetts, due to her plucky nature and exceptional looks, to marry a man with both intelligence and aspirations. Teddy McDevon received his business training in the neighboring town of Roxbury, apprenticing in the gleaming classroom of the Irish-Italian garbage business. By the age of sixteen, he was running the trucks for all of Roxbury and Dorchester. By thirty, he had tired of city grit and moved, with his wife and his own cadre of trucks, to suburban New Hampshire.

The McDevon family enjoyed the spoils of the garbage business for many years, profiting from the tree-lined towns' inexhaustible supply of trash. The business consumed Ted's every moment. Kathy busied herself with the children, returning to work in a salon—just for fun—when the children were well into school. Tom's sister was spared Tom's aching intelligence and embraced the pleasures of suburban life. But Tom was restless from an early age. How could anyone find contentment hanging out in a Dairy Queen, fulfillment on the four-mile drive to and from the video store? Parochial school provided a glimpse, however obstructed, of more enriching pursuits while the obstructions fostered a healthy desire to rebel.

It was not until college that Tom first understood the impact of his upbringing. Catholicism, he realized, explained all of his pathologies. Ten years of parochial school had taught him nothing if not self-flagellation, while daily catechism left him with a healthy fear of girls. His first encounter did little to dissuade him of this fear: an accidental glimpse of Sister Margaret's brassiere during a volleyball game in gym class. The second—an intentional glimpse of a classmate's underwear—was just as filthy and far more disturbing. By the age of twelve, the damage was done. Catholic doctrine had taken hold. In Tom's mind, suffering was synonymous with sainthood; sex with depravity.

College offered ample opportunities to reassess his past and, better yet, to reassign blame from his nuns to his parents. It was there that Tom realized that his parents' relationship mirrored an archetypal Catholic union, the one between the Virgin Mary and Joseph—one was a perennial martyr and the other, a bit of a fool. That Tom had not developed a full-blown phobia of women was nothing short of miraculous.

And yet, despite the blessed confusion of growing up Catholic, Tom suddenly felt a devastating yearning for Manchester, New Hampshire. This feeling was, of course, aggravated by a growing suspicion. But as he stood on the grass courts of the Dark Harbor Bath and Tennis Club, knees bent, racquet poised to strike, he knew he was fooling himself. His craving was not for a particular time and place. It was for a particular person. He had known what it was to feel truly at home—he had felt it in the company of one woman in his life—and unfortunately, she was not the woman he was marrying tomorrow.

But to think of her now was not only self-destructive but stupid. It was stupid enough to be funny. No, not even—it was tragic, maudlin and trite. Unfortunately, the physical exertion of tennis was failing in its promise to clear his head. A friendly game with Lila's father, William, had turned into a free-for-all when Lila's younger brother, Chip, and younger sister, Minnow, stormed the court and insisted that singles be rescheduled to make room for a long-awaited doubles grudge match. Tom had agreed willingly. The alternative was to sit with his own family in the clubhouse and smile while they complimented the grounds.

Perhaps this was what Lila had alluded to when she joked about "island fever." The cleverness and offensiveness of the joke rested in the double entendre, the notion that the Hayes family could legitimately be called "island people." Island people, Lila snobbishly meant to imply, were the colorful populace of Gauguin's paintings, natives who wore magenta-and-orange prints and frolicked with tigers and gazelles. Lila's islanders were lily-white. They eschewed orange-and-magenta sarongs for pink-and-green prints or bleached tennis attire. They grazed on golf courses, not fertile plains, hydrated with champagne instead of water, found nourishment in watercress sandwiches and lobster salad instead of coconuts and plantains.

The closest Lila's people had ever come to frolicking with a gazelle was walking with Lila herself. Her long, seemingly jointless legs had glided over every inch of Dark Harbor, moving from lesson to lesson, porch party to porch party in search of her next prey. Now, as Tom pictured Lila as a teen, he was suddenly enraged. He would happily wager that she had slept with at least ten of her tennis and sailing instructors. The total number could not be less than ten.

Surely, geography had a hand in Tom's anxious state. How could you not feel disoriented when stranded on the peak of a mountain jutting out of the ocean, a remnant of volcanic rock dressed to look like civilized society? The mainland, he reminded himself, was only seventeen miles away, technically only five if you counted the land bridge that connected Dark Harbor to Northern Isle. But channels between the many islands off the coast of Maine were traversed by all manners of dinghies and whalers. Ferries carrying cars and people were dispatched between the bigger islands every several hours. Still, even despite this constant commotion—a ferry was likely docking in the harbor this very minute—Tom felt completely adrift, as though Dark Harbor were isolated and remote. Seventeen miles of water felt intrinsically different from seventeen miles of dirt. It changed one's perception of a place to know that escape was possible, if necessary, simply by placing foot in front of foot.

Water would forever be an alien entity. The ocean, even for an adept swimmer, was intrinsically treacherous, largely unknown, and constantly subject to change. That the ocean presented the only means of egress from Dark Harbor was suddenly overwhelming. It was, in itself, more unsettling than any possible cause for escape he could conjure up. Therefore, he decided, the escape from Dark Harbor would be worse than anything he might need to escape. And somehow this deduction left Tom feeling both panic-stricken and euphoric. In all his years studying literature, he had only con-ceptually grasped the meaning of "existential dread." But now he felt he understood. When the act of escaping from a place is worse than the thing one might need to escape. This was "existential dread." He was in such a place right now.

He quickly checked himself for his melodramatic conclusion. Surely it was natural to be somewhat stressed right now. The phrase "wedding-day jitters" had been coined to explain this very state of mind. Grooms throughout history had felt this sensation thousands of times before. Furthermore, he was faced with another equally unnerving concern: bridging the communication gap between his parents and the Hayeses.

He rose to the task the moment his family stepped off Wednesday's ferry. He had served as translator for the two families, conveying the hidden meanings of one, shielding the improprieties of the other. To a casual witness, the packed schedule of activities—morning golf, afternoon tennis—might have seemed fun. But it was anything but recreation for Tom. Within hours of his family's arrival, he felt drained of energy.

At first sight, the Hayeses and McDevons appeared to be members of the same species. But closer examination revealed they had diverged sharply, much like Darwin's finches. Tom's mother, for example, had greeted Lila with a compliment about her engagement ring. It was an heirloom she'd given Tom for the proposal, an impressive rectangular emerald in a pleasing Art Deco setting. Kathy had inherited it when her own mother passed away. Mrs. Hayes secretly scorned the ring. She felt it looked far too much like a cocktail gem to be used as an engagement ring. Its inappropriate use bothered her as misplaced commas do a good editor. Frequent mention of Lila's ring had required that Augusta bite her tongue and Tom tether his mother's. Would that the communication gap lessened with silence.

Cultural discrepancies came to a head on the subject of the rehearsal dinner. As tradition dictated, the McDevons would foot the bill for the Friday night meal while the Hayeses shouldered the greater financial burden of the wedding festivities. It was tradition for the groom's parents to host this event, a conciliatory gesture to compensate the father of the bride for his bum deal. Nevertheless Augusta had offered to help with the rehearsal dinner. It would be easier for her to organize due to her familiarity with local caterers and her connections with local venues.

But soon enough, Augusta's "help" turned into supervision, her supervision into command. She insisted on the yacht club as a venue. She hired the staff, tweaked the design for the invitations, even secretly asked her florist to supplement the McDevons' order. Mrs. McDevon was enraged by Augusta's interference while Augusta was quietly horrified by Mrs. McDevon's stingy budget. These feelings only added to tensions between the two families. Tom, as always, served as the biased ambassador, empathizing with his mother, siding with Augusta, and hating himself for his duplicity.

He was comforted by the comparison to a translator. As the only "bilingual" party, he was uniquely positioned to comprehend the misunderstandings and missteps that inevitably arose between two cultures. His purpose was to predict and prevent as many as possible. He was comfortable enough in the post, having historically served this role within his group of friends, acting as liaison between those who otherwise could not communicate. He prided himself on this knack—it was a talent, really. He was like a crab, capable of living in any environment, skilled at presiding over the most makeshift camps. But for the first time in his life, he felt ill equipped for the task. Now, *he* felt like the foreign party, confused, put off, and consistently surprised.

The realization was marked by a sudden tightening in his chest, and he wondered, for a split second, if he was suffering a cardiac arrest. But panic attacks, he had learned over the years, aped the hallmarks of most fatal diseases; the key to snuffing them out was to focus on one's breath. With this in mind, he inhaled, exhaled, then inhaled again. But finding that the extra oxygen only increased his pulse, he made a brusque excuse to his doubles partner, Minnow, then called to his cousin, who was watching the game courtside, and asked him to take his place.

He excused himself with a half-truth—the rehearsal dinner was hours away, and he needed to work on his toast. Liberated, he walked briskly across the court, then waved to his relatives in the clubhouse before cutting across the golf course, the shortest distance to the nearby road. He was nearly foiled by an unforeseen obstruction on the seventh tee: a mortifyingly large constituent of McDevons had congregated on the fairway and transformed the trimmed grass into their own private picnic grounds. Tom smiled politely and did his best to convey a look of urgent tardiness, then cut across the green and turned up Harbor Road as though he were heading toward Northern Gardens. Once he was out of sight, he slowed his pace slightly. All roads in Dark Harbor eventually led to water; it was simply a matter of time.

Mercifully, the road made good on this promise before long. Pavement gave way to moist brown dirt and dirt to gravelly sand. Whiter, silvery light betrayed the nearness of the water. Finally, Tom faced two familiar landmarks: on his right, the elm-flanked drive to Northern Gardens; on his left, an ancient graveyard. Its headstones were not the typical gray but a chalky, iridescent white. Calming slightly, he checked in both directions to make sure he was alone, then ducked into the graveyard, picking up speed as he passed through the open gate. As he ran, the headstones formed a clean white ribbon in his periphery. The ocean announced itself with the rush of wind through trees.

Sprinting now, his vision was blurred by so many familiar names: Hayes, Getty, Westfield, Adams. Would he and Lila be buried here, too? What would Lila's headstone say? Lila Hayes McDevon or Lila McDevon Hayes? And as though these morbid thoughts possessed a force of their own, Tom found himself running at a desperate pace as though he was being pursued. He ran faster and faster through the sloping cemetery, past the modest graves that rose out of the earth like an endless row of perfect teeth, past the formidable mausoleums with their intricate vines. Soon enough, gravity and velocity combined to pull him toward the ground. Grabbing hold of a branch, he averted a fall and glimpsed the water beyond the trees. He remained like this for several moments, panting and wheezing, watching the afternoon ferry as it lessened into the fog.

THREE

The Gettys' house was a smaller version of Northern Gardens, but it lacked the vibrance of the Hayeses', and, of course, it lacked a name. It was built with similar materials and with only slightly smaller proportions, but it looked, particularly when seen from the water, like Northern Gardens' younger, less attractive sister. It was painfully clear the house had been shortchanged the attention and refinements Northern Gardens had enjoyed. Its defects were visible even as the group approached from across the field. Its white paint peeled noticeably near the gutters; all but one of the decorative black shutters was missing a crucial panel; the wraparound porch had been so severely damaged by termites that whole sections had been roped off. Like so many homes that have remained in one family over several generations, it had become a museum of sorts. Everything about the house bore the faint musk of 1963.

Lila had given the room assignments great consideration. She had factored in the respective needs of each guest (and her affection for that guest) before settling on the right room. Tripler and Pete, she had decided, would stay in the master bedroom, a sizable, if slightly dated suite whose red toile upholstered furniture had faded to a consistent pink. Weesie and Jake would stay in the bedroom that belonged to the Gettys' older son, a small damp room that made up for its size with a stunning view of the ocean. Annie and Oscar would stay in the younger son's bedroom, a room that made up for its inconsequential views with a charming built-in window seat. Laura would stay in the room that belonged to the Gettys' youngest daughter, a room that had remained monastically untouched since the child's tragic death from leukemia.

At Lila's insistence, the group disbanded to settle into their rooms, promising to reconvene in an hour on the porch of the Hayeses' house. The girls dispersed to compare their rooms—why did Tripler get the best one—and to assess available bathrooms, negotiating their order of entry through a series of announcements shouted across the hall. The boys dropped their bags in the appointed rooms and reassembled on the porch, arranging themselves on the wicker furniture, oblivious to its state of disrepair. Laura took advantage of the commotion to retreat to her room, hopeful that silence would work its magic on her frayed nerves.

She stood at the door before entering, unnerved by the stillness. Every attempt had been made to barricade the room from the summer sun, as though to shield the delicate soul who lived there from the outside world. The bed was sheathed in crisp white linen with a delicate pink monogram, its fraying eyelet ruffles brittle enough to break at the touch. Tulle curtains on the windows dusted the room with a confectionary shadow, and the windows themselves seemed to have been intentionally painted shut. A white wrought-iron headboard had jaundiced significantly, and red rosebuds on the wallpaper had bleached to a fleshy pink. One leg of the bed seemed to have suffered an emergency amputation, but a stack of books tucked underneath served as a prosthetic limb. Even though it was long before dusk, inside this room it looked like evening.

Scanning the room, Laura reconsidered Augusta's claims about ghosts. The room was unsettling—chilling, really—in that specific indescribable way of a haunted house. It was classic Lila to condemn her to this room. Annoyed, Laura walked toward the window and pushed her face to the glass. A thick forest of spruce ended a few feet from her window as though it had grown, untamed, past a designated perimeter. Still, Laura found it pleasant enough to stare silently into trees. It was an interesting change, if not exactly a relief, to leave the noise of the city, to forget, as she did, even with brief separation, the rhythm of her daily routine. Ben, though technically a boyfriend, suddenly seemed like a figment of her imagination, as permanent and corporeal as the girl whose bedroom she borrowed right now.

Raucous laughter in the hall jolted her from her thoughts, reminding her of her imminent obligation: a toast for the rehearsal dinner. As maid of honor, she was expected not only to propose a toast to the bride and groom but to deliver one of the most eloquent toasts of the night. Nostalgic reflection, dramatic summary, uproarious hilarity—these were merely the prerequisites of a successful wedding toast. And as though the task was not daunting enough, she was expected, while weaving a compelling narrative of the bride, to paint a secondary portrait, an equally, if not more captivating, depiction of herself.

Every time she fixed her mind on the subject, it went suddenly, totally blank. When she thought of Lila, she had nothing to say. No, not true; she had nothing *nice* to say. She had experimented with various openings during the drive up to Maine.

"I've known Lila for nearly ten years now," she considered, "but it was only when we roomed together that I grew to detest her."

But irony was better left to the groomsmen. People expected more of the bridesmaids, adulation, clear and bright. She went on to consider the brazen potshots of a roast:

"Lila Hayes is universally known as the most beautiful girl ever to attend Yale. Unfortunately, she's also known as the most promiscuous . . ."

But she quickly dismissed this concept in favor of a more traditional narrative.

"Lila and I have shared many things over the years: rooms, clothes, study notes, colds, boyfriends."

But nothing about their relationship sanctioned this kind of candor. As a last resort, she experimented with earnestness.

"Lila Hayes is, quite possibly, the luckiest girl in the world. Beauty, wealth, impeccable lineage, intelligence—the list goes on and on."

This tone felt right, even if the content was nauseatingly saccharine. If nothing else, it would please the bride.

"But in addition to her extreme good fortune in said areas," she might go on, "Lila Hayes is perhaps luckiest in love." And this, in Laura's opinion, was the thing that made this the best and worst option for a toast; best, because it segued naturally from a discussion of the bride to the groom; worst, because it revealed the very thing Laura strove most to deny, that she was envious of any stroke of Lila's good luck, let alone her groom.

The thought was so literal and banal it made Laura blush. It would have been subtler to say that she was jealous of Lila's looks. But although Laura had absentmindedly yearned for skinnier thighs or mused on the perks of life as a golden blonde, she had ultimately decided that her dark hair and thoughtful eyes were more mysterious in the final analysis, that blondes were bubbly, bodacious, and all that, but rarely did crossword puzzles with her speed and expertise. And why preclude the possibility that her own DNA hid the coveted recessive gene? For all she knew, she would one day give birth to a blond, blue-eyed child, revealing the raw potential she stored within, the untold capacity to assimilate. No, for all her self-criticism, Laura had settled on the fact that she liked her appearance, appreciating it both for aesthetic value and for its difference from her friends. She was the brooding, intelligent one, the exotic Jewess. Conceptually, boys coveted Lila, but it was Laura they wanted to possess. And she would take sultry over pretty any day.

No, if Laura was jealous of anything of Lila's, it was not her looks. But to say she was jealous of her relationship with Tom bordered on comic understatement. Jealous was not the right word, she decided. Cynical was more accurate. Or indignant. Indignant was accurate. And why wouldn't she be? She had dated Tom first, for the first two years of college. The only difference was that her relationship with Tom ended in the span of an afternoon. And as though that was not cruel enough, she had been robbed of the comforts of mourning. She had been forced to face Tom the very next day when he started dating Lila. The two roommates had merely switched places as though it were a beloved Ivy League tradition for roommates to trade boyfriends every fourth semester.

Laura had watched as a fling grew into a relationship of its own.

Throughout, she comforted herself with two predictions: Tom and Lila would go their separate ways after graduation, and she and Tom would eventually reunite, wiser and more in love. But the years after college confirmed only half of this hypothesis: Tom and Laura did reunite with renewed passion, but they did so even while Tom and Lila's relationship thrived. At the tender age of twenty-two, Laura found herself entwined in an affair.

In the beginning, it felt like most transgressions—like an experiment, a day in someone else's life. But gradually, it became commonplace, banal even. That she still spoke to Tom on the phone every day even while he went home to Lila seemed perfectly normal—unfortunate to be sure, but manageable nonetheless. They were still too young to concern themselves with the notion of permanence, and there was a certain freedom in having her nights to herself. That she pictured Tom when she was with other boys was peculiar but convenient. It softened the blow of wasting time with hopelessly incomparable replacements. Like any other habit—vice or virtue—it eventually became routine. It was simply a function of their unusual bond that they remained in love—fell deeper in love really—after their time as a couple ended, in much the same way you yearn for a family member after he dies.

Physical attraction did its part to glue them together, but something stronger than sexual attraction sealed the bond. When men and women grow apart, Laura had found, it is for the same reason they are drawn together; because they are finally, inherently too different. Friendships among women, on the other hand, were burdened by similarity. But Tom and Laura were somehow immune to the pitfalls of both relationships. They enjoyed the intrigue of opposites and the comfort of twins.

In Tom's presence, Laura felt incomparably calm, the way you feel on a rainy day when your only reasonable option is to consign yourself to sitting still, the way she had felt the moment time was called on the last exam of senior year, that a vast amount of work had been completed and the future held only excitement. In Tom's presence, time passed at an accelerated pace. They could be sitting in traffic or talking on the phone or waiting in line for a movie, and their time felt precious, important, worthwhile. Memories of Tom looked different. Their colors were sharper and richer, like grass after it rains. And she had been in love enough times to rule out the possibility that this was merely some feat of nostalgia.

With everyone else, Laura felt rushed, convinced that her companion was on the verge of being bored. She spent her life cursed by this awareness, rushing to make a point, pretending to understand someone else's. But with Tom, she felt the same pressure to finish a thought that she would if she were talking to herself. It was understood that they shared the same thresholds—the same inexhaustible appetite for wasting time, for discussing lofty ideas, for dissecting trivial things, for driving to nowhere in particular, for listening to music, for talking about books, for obsessing over pop culture, but mostly for laughing, talking, and simply being together. There was nothing one could say that the other would find too cruel or too kind. And on those rare occasions when they did tire of each other, they needed only go a day without talking before they yearned to reconnect.

Laura knew perfectly well that her friends disapproved of her friendship with Tom. But their disapproval was based on an incomplete set of facts. Unfortunately, she could never share the extent of their relationship. So she stomached the disgrace and let them think what they pleased. They were, at least, correct in thinking that she was brokenhearted. Only, she was not brokenhearted because the relationship had ended suddenly; she was brokenhearted because it had never truly ended.

Finally, new inspiration for her toast:

"Tom and Lila are two incredible people," she could begin, "who are going to have incredible lives. Unfortunately, they are not meant to spend their lives together."

Loud laughter from the hall interrupted the pleasure of this notion. Suddenly conscious of the time, she collected her things and hurried to join her friends in their customary pre-party bathroom caucus. As for the toast, she would simply have to hope for the best.

"What was that about anyway?" Tripler was saying when Laura arrived.

The bathroom had been transformed into a steamy war room. Each girl stood at the mirror in uniform, one towel wrapped around her showered body, another twisted into a turban on her head. As they dried their hair and applied makeup, they plotted the evening's strategy like top military aides.

"That *was* a little weird," Annie agreed. "It kind of felt like the beginning of a horror movie."

"Gussie's gotten a little cuckoo," Tripler said, "in her old age."

"It's not her fault," Weesie said. "You drink enough champagne, it's bound to waterlog the brain."

"That whole thing about the porch," Annie said. She extended her arm and craned her neck to inspect the state of her underarm.

"That's her way of saying they've let the house go," said Weesie. Lips pursed, she leaned into the mirror and applied a coat of sugary lip gloss.

"It's her way of saying they're not as rich as the Hayeses," Tripler corrected. Without warning, she sprayed perfume inches from Weesie's ear and stepped toward her, into the mist.

"What is that?" Weesie yelped.

"It's just perfume," Tripler sniffed.

Weesie glared her reproach at the mirror.

"She sounded awfully proud about that ghost on the roof," said Annie.

"Maybe she had a soft spot for her great-great-great-grand-mother," said Tripler.

Laughter erupted, amplified by the tight quarters.

Weesie looked up from her lips to meet Laura's gaze in the mirror. "Oh," she chirped. "There you are."

"I'm screwed for my toast," Laura declared.

"Shut up," said Weesie. "You always say that, and then you give the best toast of the night."

"I wrote mine out," Tripler bragged, pointing to a stack of index cards on the sink counter. Wielding an eyeliner pencil, she pried one eye open to reveal the pink interior of an eyelid.

Weesie held Laura's gaze then shot Tripler a murderous look.

"Your signature rhyming ode?" asked Laura.

Tripler nodded, one eye still pried open. "Guaranteed to bring down the house."

Laura and Weesie opted for silence. It was the fastest way to shut Tripler up or, at the very least, to change the subject.

"Did Lila put you in that dead girl's room?" Tripler demanded.

"That's nice," said Laura.

"Lila would only pull that shit with you," Tripler quipped. She had a knack for weaving character assassination into the most offhand comment.

"I love old houses," Laura insisted.

"Why?" Tripler asked. Satisfied with her eyes, she unraveled her towel to release a mass of stringy wet hair.

Annie shed both towels and strutted proudly across the room as though to assert the intimacy they all shared.

"I don't know," Laura said. "It's kind of fun to picture the girls who grew up here . . ."

"But who would want to?" Tripler asked.

"It makes me want to write a novel," said Laura.

"Better not write about me," said Tripler.

Laura stared at Tripler, checking the urge to say something snide.

"Well, the fascination is mutual," said Weesie, reviving the previous conversation. "Remember sophomore year when you got that tattoo, and Lila went out and got the same one . . ."

Laura offered Weesie a grateful smile. "It was only henna," she said.

Annie paused to interject, one foot out the door. "Not to get too technical, but didn't Lila steal Tom from you, too?"

Running water punctuated her question. The girls remained silent, plucking hairs, puckering lips.

Finally, Weesie spoke up, sparing everyone the discomfort. "Shit," she said. "It's ten to four. Who has the hair dryer?"

Tripler pressed the power button in response, assaulting the room with its deafening noise and precluding conversation entirely.

Laura was ready before the others and walked down to the porch to wait. The air was fresh, and the light was remarkably different from the light in New York. Calming slightly, she took the opportunity to survey the house. What was it about this house that Augusta wanted to destroy? Had she once yearned to tear down the porch at Northern Gardens too? Was that how Augusta felt when she looked at her? Now, looking across the field, she studied the profile of the elegant white house. A truckload of white chairs had been stacked by a vine-covered trellis, ready to be arranged for tomorrow's fete. The enormous white tent rustled in the breeze, as though taking a deep breath.

Suddenly, Laura was struck by the immediacy—the reality of Tom and Lila's wedding. In twenty-four hours, Tom and Lila would stand underneath that trellis. Chairs would line the lawn in neat rows. Guests would fill the chairs. Laura would stand in her horrible tin dress, beaming at Lila's side. Picturing this, Laura felt and fought the impulse to run screaming onto the lawn, to find Tom, shake him, beg him not to go through with it. Strangely, this operatic act seemed entirely sensible at the moment. It would be worth any mortification to prevent him from making this mistake. But just as quickly, she kicked herself for humoring an absurd notion. How many movies had she seen that exploited this very setup? How many soap operas had culminated in just this story arc? And more important, what made her think she wanted him for herself? She did not admire the man Tom had become. He had traded integrity for status. What was desirable about a man like that?

As she stood on the porch, a beautiful day grew even more picturesque. The full, buoyant clouds of the afternoon stretched into gauzy ribbons and hovered above the house like contrails left by a plane. A school of pristine sailboats cut across the shimmering cove. Grass turned from green to gold as the sun sifted through the clouds, lengthening the shadows of trees and the house. Across the lawn, people were starting to gather. A small contingent formed on the Hayeses' porch and filtered onto the lawn for the rehearsal. One person broke from the group and took an exuberant lead. It was Lila, swinging her arms up and down like a child on Christmas day.

The girls walked over to Northern Gardens together, arms linked, four abreast, like soldiers marching to battle. The boys followed close behind, jostling each other and occasionally bursting into a chorus of shouted insults. For everyone, distance from home and routine and the smell of fresh-cut grass played a trick on their moods, convincing them that they had retreated to a different time. Gradually, the girls loosened their grasp on one another and fell into a new formation. Tripler enlisted Weesie to listen to a practice run of her toast. Annie and Oscar walked in silence, appreciating the ocean breeze. Pete and Jake broke into an impromptu race, as though to remind the group of their athletic prowess at Yale. Laura lagged behind, forcing a merry smile that only an idiot could mistake for real cheer.

The Hayes and McDevon families were fully assembled when the group arrived. They had formed a semicircle with Augusta at its center like members of an ancient religious cult worshipping a deity. On one side of the circle, members of the Hayes contingent stood in official cocktail stance. They chatted amiably, arms propped on hips, heads tilted inquisitively. On the other side, the McDevons reunited, greeted new arrivals to the clan, but they looked slightly confused, like school children awaiting instructions. Their side of the circle had bottlenecked into an inelegant clump, causing the semicircle to resemble a snake with a curling tail. The pileup looked strangely inappropriate on the otherwise immaculate lawn. Annoyed, Augusta dispatched her younger daughter to impose order.

Lila stood apart from the circle, watching her guests arrive. She greeted the group with a high-pitched shriek that was answered with an echo. She was quickly surrounded by the wedding party and congratulated on her current ensemble. Somehow, they managed to double the excitement they had expressed only an hour earlier before subsiding into a more appropriate volume to coo about their rooms and the fit of Lila's dress. She looked perfectly radiant in a fitted navy blue silk frock. The dark blue silk offset her eyes even while allowing them to upstage it. Her golden hair provided the perfect contrast to the rich color. The dress seemed to have been designed to showcase her enviable figure, announcing her virtues in rapid succession: long legs, ample bust, beautiful face.

Laura surveyed the lawn for a moment before she spotted Tom. He was obscured by Lila's maternal grandparents, who had effectively barricaded him as though to prevent a sudden escape. When she finally caught a glimpse of his face, he looked strange, unlike himself. He stood unnaturally erect and smiled in a forced, plastic way, like a kidnapped child feigning normalcy on a ransom tape. He wore a cream-colored linen suit of a cut and color designed expressly for garden parties, the kind of suit Tom would surely have called "poncy" had he seen it on another man. He nodded and blinked more than usual, as you do when you're faking an emotion. It was immediately clear to Laura that he was miserable and scared, and the realization made her feel equal amounts of delight and despair. The paradox of emotion caused a combustive reaction in her heart that resulted in nausea.

Tom noticed Laura just as this sensation threatened to bring her to the grass. Laura stared back without smiling, forgetting propriety. Mercifully, Tripler grabbed her elbow just then, demanding that she vet the closing joke for her toast, allowing Laura enough time to slow her pulse before Augusta corralled the crowd.

"Ladies, gentlemen. I hate to interrupt, but cocktails beckon us tonight. Lila, Tom." She gestured to both and waited for them to grasp her outstretched arms.

Her muscular smile, Laura noted, was actually quite impressive. It was, in fact, a feat of stage acting. She had gauged the size and distance of her audience and made the necessary adjustments. Up close, the clenched veins in her neck betrayed anxiety. From twenty feet away, her whole effect was quite subdued.

"Now, let's get this over with, shall we?" she said. "So we can toast this fabulous pair."

A hearty cheer erupted from the lawn. Augusta encouraged it with polite applause, then silenced it with a definitive clap.

Lila, who was herself a veteran performer, smiled demurely at the crowd. This was her cue to play up the romance.

Tom performed his scheduled kiss, but a moment too late, with obvious haste, like an actor who has forgotten a line.

"If you'll forgive me," Augusta went on, "we're going to begin. If you listen." She gazed pointedly at the younger members of the crowd. "This won't take long at all." She dispensed a merciless scolding look, then, just as quickly, transformed her face into an expression of rapturous delight. "Let me introduce the Reverend Hipp. He is our dear family friend and the beloved pastor of the First Presbyterian Church on Garden Street in Cambridge. He will be performing the ceremony tomorrow."

"And drinking heavily tonight!"

Augusta turned sharply on the group. Who would say something so crass and inappropriate?

The delighted grin on the face of one of Tom's many younger cousins gave away the culprit. Augusta glared at the offender and his mother, conveying her disapproval.

"So!" she said, startling the crowd with a staccato high pitch. A natural public speaker, she understood the power of explosive utterances. "This handsome, youthful group over here. They are the wedding party." She scanned the group, offering each a cursory nod. "Tripler, Louisa, Anne. Oscar, Peter, Jake. These are the dear friends who will participate in the wedding. They are honored guests." She paused and smiled coyly. "But not until Lila says 'I do.' Until then, this wedding is work."

The wedding party assented with a good-natured round of hoots and whistles. Augusta silenced them with a sharp look. She had not meant this in jest.

"Minnow, my youngest, is also a bridesmaid," she went on.

Minnow smiled and curtsied for the crowd. Even at fourteen, she was already more of a ham than her older sister.

"And Laura and Chip," Augusta said conclusively. "Laura is Lila's maid of honor and Chip is Tom's best man. They will be the last to walk down the aisle before the bride and groom."

Laura bristled instinctively at Augusta's description. She was not Lila's anything, except perhaps her greatest critic. Still, she mustered the expected smile for the waiting eyes, trying to find the most livable balance between submission and self-respect.

Without warning, Chip snuck up from behind and grabbed her by the waist. The surprise and bad taste of the gesture nearly caused her to lose her balance.

"I knew it," he roared. "Laura Rosen. I still make you weak in the knees."

"Chip, get off me," Laura snapped, then embarrassed by her harsh tone, she quickly added. "You nearly took me down."

Chip Hayes was a strange boy that Laura loathed as much as she loved. Over the years, she had spent more time with him than she would have liked, sharing with Lila the responsibility of older, wiser sister. Like Lila's, Chip's looks, demeanor, and credentials were irreproachable. But he lacked his sister's lightness and magnetism. He had inherited, Laura could only guess, more of his father's than his mother's traits. Even more than most boys, he was plagued with an off-putting strain of restlessness. His checkered history in school and love attested to this fact.

From the age of thirteen to eighteen, he had attended no less than five prep schools, relocating whenever a new learning disability was diagnosed or new transgression discovered. Each school had been more specialized than the one before and, in turn, more ill suited; first, a traditional coed day school in Cambridge; second, after a series of suspensions, an ascetic boarding school in Connecticut; third, after the expulsion, three months at home at a smaller, alternative day school; fourth, after the second expulsion, an all-boys institution that bordered on military school, with a heralded department for challenged learners; and fifth, after he escaped from this school on the Vespa of a very attractive drama teacher (with that drama teacher), Chip completed his high-school degree at a ski school in Vermont, the only licensed institution that would accept his dossier of transcripts.

Incredibly, Chip had turned around this ten-year fiasco when he began to channel his restlessness into artistic pursuits. A compelling portfolio of mixed media collages, stellar performance on the ski team, and a small donation from his father earned the attention of the admissions director of Trinity College, landing Chip, for the first two years of college, only forty miles away from his sister. The short commute from Hartford to New Haven allowed Lila to keep the promise that she made to her parents, that she would keep an eye on her younger brother, and permitted Chip to benefit from the dating options of the Ivy League. Throughout, Laura tolerated Chip's frequent stays on their common room futon. He was always game to procrastinate, and his constant professions of lust and adoration were amusing, if not flattering.

"All right," said Augusta. "I'd like us to do one walk-through of tomorrow's procession. Members of the wedding party, I need you to break into your assigned pairs." She waved her arms with the wide, ambiguous movements of an airport traffic controller. "Everyone, line up behind Uncle Jack's tree. That's where you'll begin."

The group dutifully broke into pairs, husbands clutching wives, fiancé grasping fiancée with the relief and sweetness of wallflowers finding partners at a dance.

Laura stalled for a moment, embarrassed by the indignity of the situation. It was somehow degrading to march at Augusta's command. It hearkened back to an insult borne by her ancestors. Still, she followed the crowd toward the trunk of the majestic tree. Chip followed close behind, poking her waist like a twelve-year-old child.

"Oh boy," he said. "Tonight's the night."

"The night you finally drink yourself into oblivion?"

"The night you finally realize you're in love with me."

"But, Chip, I realized that years ago," Laura said. She had found that playing along with him was the best course of action. Defying him just provoked him to try harder, at a higher volume. "It's sad, though, about the age difference. People would talk. You don't want a bride who has to hobble down the aisle with a cane."

"Oh but I do," Chip replied. "It'll make it easier to have my way with you."

Augusta interrupted, sparing Laura the burden of another scold.

"Family members last," she said. She gestured at the McDevons with a patronizing flourish. "Flower girls will walk first. Your mothers have hung or steamed those dressed already. That silk wrinkles so easily." She turned to Lila's older cousin. "Kate, I suggest you use my time-tested trick. Don't feed your girls after eleven. Then stand at the end of the aisle with a piece of candy." She indulged in a mischievous smile, then returned to business. "Kathy and Ted, you'll walk together. Minnow, you'll walk with the bridesmaids, after Tripler but before Laura. I'll walk with Chip. Lila will walk with her father. And Tom, of course, will wait with Reverend Hipp."

For a moment, everyone remained still, too intimidated to move. But soon the group began to shuffle in the prescribed order, processing from under the gnarled, stately tree with halting, self-conscious steps.

"You would think it was our first time walking," said Jake. "Hey, Frankenstein," he called to Pete. "You all right over there?"

"I wouldn't talk," Pete quipped. "You're about as graceful as this tree."

"I hope my dress fits," Annie said, teasing too loudly.

Lila turned sharply to look at her friend, opened her mouth to reprimand her, then, realizing Annie's joke, closed her eyes and smiled.

One by one, each pair completed the journey from the tree, meeting Augusta and smiling as she nudged them into the correct positions.

Throughout, Lila remained uncharacteristically quiet, as though she had been hypnotized. Finally, a more familiar Lila seemed to wake from trance. "All right, Mother. This is a wedding. Not a marching exercise. I think we've asked enough of our guests." She shook her head with disdain and let out a peal of gay laughter, playing to the crowd as only she could, distancing herself from her mother even while channeling her.

"We'll exact our punishment tonight," Oscar teased. "At the rehearsal dinner."

Another chorus of laughter erupted, followed by louder hoots and whistles.

"If we drink enough," Jake said.

"If you drink your usual amount," Pete said, "you won't be standing when it's your turn to toast."

Finally, Tom descended upon the debate to deliver his verdict. He was the de facto judge of the group, their moral arbiter, if not their conscience.

"If I drink enough," he said, "you may both live to see me get married tomorrow."

At this, the assembled group devolved into raucous applause, their volume escalating suddenly like schoolkids' after a period bell.

Tom and Lila grasped hands in a show of unity, and Augusta surrendered, acknowledging that she had lost the group's attention.

Lila was rewarded for her gracious act with a kiss from her groom. Tom turned her toward him as though she were a large marionette, wrapped his arms around her shoulders, and deposited a polite kiss on her lips. Laura watched the elaborate performance of romance from her assigned position. She was relieved to find she was wholly unmoved. In fact, it was a great comfort to see Tom and Lila finally interact, perhaps because this kiss revealed something far worse than anything she could imagine. It was immediately apparent, not just from the kiss but from his halting step, the choreographed placement of his arm—the whole charade she had just witnessed—that Tom was not in love with Lila—in fact, he seemed mildly repulsed. Realizing this, Laura felt her lungs saturate for the first time since arriving at Northern Gardens. Odds were even that Tom would marry Lila tomorrow.

FOUR

By five o'clock, the weather seemed to have lost conviction. A beautiful day had dissolved into a foreboding evening. The wind had picked up, and the clouds had darkened to the color of a bruise. Laura could not help but smile as she pictured the consequences of an approaching storm. She imagined snapshots of the event: an immaculate satin shoe splattered with rainwater, a puddle collecting in the center of the dance floor, rows of shoulders huddled under cocktail shawls. Improbably, she thought of something her father had told her as a child: "What's good for your friends is good for you." But she dismissed it as a trite notion just as quickly as it entered her head.

When she entered the yacht club, she was greeted by a disturbing smell. It was pungent, nutty, and faintly obscene, hardly appropriate for the refined event under way. She knew, from visiting Lila over the years, that it was the stench of sulfur, rising from the marshes at low tide just in time for cocktail hour. But even after deciding on the cause, it was funny to think about other possible sources of the pungent scent. She couldn't help smiling at the thought that the guests emitted their own noxious gas. Amused, she veered away from the group and wandered toward an empty patch of grass. The detour left her dangerously far from the other bridesmaids and directly in Augusta's path.

"My Heavens," said Augusta. "Everyone's in black." She simultaneously looked past and at Laura, rapidly scanning the grounds.

Laura followed Augusta's gaze into the assembled crowd, but found only a bright bouquet of primary colors. She regarded her own dress with shame. She was better dressed for a funeral than a wedding party.

"Well, you certainly are a city girl," Augusta chirped.

Laura replied with a smile meant to convey two things: gratitude for the feigned compliment and apology for the insult of her attire.

"Now, what is that perfume?" Augusta said.

"Isn't it the marsh?" Laura asked.

"No, no," said Augusta. "Yours." She struck a contemplative pose and furrowed her brow, making it perfectly clear that she hated the fragrance before moving on to greet another guest.

It had taken Laura several years to learn the language of Lila's culture. Rooming with Lila had, of course, been a crash course in the dialect. But the language was as nuanced and subtle as the most complex Eastern tongue, cursed with its own multifaceted characters and an unpublished set of rules.

In conversation, for example, one must maintain a constant stream of chatter while avoiding emotional content at all costs.

These two requirements were, of course, in direct conflict. The exclusion of emotional content necessarily shortened response time and rendered continuous banter all the more difficult. Still, a skilled conversationalist overcame this obstacle by stockpiling pithy, interested questions and keeping them poised at the ready. All the while, the speaker maintained an air of wondrous intrigue, answering with thoughtful precision and asking with breathless curiosity.

A truly advanced speaker was capable of even greater feats. He could draw on information gathered in previous conversations, thereby displaying his impressive recall, and yet still maintain a dry and emotionally guarded mystique. Such a pro could weave a seamless ribbon of pleasantries into a factual conversation. He could summarize profound life-changing events such as deaths, births, and marriages with short superlative statements. A conversationalist of the highest level could use one phrase for two wholly disparate scenarios. For example, "How is that guy anyway?" could be used for both of the following queries: "How is your one-month-old?" and "How is your dying father?" Both were asked with the same furrowed concern and chipper aplomb.

God forbid one answer a question with too much gravity. Earnest expressions of sorrow or distress were best left for one's diary. Of course, the uninitiated might hear the question, "How is your dying father" and mistake it for a sincere query. But the distinction between the words and the questioner's intent, though subtle, was all-important, for it spared the cocktail realm incongruous heaviness—subjects better saved for private talks on the porch— and it enabled good manners to be mistaken for sincere compassion.

This, of course, was a dangerous mistake should you ever find your-self in need of a confidante.

Laura had first encountered the language freshman year in col-lege when she and Lila together took on Yale's secret society punch. Never mind that they were conversing with a population that was almost exclusively drunk, these people were incomprehensible to Laura. For months, she struggled to understand; Lila was fluent from the start.

Nearly ten years later, Laura was finally conversant. She had, of course, been subject to an immersion course while living with Lila, and she had honed the ear of a foreigner from the day she was born. Her own parents were members of the caste known most af-fectionately as reformed Jews, in other words, Jews who had all but converted to another religion. They were people who summered in the Hamptons and lived on the Upper East Side, or resided in Brookline and summered on the Vineyard. They were people who sought membership at Bath and Tennis Clubs all over the New England seaboard in spite of their well-known membership policies. They were the people who supported a multibillion-dollar industry of retail modeled on yachting attire. They were people Laura had come to think of in the most simplistic way: Jews were black and Wasps were white, and she was some shade of gray in between.

Boarding school was the defining turn in her religious educa-tion. As one of four Jews in her grade-school class, she had always been outnumbered. But at boarding school, she was marooned, finally far enough from her city roots to forget her urban identity. Quickly and quietly, thirteen-year-old Laura had completed a total make-over, trading in the Doc Martens in which she arrived for tasseled moccasins. The pictures she tacked on her wall still revealed the stylish iconoclast of her younger years; the foray into rubber bracelets, a short affair with side ponytails. But, without this evidence, her classmates would never have known her secret history. By the time she returned from Thanksgiving break, the transformation was complete; her room was stocked with J. Crew catalogs, her drawers filled with plaid flannel shirts. Only a genealogical expert would have guessed her ethnicity.

She sometimes blamed her parents for this disgrace. It was their job to instill pride in her heritage. Instead, they had confused her with a surplus of cultural identities, as though religion were something you could change at will to match a new pair of pants. Her family's Chanukah tradition typified the problem. On the first night, her mother unveiled a dusty menorah, assembled the family in the kitchen, lit a candle from the burner in the stove, and sang a dirge-like Hebrew prayer. The custom was entirely devoid of joy and magic. It felt both cursory and compulsory, like the stats class required of all freshman at Yale, which no one really studied for, but everyone eventually passed. On the five remaining nights, the menorah was lit, but the somber songs were dropped. Hastily wrapped presents were exchanged over a take-out meal.

Her mother's approach to Christmas was ebullient, by contrast. Mrs. Rosen, a Jew on both sides, decked her halls with holly and filled the house with an abundance of presents as though striving to destroy her credit in a single month. Her one nod to Judaism was the color of the lights on her Christmas tree. The tree was festooned, not with tasteful white bulbs, but tacky colored ones, a sign to God or Moses or Abraham, much like lamb's blood smeared on the doorway Passover night, that hers was a family of believers.

The confusion had started early. From the age of five, Laura attended an Episcopal school. At daily assembly, she whispered the Lord's Prayer alongside her blond classmates, hands clasped, eyes closed piously. When they braided each other's hair, she prayed no one would notice her darker, coarser strands.

"You're Jewish, right," a classmate demanded sometime around sixth grade.

"Yeah." Laura shrugged. For some reason, assent felt like a confession.

"I thought so," the classmate said, "because of your last name." And then by way of consolation, she added, "But don't worry, you'd never know."

Laura smiled her thanks, torn between relief and humiliation. She was utterly confused: Had this been a compliment or a slight?

By the time she got to college, she was anxious to end the debate. But a strange cultural trend coincided with her predicament. Suddenly, it became fashionable to be Jewish. College kids who had spent their childhoods downplaying their cultural heritage embraced their Judaism with the sudden fervor of sinners accepting God on their deathbeds. It was a happy occurrence for Laura, bridging the gap between her heritage and her persona, a comforting option even despite the kitschiness of the new schtick. She was half-and-half, part Jew, part Wasp, a beautiful anomaly. And the success of the new persona only reinforced her reductive view of the world. There were two types of people: Wasps and Jews. It was a crude and polarized way of looking at the world, but it was *her* polarity, her north and south, her guiding principle, and she relied on it to describe and decode the world just as sailors relied on the stars.

Only later did she consider the implications of her dual citizenship. Junior year, she needed to fulfill a core requirement in world history and searched for the easiest class that fit into her schedule. "Jews, from Jesus to Hitler," was only a cursory survey, but it jogged Laura's memory, detailing the persecution permitted by neglect, the atrocities condoned by silence. Now, the shame of her first offense was matched by the disgrace of her second: being Jewish and failing to observe her religion and being Jewish and failing to admit it. Faced with the dates, the names, the pictures of the Jews' most recent persecution, Laura finally fathomed the damage caused by her omissions, every compliment she had accepted, every utterance of the Lord's Prayer. It was this very complacence that allowed a generation to be murdered in sight of civilization.

Rattled, she scanned the lawn for her friends, eager for distraction. She crossed the lawn, taking special care to avoid Augusta.

Tripler, Pete, Weesie, and Jake had formed a human barricade by the buffet, thwarting other guests from enjoying the crudités. Tripler, as usual, had monopolized the conversation and betrayed her early buzz with sharp, sporadic peals of laughter. Annie and Oscar were preoccupied, mocking the attire of a nearby guest. Laura was comforted by the sight of her friends, but not enough to join them. She wandered toward the edge of the lawn for a better view of the bay. The view offered the distraction she craved, its constellation of sailboats providing a welcome shock of color.

"Laura? Are you okay?"

The compassionate query was quickly followed by a more caustic one.

"Laura!" Tripler barked.

Laura turned to find Tripler and Weesie at her back. She felt immediately defensive, as you do when you are awakened by the ringing phone and attempt to convince the caller you've been up for hours.

"What are you doing here?" Tripler demanded. "Why so reclusive?"

"No," Laura mustered. "I'm just . . ." She couldn't believe it when it came out of her mouth. "Admiring the view."

"Um okay . . ." said Tripler. "Admiring the view?" She scolded Laura for the cliché with an indignant snort, punishment for denying their intimacy.

"Laura's just getting her bearings," Weesie explained. If Tripler's typical mode was speaker, Weesie's was interpreter.

Laura smiled. It was a flaw of hers that she was so guarded with her best friends. A failure to trust these people was a sign of deep paranoia.

"You don't have to be 'on' with us," said Tripler. "We know this is hard for you."

"Hard for me?" Laura said. The defensive feeling returned, this time coupled with anger. "Why would this be hard for me?"

Tripler said nothing. She locked eyes with Laura, challenging her to defy the assertion.

"I think Tripler just means being here without Ben."

"Oh," said Laura. But she kept staring at Tripler. This was not what Tripler had meant. "No, it's fine," she said, deciding to play along. "It's actually nice to be on my own. Our apartment is so small."

"Yeah," said Weesie. "Tell me about it. Remind me again why we live in New York."

"So you can pay a million dollars to live in a two-hundred-square-foot box," Tripler quipped.

"Why don't we all chip in and buy the house we're staying in. Then we can gut it and start a commune up here in Dark Harbor." Weesie smiled, tickled by the thought.

"Now that would be a horror movie," said Tripler. "We'd cannibalize each other."

"No, we wouldn't," said Weesie. "We all lived in the same house in college."

"Exactly," said Tripler. "And we nearly killed each other. Which reminds me. Did you guys make the offer on that apartment?"

"No," said Weesie. "Now we're thinking it may not make sense to buy in this market. It's going to be more expensive than we thought to break through that wall."

"That sucks," said Tripler. "That room would make the most amazing nursery. What are you guys waiting for anyway?"

Weesie prepared a heated response—Tripler pushed the baby thing like some Bible-toting fundamentalist. But noting Laura's tuned-out stare, Weesie checked the impulse to engage Tripler. They had plenty of time to bicker over the weekend. She changed the subject with a conspiratorial smirk. "I kind of wish the boys weren't here. We could go skinny-dipping in the bay like we used to."

"We can still do that," Tripler said. "Hasn't your husband ever seen you naked?"

"Shut up, Trip. You know what I mean."

"So that's why you're not pregnant yet," Tripler teased.

Weesie rolled her eyes, refusing to dignify the joke with more strenuous muscle movement.

Tripler took the cue and disengaged. "Anyone need another drink? I'm fueling up for my toast."

"Good idea," said Weesie, relenting.

Tension evaporated between the two as they focused on the new task.

Laura stood still for another moment, staring at the sparkling bay as though she was trying to memorize the face of a loved one before saying good-bye.

The dinner announcement was followed by a mad rush to the tent. Guests hustled to find empty tables, then to secure the seat that would yield the most enjoyable conversation. The wedding party simply rushed to find the best table. They were so accustomed to being seated together that their criterion was different from other guests', they wanted the table with the best view of the festivities, the best vantage point from which to watch and mock the parade of speakers. It was customary for them to transform themselves into a panel of judges. Speakers were measured on the bases of originality, delivery, and humor, and quietly booed for use of cliché, sentimentality, and bad grammar.

Upon entering the tent, it was immediately apparent that the party was being thrown by the McDevons. It lacked the organization, color scheme, and sophistication of a Hayes affair. Tables had been assembled in a slightly haphazard manner just beyond the lawn where cocktails were served. Green tablecloths picked up the color of the grass, but in a neon hue. A stream of peach ribbons hung from the rim of the tent at the entrance, connoting a disco parlor. Guests were encouraged to root through these hanging ribbons to find a small card with their name and table number attached. It was a sweet idea, poorly executed—it caused a bottleneck of guests to accumulate at the entrance.

The color peach proved an unfortunate complement to the ubiquitous green. The shade Mrs. McDevon had chosen consisted of more yellow than pink and had the odd effect of vibrating slightly when seen in the periphery. The pairing of green and peach also caused the room to resemble a golf function or a bar on St. Patrick's Day. Worse still, the two colors clashed with the club's nautical blue-and-white scheme, creating the effect of a child's art project whenever all four colors intersected.

The cocktail hour had been presented tastefully enough. Perhaps the number and selection of hors d'oeuvres had been on the sparse side and veered slightly from the standard premium choices expected of such a momentous affair. Water crackers smeared with fondue shared space with a pallid array of crudités while uniformed staff passed congealed smoked salmon on pumpernickel squares. Certainly, there was no horrible offender on the menu—no pigs-in-blankets, no sour-cream-and-onion dip—but the whole spread bore a strong resemblance to the buffet one of Chip's prep schools had trotted out on Parents' Day, a smorgasbord that prompted jeers from students and parents alike.

Mrs. Hayes had warned Mrs. McDevon about all of these flaws—hors d'oeuvres, color scheme, staging. She had done her best to share knowledge of the yacht club venue. But now, as she stood watching the guests all but tackle each other in their search for seating, her worst fears were confirmed. Mrs. McDevon was utterly incompetent. The event was an embarrassment. Augusta was not surprised, of course. Taste was an inborn thing, and Mrs. McDevon could not be faulted for lacking it. She could be faulted, however, for refusing to heed Augusta's good advice, and worse, for her seeming satisfaction with the end result. Her inferior taste spoke to the inferior nature of her family. It was distressing to think that Lila was marrying into this mediocrity.

Just as she suppressed this thought, Augusta spotted Lila. Her daughter was trying to advance toward her seat but had been slowed by oncoming traffic; a moving huddle of Tom's older relatives had glommed on to her like a virus.

Augusta grabbed Lila's arm as she passed, as though offering a hand to a drowning swimmer.

Lila gripped her mother with the same force, attempting to quell her gripe before she uttered it.

"I warned her," Augusta hissed.

"I know," whispered Lila.

"She might as well have done a picnic on the grass. Served ribs on paper plates."

"Mother," said Lila. "I don't understand what you have against new money. It's still money." With a smile, she signaled her teasing tone and succeeded at diffusing Augusta's anger. Lila had an amazing knack for speaking her mother's language while providing a modern translation.

"I told her I'd do it for her," said Augusta.

"I know," said Lila. "But it doesn't matter. Everyone's having a wonderful time." The few inches Lila had over her mother in heels provided an automatic edge. "You should try to do the same thing."

Augusta sighed with all the distress of a deposed queen. "I will try," she said. Then, as though remembering the appropriate posture for a mother of the bride, she took a step back so that she faced Lila. She grasped both of her shoulders, at once scanning for imperfections and admiring her beauty. "You look stunning, darling," she decided.

"Thank you, Mother," said Lila.

"Now, if we can only find your groom."

Together, Lila and Augusta scanned the tent. But the commotion of guests finding seating and the flood of peach ribbons obscuring their view made this a difficult project. Finally, Augusta spotted him. Her frown revealed it before she did. Tom stood at the edge of the lawn, where Laura had stood earlier, staring out at the bay in a maudlin impersonation of a sailor's widow.

"What has gotten into him?" Augusta barked.

"Leave him alone, Mother," said Lila. But she couldn't help agreeing with the sentiment. Tom's behavior over the last few days had been odd. He had been cold, distracted, not at all his usual self. Of course, it was well-known that grooms suffered a particular pathology and that the planning of a wedding could snuff the fire of even the most passionate romance. But there was no excuse for behaving like a pariah in front of their guests. Checking her annoyance, she took a quick, deep breath, tapped her mother definitively, and set off across the damp grass, stepping gingerly to prevent her heels from sinking into the dirt.

She arrived behind Tom and slipped her hands into his pockets without saying a word, then stood for a moment as his body tensed, then relaxed upon recognition.

"Honey?" she said.

"So quiet," he whispered. He did not turn to acknowledge her, just continued to stare at the water.

Lila followed his gaze into the harbor and stared with him in silence, as though trying to perceive something he had pointed out in the distance.

"We're going to have a good life," he said.

"Yes, we are," she confirmed.

Another moment passed as they stared at the darkening water. Suddenly, it occurred to Lila that Tom's comment had been a question. Annoyed, she removed her hands from his pockets and stepped to stand at his side.

Finally, Tom appeared to notice Lila's presence. Breaking out of his trance, he pivoted her shoulders so that she faced him. He gazed into her eyes as though to confirm their intense beauty. Satisfied, he kissed her forehead.

"How's your mother doing?" he asked.

"She'll be fine," said Lila. She fluttered her lashes in a patent request for another kiss. "You know how she is. She doesn't do so well with peach."

Tom smiled and kissed her, this time on the lips. She was undeniably beautiful, and worse, impossible to resist.

Tradition held that toasts began during the salad course. How and when this tradition arose was difficult to say. But it was understood that rehearsal dinners were subject to this rule, that the dinner itself was secondary in importance to the performance of the toasts. The tradition was treated with the same reverence as any other universal custom, that gifts were exchanged on Christmas morning, turkey eaten on Thanksgiving. Every rehearsal dinner Laura had ever attended abided by these same rules. It was a genre of its own, much like the wedding proposal, with its own discrete set of criteria. And Lila's wedding party was perhaps the most stringent set of judges ever to gather for the spectacle. They had spent their college years honing the art of the toast. With the constant stream of athletic team and secret society banquets they had attended over the years, it was practically a graduation requirement to know how to command a room.

Lila's maternal grandmother, Evelyn Westfield, gave the first toast of the evening, a surprising piece of good luck for subsequent speakers because her toast was inordinately bad. Most toasts made by elders are automatically buoyed by wisdom and perspective. But Mrs. Westfield's was dry and boring, two cardinal sins in a wedding toast. And worse, it was laden with snobbery that made all but the most staid guests ill at ease. The flaws in her toast, in Laura's opinion, confirmed that she was Augusta's mother.

Perhaps it was unfair to fault an older woman for antiquated thinking. Why wouldn't she see the world through the lens of her generation? But the excuse did not satisfy Laura. This same argument had been used to absolve generations of racists. Peer pressure was not a valid excuse for an act of discrimination. To this day, the only nonwhite people Evelyn had addressed were her driver and maid.

"The McDevons and the Westfields were neighbors," she began, "and yet we never met until this week. And what a lovely week it's been. Though I daresay Grandpa Westfield may disagree after Timothy McDevon beat him handily in tennis."

This joke was met with an obligatory giggle.

The wedding party exchanged a flurry of eye rolls in the privacy of their own table.

"That's because the Westfields blocked the McDevons' application to the club," Pete whispered.

"Oh, the McDevons got in the club all right," Tripler quipped. "Every morning when they rolled the tennis courts and every night when they swept the floors."

Laura inhaled sharply. Tripler had only just drained her second drink and she was already out of control.

"In 1964," Evelyn went on, "William Hayes came up from Philadelphia to Boston and captured my daughter, Augusta, who was widely known as the city's greatest beauty. In 1965, Robert Barclay came up from Providence to Boston and captured her little sister, Eliza. Now, it seems, Tom McDevon has reversed the trade route. He came down from Manchester to win Lila's heart in New Haven. Let's raise our glasses to the latest capture. New Haven, Manchester, terrific!"

The toast was met with polite applause and followed by a clumsy huddle as Lila and Tom maneuvered through the narrow corridor between folding chairs and tables. It took at least a minute for them to hike across the grass to share a theatrical embrace with the stately matron.

Before they had returned to their seats, an already-drunk Timothy McDevon rose from his chair. Tom's paternal grandfather batted at a tumbler of whiskey with short, violent swings, causing the guests nearest him to brace for broken glass.

"Hear, hear," he said. He had apparently forgotten that this was an appropriate response to his speech as opposed to an opening.

The guests regarded him with some confusion, exchanging the forgiving and patronizing chuckle afforded to the elderly.

Timothy McDevon was already so drunk as to be dangerously off-balance. He stood, holding the chair in front of him, rocking slightly for several seconds before he started speaking.

"When Tommy told me he was marrying Leila."

A sharp gasp arose from the Hayeses' table, but Mr. McDevon was unfazed.

"I said to him—"

A consort of distant relatives raced to prevent further indiscretions. Someone yelled "Lila" with the volume and intensity of a catcall.

Augusta fought the urge to stand up and silence the drunken man. But she remained sitting, braced to leap from her chair if the situation demanded.

Timothy paused, confused by the commotion in the tent. He offered the crowd a scolding look, then went on enthusiastically. "I told him." Here he paused again, this time for dramatic effect. "I said . . . 'You lucky son of a bitch.'"

Hearty laughter exploded from every corner of the tent.

"I mean, 'Tom,' I said, 'how on earth did you trap a woman like that!?'"

More laughter, but this time it subsided with a relieved exhalation.

Laura had seen so many toasts like this one it barely registered as worthy of satire. It was far more interesting to watch her friends; their jaded sneers betrayed dirtier secrets.

With the exception of Augusta, the Hayes family was enjoying the evening immensely. Mr. Hayes was particularly chipper, buoyed by a constant stream of alcohol in his bloodstream. Lila's sister, Minnow, was happy to bask in the celebrity of her role as sister of the bride. She reveled in the special distinction of being the second prettiest girl in the room and, as of tomorrow, the most available. Her lavender dress was a perfect rendering of the color "sugarplum." Chip also seemed to relish his supporting role in the cast. Congratulations for his sister, he felt, were congratulations for him. He took full responsibility for preventing her from being as boring and predictable as Augusta.

William rose to speak as soon as Mr. McDevon sat down, prompted by a nudge from Augusta.

"Well," he said, "what a joyous occasion." He scanned the room in a regal, fatherly way, endowing his banal declaration with more importance than it deserved.

"He's tossed," Tripler said.

"Completely," said Weesie.

"This should be interesting," said Pete.

In certain circles, William Hayes had become the stuff of legend. He had graduated from Yale, admitted easily enough like so many of his generation. He went on to accept a job at a prestigious bank that ensured the purchase of a Beacon Hill apartment and a summerhouse on Nantucket. He proceeded for a few years on the path of least resistance. Then, without warning or explanation, at the age of twenty-five, he gave his notice at Merrill and summarily quit his job. His plan: to pursue a lifelong aspiration of writing a musical. He spent the next several years developing the libretto. But to this day, he had never shared a tune with any friend or family member. Over time, his commitment to the project dwindled, though he never returned to work. Throughout, he was consistent in his threat: One day, he would put up the show on Broadway, or, at least, at the yacht club's summer talent show.

One would think that a man who had devoted thirty-odd years to the composition of musical theater would have a more gleeful disposition. But his eyes betrayed a deep sadness. They were glassy and wet at all times of day and oozed at the corners like a shucked oyster. His mood could be gauged by their fluctuation and viscosity. Even when he was totally sober—which was rare—they appeared to be waterlogged. Laura had always noted his eyes but resisted the urge to blame alcohol. It almost made more sense, given his marital situation, to assume that the poor man had been weeping.

"Let me begin by thanking the McDevons for a magnificent party," he said. "Kathy, Ted, you've outdone yourselves. What a perfect night."

Like Augusta, Mr. Hayes spoke in a dated, overly formal manner, with the heightened diction of an Englishman and the sentimental jolliness of a fifties television dad.

"Now, I promise to keep this quick, because I know how many fans these two have. But if I may, I'd like to say a few words about the bride and groom. Lila . . ." He gazed into the crowd at his daughter, as though beholding her lovely face for the first time. "Lila and I have always been tight. Even when she was a little girl, we were thick as thieves. We were living in Brookline at the time, and our house had a wonderful driveway, the kind of driveway that seemed to have been designed for learning how to ride a bike. You should have seen her riding that bike of hers—it was pink with tassels on the handlebars, a great big wicker basket, and a bell. Lila was fearless. Unstoppable. She would ride up and down the driveway for hours, with me trailing on foot. Once in a while, she would get going a little too fast and veer dangerously to one side. And I would be there." He trailed off, swallowed, blinked several times. "I would be there just in case," he went on, his voice cracking, "she needed someone to break her fall."

This statement was met with a collective sigh from the assembled guests. The members of the wedding party exchanged dismissive looks. The only thing that bothered them more than sentimentality was cliché.

"We had some fun," he concluded. He deepened his gaze at Lila, his eyes wet as melted ice. "But you're not here to watch me get all choked up. You're here to celebrate an auspicious union. My daughter is marrying a man whom I have come to admire and respect."

This drew a second round of scathing looks from the wedding party.

"*Come* to?" Weesie whispered.

Tripler confirmed with pursed lips.

"In fact, I cannot imagine a better man for my daughter than Tom McDevon. And Augusta and I cannot imagine joining hands with a more wonderful family than the McDevons."

The wedding party raised a collective brow.

"So let's raise a glass to Lila and Tom. Here's to the many bike rides in your glorious future. And Tom, don't forget, I'm counting on you. You have the most important job. Now, it's your turn to catch Lila when she falls."

His conclusion was met with a swoon that was even louder and more saccharine than the first. The delight of the sentiment was paired with relief as the guests looked down to find that the salad course had arrived.

Volume swelled to a festive hum as the guests tore into their food. Once again, Augusta fought a surge of rage. Kathy McDevon had skimped on the menu. Flimsy iceberg lettuce drizzled with blue cheese chunks and thawing cherry tomatoes was well-known among club members as the yacht club's budget option. She shuddered as she imagined the corners that had been cut on the main course. With any luck, she could look forward to a brittle roast hidden by a dollop of stiff mashed potatoes and a dropping of wilted spinach.

Toasts continued at intervals of five minutes throughout the next course, distracting the guests from the dismal selection and the paltry servings. Throughout, the speakers followed an unwritten law that guided order of appearance. All obeyed the tacit understanding that speakers should proceed from most important to least, a convention that ensured that toasts grew more interesting as the night progressed. But before the guests could enjoy the benefit of this trend, an assortment of random family members took the stump, compiling a heartfelt, if repetitive collection of tearful odes. Each one extolled Lila's beauty and brilliance; each one lauded Tom's brilliance and beauty. Each one congratulated the couple on their unbearable good luck and the certainty of their eternal bliss. The phrases "perfect pair" and "meant for each other" were used so many times that even the most intoxicated speaker apologized for the redundancy. The adjectives "excellent" and "amazing" were used so frequently—sometimes twice within the same sentence—that even the least discerning listener began to yearn for variety.

A handful of female McDevons joined forces for a three-part tribute to Tom. Minnow delivered an earnest and moving paean to her sister, ending with a plea to her parents to convert Lila's bedroom into the clubhouse she'd been promised. Jake spoke eloquently about Tom's prowess on the soccer field; Pete spoke eloquently about Tom's prowess on the swim team; both extolled Tom's legendary status among Yale freshman girls. Tripler delivered a poem in the Homeric tradition, a narrative tale, in rhyming couplets, of Tom and Lila's epic courtship. Weesie began with a characteristically earnest anecdote and ended with an uncharacteristically bawdy vignette, mumbling something about a banana, Martha's Vineyard, and a boy who shall forever remain nameless before hastily sitting back down.

Throughout, Laura remained in her seat, waiting for the right moment. But as the crowd grew drunker and relatives grew more distant, the toasts grew increasingly candid. Finally, Laura acknowledged that she had lost her opportunity to follow a terrible toast and improve her own by comparison. She accepted the dire reality that it was permissible, maybe even imperative, for her to speak right away. Eyeing her friends for a boost of encouragement, she took a last gulp of wine and stood.

"Lila," said Laura. She surveyed the crowd in search of a comforting smile, but found instead only open mouths, wide, expectant eyes. Typically, this was the moment when words rushed in. Now, her mind was cruelly blank.

"Lila and I were assigned to each other the fall of freshman year," Laura managed. "We hated each other at first. But by the end of the year, we decided to room together again."

Surprised laughter resounded through the tent followed by awkward silence.

Laura blushed as she realized her unintentional joke, that these two statements would have been served by a transition explaining the phase in between hatred and adoration.

"By sophomore year, we were inseparable," she went on, "so much so that our friends came up with one name for us both: La-la. I was so proud of the association. I'm not sure Lila was as happy about it."

Laura paused. She had hoped and expected to be graced with her natural eloquence in the pinch, to convey confidence, detached admiration, and, inadvertently, her own intelligence. Instead, she had already succeeded at betraying her deep ambivalence for the bride and a more pathetic than endearing amount of self-doubt. She cast a desperate glance toward her table, seeking a friendly face. Weesie smiled and nodded encouragingly, like a parent at a stage-struck toddler. Laura smiled back and inhaled, bolstering herself to continue. But something in the periphery distracted her. Tom sat in his place next to Lila, staring at Laura with the strangest combination of sorrow, pity, and regret.

"We spent most of our time finding ways to avoid doing work. Somehow, Lila still managed to graduate summa. But this said more about her influence over her thesis advisor than the thesis itself. Like most boys at Yale, Lila's thesis advisor was under Lila's spell. We did, however, learn an awful lot about the Connecticut shoreline, which we studied intensively from the front seat of Lila's brand-new convertible."

A quick scan of the crowd confirmed Laura's deepest fear: The audience had turned the corner from boredom to concern. A swift conclusion was her only hope of retaining her dignity.

"Today, I watched Lila begin a new chapter in her life. She was walking alone in the field behind her house, swinging her arms like a little girl. She looked so happy." Laura paused, surveyed the room. Had she just betrayed all the bitterness she felt? "It was the most joyful thing I have ever seen. And I wish her all the joy in the world."

When she finally took her seat, she was overwhelmed by the surge of adrenaline that follows any public address. Fumbling for something to do with her hands, she removed a dirty napkin from the table and unfolded it on her lap. When she looked up, Lila stood above her, tears streaking her face.

"Sweetie," Lila gushed, "you're the first person who's made me cry all night." She beamed at Laura, an offer of sincere congratulations.

"Oh good," said Laura, standing awkwardly. Her napkin dropped to the grass.

"But I was waving at my dad," Lila said. "That's our secret wave." She paused. "When we're far away. On the grounds."

"Oh," said Laura. "Well, don't tell anyone."

"I won't," whispered Lila. "I won't."

The girls embraced and parted just in time for Lila to rustle back through the huddle of chairs and take her seat for the next speech.

Laura turned to Tripler for moral support once her pulse had resumed its normal rate. "Did it seem like I was overcome with emotion or on the verge of a nervous breakdown?"

"Maybe a little bit of both," Tripler whispered.

Laura was mercifully saved from further discussion by a clinking glass.

Chip stood next to his younger sister in the center of the tent. His eyes were wild, his intoxication clearly due to something more potent than alcohol.

"Let's face it, my sister is perfect," he began. "Everyone here knows this."

His statement was met with a small chorus of gasps and followed by the hush of attention.

"If you're a chick, you've spent your life fighting the urge to kill her in her sleep. If you're a guy, you've spent your life trying to sleep with her."

Gasps were replaced with guilty laughter and a sprinkle of hoots and cheers. The guests were now drunk enough to value humor over sentimentality.

"Admit it, Jake," Chip said, directing a defiant gaze toward the wedding party's table.

Weesie turned to her husband in shock, as though he, not Chip had been the one to utter the insult.

"Don't worry, Weesie," Chip concluded. "He never got any-where."

Surprise turned to anger as Weesie registered the public attack. Mortified, she attempted to inch her chair away from her husband.

"As far as Tom is concerned. He ain't so shabby himself. Lila's best friends can attest to that. Let's just say those were not tears of joy when they heard he and Lila had gotten engaged."

Laura, unlike Weesie, had forecast this kind of behavior from Chip. Still, it was a challenge to retain a look of detached amusement as heat rose from her neck to her cheeks.

"Tom," said Chip. "Congratulations. You've social-climbed your first Everest."

The guests gasped audibly.

Augusta sat, braced for an emergency removal. Every muscle in her face clenched with anticipatory panic. Lila glared hatefully at her brother. Tom grasped her elbow with a firm grip. Chip smiled proudly at the shocked guests, thriving on the tension.

"Mom, Dad, I know it's been hard to embrace the new in-laws. But don't worry, we only have to see them on Thanksgiving and Christmas." He lowered his voice to resemble a horror-movie de-mon. "Every year. For the rest of our lives."

A rebellious chirp of laughter emerged from the increasingly somber audience.

"Wait a second. Do Irish people celebrate Christmas or Chanukah?"

His quip was met with grave silence.

"Anyway, here's to a perfect couple. A perfect C cup-ple." He grinned and waited for his punch line to sink in.

Every guest looked to Lila, mouths agape.

"No? Nothing?" Chip asked. "I thought it was punny." He stood for a moment, scanning the crowd in utter bewilderment, like a valedictorian whose index cards have blown away in the breeze.

The guests looked back with unabashed shame. Chip had put them in the uncomfortable position of having to hide their amusement.

"In closing, let me just say one last thing: Tomorrow is going to be perfect."

He paused, riding the crest of his well-earned comic crescendo.

"If it's not, my mother's going to bust a nad."

Another pause, this time to laugh at his joke.

"That is, if they even make it to the altar." At this, he whipped his head around to face the wedding party, singling out Laura with his gaze.

She returned the gaze with her best impersonation of disinterest as Chip fell onto his chair.

A hacking cough and the clearing of throats punctuated the silence that followed the toast. The arrival of the dessert course offered welcome relief. It was not until the fourth, even fifth bite of chocolate cake that conversation resumed its previous volume.

FIVE

All in all, the wedding festivities had been very disappointing so far. The rehearsal dinner was mediocre at best. The food had been fair to poor. The toasts, with the exception of Chip's, were predictable. And whatever fun was to be gleaned from so much praise was canceled out by Chip's little outburst. As Lila poked at her slice of cake, watching the umpteenth relative enumerate her attributes, she couldn't help but suppress a yawn. There were only so many times a girl could be paid the exact same compliment.

Certainly, Chip had not done the evening any favors. After twenty-six years of destructive behavior, he had finally crossed the line from stupid to sociopathic. What aspect of his charmed childhood had caused him to snap? And more importantly, why had years of therapy failed to cure this bug? These and other similar questions consumed Lila for the duration of dessert. By the time coffee was served, she had absentmindedly eviscerated her cake.

She did all she could to rise to the occasion and join her guests' collective effort at denial. Somehow, they had managed to pretend Chip's speech had never happened. But the forced frivolity and excessive praise of the closing toasts felt gratuitous and defensive, overcompensations for Chip's attacks, and somehow seemed to dignify his outrageous claims. Furious, Lila tuned out the accolades and resigned herself to anger. She spent the final hour of the event composing a kiss-off to her brother. She relished the chance to deliver it the first moment she could corner him in private.

But even the comfort she took from this plan was soon replaced by a new irritation: The breeze rustling her cashmere shawl bore a distinct, undeniable dampness. She entertained an irrational thought: Chip had somehow planned for this—he had found a way to ensure rain on her wedding day. It was an absurd notion, to be sure, but at the moment, seemed entirely plausible. Rattled, Lila gave up on the pretense of contentment and waited for the first acceptable moment to leave. Finally, after a toast by a fifth cousin of Tom's—had he ever even mentioned this person?—she bolted from her seat and made her way out of the tent. She made only the necessary good-byes to those relatives who stood between her and the exit.

Just before leaving, she stopped by the table where her wedding party was seated to commiserate about Chip's toast—it was hilarious, they assured her; the perfect antidote to the grandparents, permission to get totally trashed. And indeed, every one of them seemed hopelessly drunk. Annoyed, she blew a collective kiss at the table and offered a brusque thanks for their tributes, then secured a promise from her bridesmaids that they would honor their commitment to meet in her bedroom at midnight. At the strike of twelve, the five friends would reunite for a sacred, if saccharine, rite of passage during which the bridesmaids would treat the bride to a last outpouring of tears and nostalgia before tucking her into bed. The overwrought dramatization of the "end of innocence" was one in a series of nuptial rituals Lila intended to observe even if it was quickly becoming clear that each was more overrated than the next.

With new resolve, she uttered a hasty thanks to Tom's parents for the party. She made a public show of kissing Tom good night and reluctantly tearing herself away. Then, she hurried away from the yacht club, gaining speed as she cut across the seventh tee. As she walked, she hopped to remove her shoes. She dangled them between two fingers in one hand in a manner that conveyed lightheartedness—the opposite of what she was actually feeling. Thankfully, distance from the tent restored her spirit slightly. The cool, wet grass was comforting, as was the fading sound of laughter.

Weeks ago, Lila had decided to heed the old-fashioned superstition that required a bride and groom to spend the night before their wedding in different beds. It just seemed wise to honor those customs designed to instill good luck, particularly in light of her abundance. Oddly, she was not entirely daunted by the prospect of a night away from Tom. After the emotional drain of the rehearsal dinner, she was all too happy to be alone. She needed to process the experience by spending at least an hour in complete silence.

How could she have known how tiring it would be to be the object of so much attention? She had spent every day since the age of two owning the spotlight of every room she occupied, so the idea of consolidating the focus of so many people simply seemed efficient. To her surprise, it had been tiresome, uncomfortable even, to be stared at and talked to by so many people. She finally understood why celebrities complained about being recognized and signing autographs. It was exhausting to sustain a smile for that long; it was difficult to assume a look of curious intrigue during dull conversations. It took a certain talent to appear interested in a fool.

In fact, by the end of the night, she had begun to feel strangely toward her guests. And she could imagine that celebrities felt the same way about regular people. There was something tragic about her guests' ignorance of their redundancy. Wouldn't they cringe, Lila wondered, if they knew how many before them had complimented the fit of her dress? Wouldn't they bristle to learn how many people had gushed about the color of her eyes? Wouldn't they die to find out that they all conveyed the same desperate anxiety, that their nervous obsequiousness was as distinct and repellent as the spray of a skunk?

Their repetition couldn't help but ignite a measure of her disdain. And disdain, on a night designed for delight, was a tremendous burden. The eve of her wedding should not be cluttered with an emotion as ugly as pity. It should be spared from all pettiness, secured exclusively for lovely sentiments. To this end, Lila decided on a strict schedule for the rest of the night. Upon her return to Northern Gardens, she would do the following: edit the choice of clothes she had packed for her honeymoon, decide on the departure dress between the two she was debating—an audacious red shift and a classic honeymoon suit in a demure shade of blue. She would take a hot bath, soak until she was fully renewed, and, afterward, apply every potion in her cabinet to faded and future blemishes. This would leave just enough time to receive her friends at midnight. If all else failed, they would succeed in restoring her good mood.

Lila's room provided a measure of soothing, if superficial, relief.

Despite her gripes with her mother, there was no denying the house had benefited from Augusta's impeccable taste. Lila's room had been redone during the most recent redecoration, a triennial occurrence as reliable as the return of gypsy moths. The makeover was characterized by Augusta's usual staples: Clarence House chintz, Rosecore carpets, Brunschwig and Fils wallpaper. But it diverged delightfully from earlier interpretations of the perfect seaside mansion, incorporating a color palette that could only be described as Archipelago Chic.

The combination of the two styles—Classic Wasp and Indonesian—was surprisingly agreeable, reinvigorating the ancient summerhouse aesthetic with the feel of a thatched-roof hut. A citrus yellow pillow infused a white linen eyelet duvet with a welcome shot of color; a brown throw made an otherwise dainty pink floral chintz sofa seem suddenly sumptuous; a woven straw wallpaper provided a seamless segue from an indoor dressing room to an outdoor terrace; a sisal rug provided a welcome antidote to the formal carpeting downstairs, while batik pillows dotting the bed and settee gave the room an inviting whimsy. Every corner of the room offered a new and more pleasing vignette. It was no surprise that the house had been photographed by *House and Garden* three times.

But even this pastoral refuge failed to revive Lila's mood. She was plagued with a vague inexplicable feeling as she settled into the room. It was the same feeling that she had when she left the house at the end of August every summer, that nine months of dreariness stood before her next breath of bright sunny air. Discouraged, she took a seat at her vanity and hastily unzipped her dress. She eyed herself in the mirror as though challenging her mind to reveal the source of her discontentment. It was always this way, she decided, with something you've awaited too eagerly. It was simply impossible for the world to live up to one's expectations. She had spent her life trying to challenge this notion—to match expectation and experience—but this was no small feat given the standards set by such a lovely childhood.

She had intended, for example, to look a certain way on her wedding day. Her dress fit her best when she was 120 pounds. It clung to her hips just enough, her collarbones protruded the ideal amount, and best of all, her bust at that weight was a perfect 32-C. Here, she had pulled off a clear victory. When she weighed herself earlier this morning, she was 117 pounds, three pounds less than she had weighed the summer after senior year. But herein lay the problem: Unfortunately, she could not control the rest of the world as precisely as she could her weight. Tonight was proof, if anything was, that the world will always—it can only—disappoint.

Lila's mood improved slightly as she studied her reflection in the mirror. There was no denying this was the right weight for her. Her collarbone formed a dramatic line just underneath her neck, as though to underline the incredible beauty of her face. Her waist had never been smaller; her stomach had never been more taut. But she had not gone too far and become annoyingly skinny. Her legs, as always, descended from her hips like pulled taffy, decreasing their circumference at a constant gradation down to her ankles. Her hair was the same honeyed blond it had been when she was two years old. But she had recently made the jump from elegant to sexy with a cut inspired by Brigitte Bardot. It almost made her wish she'd experimented with bangs sooner. All in all, Lila had never looked better. So why did she feel so gloomy?

When she got engaged, she had made a vow never to become one of those brides. And she was proud to say she had kept her promise. She had not bored her friends with endless discussion of her dress. On the contrary, she had been astonishingly blasé about the whole endeavor, selecting her dress from the very first batch she tried on. She had not asked her bridesmaids to suffer through an inordinate number of parties. There had only been two bridal showers, one of which Letty Bayer had insisted on throwing for Augusta's friends and the older relatives, and one bachelorette party which, in all candor, was not terribly well planned. Furthermore, Lila had been very understanding about the slipshod party—the lack of reservations, the nonexistent schedule, the misguided episode with the stripper—never once scolding the maid of honor, whose duty it was to plan these things.

She had not asked her bridesmaids to wear something that compromised their dignity. Rather, she had gone out of her way to choose something that satisfied everyone in the group. She had been admirably tolerant when Tripler demanded that they switch from a strapless to an off-the-shoulder style, and very sympathetic to Annie's request to change to a color that was more flattering to her skin tone. She had decided on "sterling silver" only after everyone had weighed in with her personal preference, an exercise that had every single bridesmaid demanding a different color of the rainbow. Even silver had been a selfless choice; it promised to accentuate the many blue eyes in the group, pick up the metallic glint of the ocean, and was the most forgiving, second to black, to the girls' varying physiques.

Lila held her tongue when Weesie insisted on ordering her dress a size too small, a strategy that she claimed would motivate her to lose weight in time for the wedding. Though Lila had bristled at the notion, she did not oppose her at the atelier nor call and arrange for the larger size to be ordered behind her back. As a result, she had suffered terrifying nightmares until this past Thursday night, envisioning a hideous bridal procession in which bridesmaids waddled down the aisle like overstuffed sausages.

But of all her generous acts as a bride, Lila felt her greatest was her treatment of Laura. From the moment she got engaged, she had been highly sensitive to Laura's prickly spots. She had delayed telling Laura about the engagement as long as humanly possible and, when she did, downplayed her excitement an enormous amount. She might as well have been saying she had finally found the perfect winter scarf—she was that nonchalant. She had made a special effort not to bother her with any of the frivolous girly stuff. She was unbelievably forgiving when Laura flubbed the bachelorette party. And even after Lila found out how little Laura contributed to the planning of the bridal shower—Weesie and Tripler did the invitations, for God's sake, and they were just regular bridesmaids—still, she said nothing. In her humble estimation, she had been more selfless than a saint.

Incredibly, Laura's behavior had worsened in the last twelve hours. She had arrived a day late, making absolutely no apology for her tardiness. The comment about the bridesmaids' dress was passive-aggressive to say the least. Was it Lila's job to attend to the needs of her bridesmaids? No, it was their job to attend to hers. And her toast, though sweet, had been unmistakably downhearted. She had seemed downright unhinged by the end. It was not like Laura, valedictorian of her high-school class, to fold in front of a crowd. No, Lila decided, she had spent too long denying the truth about her friend, shielding herself from the thing that had roiled their ten-year relationship. Even when she told Laura the news of her engagement, it was obvious she was perplexed. The tone of her voice was forced—congratulatory, but not truly happy. Her jealousy, though hardly a new thing, had finally gotten out of hand.

It would be one thing if Laura were just a measly bridesmaid, the title Lila forked out to everyone in the rooming group. But the "maid of honor" title was the venerable post given to one's best friend, and it was given not only to acknowledge the friendship but to ensure a certain amount of work. It was one thing for her to fall short during the preliminary phase, but to be so distracted the day before her wedding was horribly insulting. For a maid of honor to be so remiss was truly unacceptable.

Now that she focused on the subject, Lila wondered if she had appointed Laura her maid of honor expressly for this reason, to provide Laura with a means of participating in Lila's happiness, to draw Laura's attention away from her own bad luck. Certainly, she could sympathize with the fact that Laura was put off by weddings. Her lack of marital prospects and her own parents' troubled marriage justified an aversion to the institution. But still, she felt, had the roles been reversed, she would have put on a good face. She would have set aside her needs for the sake of the bride. It was just good manners.

And so it was this, Lila realized, that was riling her tonight. She took some comfort in this realization—at least the bad mood did not reflect some horrible defect in her. But there was another yet more insidious component to Laura's jealousy. Any friendship between two women might suffer when one of the two graduated to a new phase, especially if the other trailed so far behind. This specific situation somehow exceeded the limits of healthy rivalry. It was not simply that Laura resented Lila for getting married first, but rather—why not be completely honest—that she resented her for marrying Tom.

That Laura still harbored feelings for Tom was not a revelation. To be fair, she had dated him long enough to justify a proprietary attitude, at least in the beginning. Laura and Tom shared a portion of their youth and a bank of memories, and they referred to them with the same easy familiarity with which you might quote a movie you've seen too many times. Lila had never been threatened by this—not when she first started dating Tom, nor as their romance progressed. In some strange way, it was comforting to know that Laura seconded her opinion. Subconsciously, competition made him more precious.

Not that her love for Tom needed any augmenting. Tom was, of course, unanimously considered to be a superlative catch. But truth be told, their rapport was not the most effortless she had ever enjoyed with a man. Occasionally, she wondered if all couples struggled so much to understand one another, spoke so little at dinner together, spent so much time camped out in front of the TV. Did all women sometimes feel distanced from their man while they were making love? Just last week, she had looked up at Tom while they were having sex and forgotten, for a split second—it was the strangest thing—who in God's name he was.

But this was surely a common symptom of wedding preparation, a casualty of the heightened stakes built up around one single day. What relationship wouldn't buckle slightly under the pressure? What couple would not be strained by so many inconsequential disputes? Over the past several months, she herself had reached her breaking point at least seventeen times. It seemed fair to multiply that number by ten to approximate Tom's annoyance.

For the most part, he had been a very good sport. He had indulged her "suggestions" about the engagement ring, procuring a substantial stone, if not the one she had in mind. He had pacified Augusta at her planning sessions, supplying the right mixture of submission and scorn. He had behaved affably at the parties, attended his fittings without too much grumbling—had helped just enough to seem interested but not so much as to seem effete. In short, he had showered her with all the love and attention befitting a princess, displaying a tasteful amount of affection when they were in public and ravishing her when they were alone. Yes, if there was one thing in which to take solace, it was that Tom had been a good boy.

Then why was she suddenly gripped with doubt about the merits of their union? She cursed her moronic brother for putting these thoughts in her head. Still, as she sat, staring at herself in her grandmother's white lacquer vanity, she couldn't help but obsess over the very themes Chip had touched upon. Was it possible there was some fatal flaw in their matching, that they were ultimately, impossibly different—dissimilar enough to fall in love, but too fundamentally distinct to stay together?

She had heard it said once by an aging aunt at a Christmas party when she was a child that marriages cannot work unless both members are from the same class. Instinctively, she had bristled at this notion. Even by the age of five, she understood the small-mindedness of certain relatives. Still, Aunt Caroline's comment took root in her mind. She remembered her parents' conversation in the car on the way home from the party. Aunt Caroline was rude and provincial, they had hissed, an embarrassment to the family. But they never said Aunt Caroline was wrong.

Now Lila dared to consider the validity of Aunt Caroline's thesis. Certainly, things had changed since Grandmother Westfield's time. Even Gussie described a time when Hayeses, Bayers, McCarthys, and Kennedys played doubles together at the club. No Rosensweigs or Rosenfelds were present. But perhaps one day, even they might be inducted, or at the very least, invited as guests. Whether Gussie realized that the road to that club was paved for the McCarthys and

Kennedys by a president by the same name was of little consequence anymore. Just as Bouviers had married Kennedys, Hayeses would marry McDevons. Much to Aunt Caroline's confusion, all these families were indistinguishable now. They had blended and mixed as compatibly as horses and donkeys. Only people like Gussie and Lila could tell which ones were mules.

In some way, Lila relished the opportunity to botch the bloodline, to exercise the power bequeathed to her by Darwin. It would be unfair to call her a snob. She was not a reactionary either. She was simply happy to view the world from the enviable position of membership. She welcomed her friends as guests to her club, so long as they remembered who was the member.

The subtleties of her choice of husband were not lost on her. Marrying Tom was a safe rebellion, much like smoking from the window of her childhood bedroom or sneaking out of that same window to meet Charlie Bayer at the dock. She could not count the times she had sat on that ledge, her feet dangling dangerously as though she might propel herself onto the lawn at any moment. Reforming from within was Lila's preferred mode, a strategy that allowed her to change the rules of the club while retaining membership. Even she could not deny the intricacy of her maneuver: She was marrying a McDevon who passed for a Hayes, a trick of camouflage that allowed her simultaneously to fulfill and flout everything she held dear.

Inspired, she moved from her seat at the mirror and crossed the room with purpose, determined to indulge in this favorite childhood pastime. She walked to the window at the side of her room closest to the ocean, parted the rosebud curtains, and pushed it open as far as it would go—not quite to the top—fighting the rigidity of fresh paint and infrequent use. Refreshed by the air, she removed the screen and placed it on the floor. Then she lifted one leg to the sash, drew the other through the open window, and shimmied head and torso under so that all but 5 percent of her body was in open air. In the ten years since her last perch, her body had not changed, but her stomach had, making the distance to the ground seem suddenly like a much greater drop. Still, she felt slightly calmer, even without the aid of cigarettes. She stared out at the black bay and focused on the sound of waves. Their arrival was louder and more frequent than usual, clear evidence of an approaching storm.

As she sat, she continued an honest assessment of her relationship with Tom. The crux of the problem was this: He was at once everything and nothing she needed. Seen from afar, they were picturesque, a symphony of superior genes, a study in storybook promise. But when they were alone together, they were curiously ill suited, sometimes mortifyingly lacking in secrets to share and things to talk about. But common wisdom condoned this, did it not? Was this not the basis of a great partnership: opposition, difference of opinion. Pairing up with someone as practical as she would be terribly boring, just as coupling Tom with another dreamer would result in incompetence; that pair would never make it out of the house. Both combinations would amount to deadening and impractical redundancy. But what if it was equally dangerous to pair up two people who were so different? Were they not signing up for a lifetime of silent dinners or, worse, after-dinner spats?

No, she had settled this debate long ago. Their differences were essential to their attraction. And when these differences created repulsion, there were solutions for that as well. In some way, this was the reason that Lila tolerated Tom's friendship with Laura. It was like a daily cigarette for a former smoker; just enough to ensure the addict did not regress to several packs a day. Laura quelled Tom's thirst for drama and dysfunction, the part that his Irish heritage made him crave, the part his upbringing made familiar. Conversely, Lila was perfectly happy to discuss literature in bed, but she had absolutely no interest in re-creating its drama in her life. The compulsion to live out this chaos, she felt, was a weakness of the lower classes. And it was a weakness that Tom and Laura shared.

And so she adopted a permissive policy toward the friendship, allowing it to thrive so long as it never grew out of hand. She monitored it sporadically like a mother does a child in a fenced yard, comforted by her knowledge of the fence and yet still suspicious of its height. She resisted the urge to break into Tom's e-mail account, refrained from checking the phone bill too closely. Instead, she looked to other more meaningful markers of Tom's devotion. She paid close attention to the tone in his voice when he greeted her at the end of the day. She counted the number of times he said "I love you" or told her she was beautiful. She measured his energy in bed, his eagerness to please her family. And throughout, she took comfort in her understanding of Tom's psyche; Tom wanted beauty more than he wanted art in his life. This knowledge made it easy for Lila to tolerate his vagaries. There was no use concerning herself with the minutiae of battles. At the end of the day, she would win the war.

But tonight she had witnessed something that caused her to doubt this assertion. To see Tom and Laura in her milieu was to recognize a sacred bond they shared—something she had overlooked until this very moment. They were both outsiders, torn between two equally strong forces: desperation to be included and disdain for the institution. She had been naïve to think their only tie was a decade-old crush. They were glued by something far more intrinsic to their personalities. Both were terrified of spending their lives just beyond the trimmed hedges of the club, trapped in the shadows of their contempt and aspiration. And both were equally panicked by the prospect of being trapped within.

Now, as she sat, perched on the ledge of her bedroom window, she felt dangerously unstable. She was overwhelmed by vertigo and it threatened to pull her to the ground—or was it a reckless urge to leap to the grass and sprint toward the ocean? Alarmed by both alternatives, she shimmied back through the window and retreated to the safety of her bedroom, anxious for her friends to arrive and spare her from this silly mood.

After some debate, the wedding party decided to migrate to the Hayeses' dock. Despite the interminable toasts, it was early yet, and they were eager to begin more concerted celebration. There had been some talk of ghost-hunting in Augusta's attic, but this motion was quickly defeated by a vocal majority who felt the need to purge themselves after the rehearsal dinner.

Before leaving the yacht club, Pete and Jake stopped at the bar to replenish their resources. Jake distracted the bartender while Pete raided his cache, stuffing bottles into sleeves and pockets until he looked like an inflatable toy. They emerged with an impressive stash of smuggled wine and tequila, enough for every pair to split its own bottle and for the singletons to enjoy one to themselves. This meant Laura, Chip, and Tom were allotted twice as much as everyone else. Bottles were opened even before the group emerged from the parking lot. As a result, they were unanimously drunk as they made their way down to the water.

With the exception of Lila, the whole group was in attendance:

Tripler, Pete, Weesie, Jake, Annie, Oscar, Tom, and Laura. Chip, too, tagged along, at his own invitation. He had sobered up slightly since dinner and brought up the rear, singing a loud, out-of-key rendition of "It's My Party." It was now widely accepted among the group that the wedding would be cursed with rain. The air was fraught with the strange electrical current of an imminent storm.

In Lila's absence, the group's volume increased several notches. They relaxed just knowing she was not around. Now, as they hurried down the endless lawn of the Hayeses' estate—some walking, some running—the wedding party was finally swept up in the careless joy of the occasion and the thrill of being together without any obligations. The freedom of this moment, however ephemeral, was intoxicating in itself.

"You still want to go skinny-dipping, Weez?" Tripler demanded. She ran ahead of the group, making wide zigzags on the lawn.

"Absolutely not," said Weesie. "Unless it's a group movement."

Chip sprinted to catch up with the two girls and contribute his thoughts on the matter. "I'm game," he shouted. "And so is Tom. I guarantee he wants one more glimpse of ass before his wedding day."

"I think he got his fill at his bachelor party," Pete said.

"Oh please," shouted Tom. "The last time I saw you that night, you were surrounded by naked women."

"Pete," snapped Tripler. "You filthy pig." She stopped running and turned to Tom. "Tell me right this second. Do I need to divorce my husband?"

"Sadly, no," Tom replied. "The strippers wouldn't have him."

"You bastard," Pete said. He interrupted himself to take a running start. But four years on the Yale lacrosse team meant very little after ten years.

Hearing the footsteps, Tom anticipated Pete's approach and sprinted ahead, putting several feet between him and the group. Pete persevered, keeping his pace while Tom circled back toward the house. By the time they were halfway up the lawn again, both were out of breath and had forgotten the reason for the chase. Pete ran, squealing, into Tripler's arms as Tom fell behind the group. It was only now, as Tom came to a stop, and stood gasping in the middle of the lawn, that he and Laura finally stood near enough that it seemed foolish not to speak. Not to speak would have infused the moment with more meaning than it deserved.

"I liked your speech," Tom said. It had been over a year since they had spoken, but he addressed her with incongruous ease, as though continuing a conversation they had begun before the rehearsal dinner.

"Thanks," said Laura. The sound of his voice was an overwhelming relief, like remembering the name of a beloved song or returning to a childhood haunt to find it totally unchanged. Did he not feel the same swell of relief? Or was he just better at hiding it?

"It was excellent and amazing," he said.

Laura paused before realizing he was quoting the banal epithets from the speeches that night.

They walked in silence for a moment, Tom trying to catch his breath, Laura trying to remember the anger she had felt in his absence. Instead, she felt a palpable fluttering in her throat. Two things seemed equally plausible—that she would vomit on the grass or spontaneously take flight.

"I'm sorry," he said finally.

"It's fine," she said. "I understand." And she did in that moment. But a moment passed, and with it, the sentiment of forgiveness. She rushed to say something that sounded more indifferent. "It was actually good," she managed.

"It was necessary," he agreed.

But the comment rang false, striking Laura as inappropriately formal, patronizing. She fought the urge, that specifically female one to declare the number of men that she had slept with since they'd last spoken.

"It was easier than I expected," she tried.

"It was harder than I thought it would be," he said.

Again, she paused, registering the subtle, embedded insult. Finally, she lashed out, inadvertently combining her reprimand and her confession. "I still don't believe it," she said.

But Tom refused the chance to console, to repent. "I don't either," he could have said. "It's not over. I'm not hers until tomorrow." But instead, he looked away guiltily, and said, "I'm so sorry."

"You should be," she said. She had botched her chance—she was back on the defensive. But it was comforting, at least, to be honest, even if it was a concession. Both options were trite—understatement and indignation—but at least one was true.

They walked several paces in silence, listening to the grass crushing under their feet. As they did, Laura grew increasingly convinced this was the last time they would ever speak.

"Have you missed me?" he asked.

This threw her off guard. It was, of course, a trick question. When a man says something like this to woman, there is only one correct answer.

"Of course," she answered. And only then, it occurred to her that he hadn't said "I missed you."

Then he switched subjects inexplicably. "I don't think I can do it."

The implication of the switch was not lost on Laura. "It" could mean "marrying Lila," in which case he had used the verb tense correctly. Or "it" could mean "being away from her when he married

Lila," in which case it stood to reason that he was considering the consequences of not going through with his wedding tomorrow.

But rather than question what he had meant, or worse, get the wrong answer, Laura nodded and kept up her pace, reaching her friends just as they approached the dock. She attached herself to Tripler, resolving not to be found alone again. It was just too dangerous.

The Hayeses' private beach extended the full length of their property. But the coast of Maine and its surrounding islands nearly canceled out the luxury of this fact. With the exception of a few sandy anomalies, the Maine shoreline was rocky and harsh, country designed for those who appreciated the beauty of the ocean, as opposed to those who actually wanted to swim in it. In practice, the water was at its most swimmable during this last week in August. But the chill in the air at the moment made swimming seem like a masochistic act.

Still, the friends proceeded toward the water with cheerful obliviousness, tripping down the lawn and racing to be the first to reach the water. A small gangplank extended into the cove from the rocks that lined the Hayeses' lawn. The gangplank led to a wooden dock and a floating wooden raft that was moored to the dock with rope.

"Let's all get on and unmoor it," Tripler said.

"Don't be an idiot, Trip," said Pete. "That thing was built in 1954. We'll sink it in ten seconds."

"Ooh, that would be scary," Tripler said, assuming a mock-terrified voice. "How would we ever survive drowning in a bay that's four feet deep?"

"Let me settle the debate," Chip interrupted. "That thing is moored to the dock. And it has been since I was three. But for real excitement, why not consider Weesie's plan? Let's get naked and go crabbing!"

Chip's joke was met with a chorus of disappointed revulsion.

"Hey, Chip," said Jake. "Who invited you?"

"Jake," snapped Weesie. "Don't be an asshole."

"Listen to your wife," Chip agreed, "or I might have to enlist the famous Hayes ghost against you."

The group reprised their moan of exasperation, but after years as the group's favorite punching bag, Chip had come to interpret this sentiment as grudging acceptance.

Moments later, the fledgling plan turned into a motion. Before the subject could be discussed any further, the entire group lined up on the rocks and filed down the corroding gangplank, laughing and shrieking. They clutched one another to keep their balance as they teetered down the rickety pier. At the bottom they removed dress shoes and heels and left them in a messy clump. One by one, they leapt over the foot of water that separated them from the raft and arranged themselves at equal intervals around the perimeter. Once situated, they looked like a band of stowaways, waiting for a rescue mission.

"Let's play a drinking game," someone called out.

"Drinking games are for people who are trying to get drunk. We're already shit-faced," said Pete.

"Let's play 'two truths and a lie,'" said Jake. "That always yields some interesting confessions."

"What could anyone possibly confess," said Oscar, "that we don't know about each other already?"

"I never understood that game," said Weesie.

"Of course you do," said Jake. "The idea is to bury an embarrassing confession in a series of implausible statements. The more implausible the lie, the more invisible the confession."

"Here," said Chip. "I'll go first."

A chorus of no's emerged from the group.

"No, thank you," said Tripler. "We love you, Chip, but we don't want to hear about the time you date-raped Sarah Bennett."

Laughter and jeers sufficed to censor Chip for a moment.

"I've got one," said Tom.

The group cheered, then quieted to focus. A confession from Tom was perhaps the only thing that could capture their attention.

"This should be interesting," said Jake.

"I want to hear this," said Pete.

Tom smiled and paused, relishing his control over the group. Laura couldn't be sure, but she thought he glanced at her as though to gain her approval.

"I hated the food at the rehearsal dinner tonight," he declared.

"I'll drink to that," said Jake.

"I can't stand you phony motherfuckers," Tom went on.

"Truth number two," Pete shouted.

Tom bowed chivalrously. "And I'm still fifty-fifty on this whole wedding thing. I may or may not show up tomorrow. I haven't decided."

Silence again as the group struggled to decode Tom's tone.

Laura fixed her eyes on him. This was a ploy for attention, nothing more. But she sensed, in this performance, something else: a cry for help?

"Obviously, the lie is the second one," Tripler said. "Since we're his only friends in the world."

Tom arched his eyebrow and smiled mysteriously.

Laura fixed her gaze on Tom as the group veered off on a new tangent.

"That would be funny," Jake said. "Can you imagine Augusta's reaction? If you didn't like the roast, how would you like your head on a platter?"

Volume reached a new level as the group traded theories on Augusta's response to such a glitch.

"You think she'd be pissed about rain," Tripler quipped.

"I wonder how she would do it," said Jake. "Smother him in his sleep or just a simple knife to the neck."

"Neither," Tripler decided. "She'd run him down with the Volvo."

"Nah," said Chip, joining in. "She wouldn't want to hurt the fender."

The debate over Augusta's preferred method of execution raged for several minutes until someone tired of the subject and started singing very loud and off-key.

The next several minutes were devoted to recalling every word of "Smells Like Teen Spirit." They were stalwart in their effort to piece together the lyrics but failed miserably. They settled for a deafening repetition of the chorus, as though they were trying to summon its doomed singer from the grave.

"Here we are now. Entertain us. I feel stupid and contagious."

After they'd exhausted their vocal cords and drained several bottles, they reverted to a spirited postmortem of the evening's toasts. It was unanimously agreed that Chip's was both the best and worst of the night, that Laura's was subpar for her but still better than Tripler's, and that every member of the McDevon family, even the twelve-year-old cousin, had been embarrassingly drunk. The subject of skinny-dipping was introduced several more times. Each time there were more takers, but never quite enough to overrule the opposition.

For hours or minutes—it was too hard to tell as alcohol loosened her grasp on time—Laura did her best to ignore Tom's presence. But every part of her conscious mind was focused on the incredible nearness of him—the shape of his legs pressed against the wooden planks, the grip of his hands on the wood, a sliver of neck that widened or lessened depending on the tilt of the raft.

For hours or minutes—no one knew at this point—the group caroused, laughed, and sang, oblivious to the worsening weather. The occasional shocks of cold, and the brown clouds gathering overhead only added to the night's excitement, lending everything an aura of menace.

Abundant alcohol consumption dulled their typically acute awareness. As a result, there was only a pang of terror when they realized they had come unmoored.

"Wait a second," said Weesie. "Weren't those lights closer a minute ago?"

The group followed her gaze to the house and found that she was right—its scatter of lights had drifted significantly since they'd boarded the raft. Group consensus was followed by the unmistakable silence of dread.

"Chip, you little fuck," said Tom.

"Dude. It wasn't me," said Chip.

But whether or not Chip had untied the rope was forgotten in the moments that followed.

They had more pressing things to consider: the strength of the tide, the temperature of the water, the roughness of the waves, the possibility of whales, sharks, jellyfish, the presence of a coast guard or a lighthouse, the ending of a movie they had watched together, and of course, the deadening weight of water as it smothers your lungs. But soon enough, all these thoughts rushed out and everyone was laughing again, cheerfully following the directions of the more sober people in the group. Within thirty seconds, they had devised a plan, counted heads, assigned partners, and started swimming toward shore. It was not until they surfaced, two by two, on the windy lawn, that anyone dared to make a joke.

"It's the curse of the Ghost of Northern Gardens," Pete said in a poltergeist voice.

And everyone laughed until a final headcount revealed they were short by one.

SIX

The first phase of the search for Tom proceeded with incongruously good cheer as though it were a whimsical party game the hosts had dreamed up for the guests' entertainment. The group tackled the problem with the same chipper aplomb that they had the temperature of the water or the equitable distribution of liquor.

The possibility that Tom had drowned was never voiced out loud. It was simply pushed to the side of the conversation. The group's major source of comfort—or denial—was Tom's exceptional swimming record. It was inconceivable that such a trivial swim could have overwhelmed such a competent athlete. Not only was Tom a championship swimmer—he had boasted, at a time, one of the best butterflies in the Ivy League. And before college, he had whiled away many a summer on the lifeguard chair, honing his survival skills with water and women alike.

For these reasons alone, the group felt nonchalance was merited, admirable even, and, conversely, that concern was foolish and alarmist. It was, of course, a convenient deduction. They were currently in a realm in which anxiety of any kind was considered tacky and they abided by this rule like tourists attempting to fit into a foreign culture. No, tragedy was far too maudlin and improbable for such a charmed bunch. It was more likely that Augusta's ghosts had risen from the attic, put off by the ruckus of the wedding guests, than that Tom had drowned in the bay on a swim of a few hundred feet. It was much more in keeping with Tom, the group decided, that he had swum at race pace to beat them to the shore, had hoisted himself to the rocky ledge, sprinted across the lawn mischievously, and now sat, showered and dressed, calmly awaiting their return, eager to lord his superior athletic prowess over them.

Unfortunately, certain niggling facts competed with this comforting conclusion. First and, perhaps, most disturbingly, Tom had been visibly drunk. Even before the last bottle of wine—one he consumed by himself—his speech had been halting and slurred, his behavior outside the norm. It was clearly intoxication that spurred his scandalous and absurd claim that he had yet to decide whether or not to attend his own wedding. Second, there was, of course, said bizarre claim, which, in light of his disappearance, now seemed like a veiled threat. But the idea that Tom would stage a disappearance or, worse, take his own life so as to avoid his wedding was simply too far-fetched and melodramatic to consider in earnest.

Third, the approaching storm was impossible to ignore. The water was undeniably rough or, at least, rougher than usual. The time it took the group to swim back to the shore was arguably doubled by the undertow. Everyone had felt it—a constant tug against their strokes. Fourth, it was somewhat unlikely that Tom had surpassed Pete by such a great distance. Pete swam second to Tom every one of their four years on the Yale team, and for every one of those four years, Pete had finished precisely one-half second behind Tom in the butterfly, a quarter second in the crawl. As far as they knew, Pete was the first to emerge from the water, but he had not seen so much as a shadow on the dark lawn. Given their historically similar pace, the apparent distance between them was odd. Fifth, and perhaps most alarming of all: Tom himself was the one who suggested the buddy system to ensure the group's safe and simultaneous return. Why would the principal organizer diverge so sharply from the plan?

But as the group assembled on the lawn, they did their best to push these and other disquieting facts from their minds. Instead, they indulged in the cheerful certainty that they were the unlucky and gullible victims of a practical joke, a last puerile prank from Tom before tomorrow's ceremony closed the door on boyhood. The longer it took to find him, they decided, the heartier Tom would laugh at their expense. They must divide and conquer, scour the property, and locate him before he gained further ground for taunting. Excited by the challenge, they cheerfully wrung out their wet clothes. They attempted a fair distribution of the assorted shawls and jackets they had left on the dock. They suppressed a charge of excitement as they abandoned dress shoes and high heels where they had ditched them on the dock, and prayed for the temperature to return to that of a typical August evening.

A list of directives was agreed upon without too much dissent. They would break into pairs, and each would canvass a separate area of the grounds. One pair would search the Gettys', braced for Tom's leap from a mothballed closet. Another pair would search the Hayses' house in case Tom had beelined for Lila's room. A third pair would circle the lawn, attuned to movement at every tree and, after exhausting the area, venture toward the town harbor on the off chance that Tom had wandered down for a solitary drink at a lobsterman's bar. The last pair would camp out on the shore in the event that Tom had overshot the house and now meandered leisurely back, oblivious to the stir he had caused. Everyone would reconvene on the Gettys' porch at ten of midnight to share their findings and, in all likelihood, resume drinking with Tom in tow.

This would give the girls ample time to cross the lawn to the Hayeses' house and keep their commitment to tuck Lila into bed at midnight. For the time being, they would not alert Lila or anyone in the Hayes family; by the time everyone had been informed, Tom would already be found. Why worry them unnecessarily?

"You people watch too much TV," Tom would tease as soon as they reunited.

And they would quickly surround him, smother him with a group hug, and recount the fears they had secretly harbored since they had seen him last.

Instinctively, the group paired off into the predictable permutations. Tripler, Weesie, and Annie inched toward their respective partners until they stood in a trio of couples, making Laura and Chip a couple by default.

"Oh, come on," Laura said, once she'd realized the consequence of the arrangement. "You people spend plenty of time together. Chip and I need some time apart."

Chip responded with an elaborate pantomime of brokenheartedness in which he received an arrow to the heart and fell to the ground in a wounded heap.

"Poor Chip," Tripler cooed. "Laura's so mean to him."

Laura flashed Tripler an angry look. It was Tripler's compulsion to take the opposing side in every dispute. "Why don't *you* take him," she quipped.

"You know what, Laura's right," said Weesie. Just as Tripler sought to amplify tension, Weesie sought to dissipate it. "Let's mix things up. Girl, boy, girl, boy. Like a dinner party."

"You mean a key party," said Jake.

The group considered this notion halfheartedly before rejecting it out of hand.

But Tripler, sensing an opportunity for drama, jumped uncharacteristically to Weesie's defense. She was drawn to confrontation with the same force by which most people were repelled by it. "Pete and I are sick of each other anyway. Weesie," she barked, "I want Jake."

Now Weesie froze as she sought a plausible excuse.

Laura offered a commiserative sigh. It was classic Tripler to turn Weesie's kindness against her.

The group's collective romantic history was ingrained in everyone's mind; they could complete the permutations of the various interrelationships as easily as their basic multiplication tables. Laura and Tom had dated, of course, prior to Lila and Tom. Pete flirted with every female member of the group, and those he didn't flirt with, he had slept with already. Tripler and Jake had a brief fling before Weesie and Jake started going out. But far more troubling than this brief stint was Tripler's incurable flirtatiousness, a trait whose intensity seemed to increase as she got older. Worse still, it was obvious that Tripler and Pete's marriage had hit a rough spot. If this wasn't clear from their acid exchanges, it was proven by a little-known fact: Six months ago, Tripler had asked Annie for the name of a good couples counselor.

Still, Weesie did her best to set aside her suspicion. It only degraded her own marriage to acknowledge that Tripler posed any threat.

"Fine by me," Weesie chirped, forcing frivolity into her voice.

"Wait," said Annie, "that's no fun. Oscar and I are still together."

"That's true!" said Weesie then, too quickly, she offered a new solution. "Annie, why don't you go with Jake. Oscar and I will be a pair."

"No," snapped Tripler. "I called Jake first."

"So?" snapped Annie.

"So, I have dibs."

Jake smiled sheepishly at the three women, a humble apology for inciting competition.

"Believe it or not," Oscar interrupted, "I want to be with my fiancée. Unlike you sad married couples, we're not sick of each other yet."

"Yeah," Annie nodded. She stepped toward her fiancé and slipped her arm into his.

"Wait," said Laura. "That doesn't help me." She surveyed her friends' new pairings and their insufferable smirks.

"Oh, come on," said Chip. He transposed his expression from injured to coy. "You know you want me."

Laura said nothing in response. She just stared blankly at Chip, studying his manufactured emotion and his disturbing lips. The Hayes lip was a dominant trait, a fact proven by its recurrence in all three siblings. But the full, curling lip was far more suited to a female face, serving Lila and Minnow, but cursing William and Chip.

Disgusted, Laura turned to appeal to her friends' kindness, but she found them apathetic. The new pairs mingled, enjoying the kitschy novelty of the switch with more giddy abandon than a group of seventies suburbanites. She could have burst into a loud coughing fit, frantically signaled the choking sign, and still failed to attract their attention. Giving up on her friends once again, she turned and headed down the grass toward the water.

The group noticed her departure sooner than she expected.

"Wait," said Tripler. "Where are you going?"

Laura kept her pace, said nothing.

"You can't leave until everyone's clear on their specific mission."

Laura slowed her pace but only slightly, as Tripler repeated the plan. She took an immense and almost endearing amount of pleasure in the task, much like a playwright finally given the chance to direct. As Laura listened, she made no effort to suppress her disdain for her friend. It was so like Tripler to co-opt an emergency. And this *was* an emergency in Laura's mind, if no one else's.

"Jake and I will search the main house,'" said Tripler.

"Pete and I will search the Gettys'," said Weesie.

"Oscar and I will look outside," said Annie. "We'll do the lawn, the grounds." She trailed off. "And, if necessary, the graveyard."

The comment was met with the inevitable sound effect, a chorus of ghoulish moaning.

"Which leaves the beach for Laura and Chip," said Tripler, staying on message.

"What's the point of that," Laura snapped. "We were just there, and he wasn't."

"Just in case," said Tripler.

"In case what," said Laura.

"In case he emerges from the deep, covered with seaweed and blood," Chip volunteered. He repeated the graveyard sound effect, infusing his voice with a spooky tremble.

"Whatever," said Laura. She closed her eyes and inhaled deeply. At the top of the breath, she felt a slight sting in her chest, the same cold prickle one feels at the beginning of the flu. It was impressive, she decided, how potent emotions could be in the physical realm. They always seemed to produce an apt physical sensation.

Deciding that a fight would only expend her dwindling energy, she turned back toward the water and regained her pace, determined to put some distance between her and Chip. The wind helped her cause, blowing emphatically in the same direction, forcing her to take larger, grander steps than she otherwise would have on the sloping hill. As she walked, she took comfort in one thing: Her friends were most likely watching her walk away, mired in wretched guilt.

The group was watching, but they felt no guilt as Laura walked away. They were too busy evaluating the new threat to their evening. It was such a downer when intra-group arguments bubbled among the former rooming block, and even worse when these arguments exploded into fights. As close as the five girls were—Lila, Laura, Tripler, Weesie, and Annie—their friendships were combustible. And they fought with the same intensity that they loved one another. Determined to protect the quality of their already-challenged evening, they quickly dismissed Laura's dissatisfaction and returned to the task at hand.

Chip, at least, experienced some version of empathy. As he watched Laura head toward the beach, he felt the same condescending compassion he had when shooting bunnies with BBs as a child, the same inexplicable pity he felt at the first glimpse of his target. Unnerved, he roused himself from a comfortable trance, then turned and sprinted down the lawn after Laura, yelling incomprehensibly.

Weesie and Annie stared for a moment.

"Maybe we should take her with us," said Weesie.

Annie winced. "Maybe you're right."

"She'll be fine," said Tripler, and she corralled her friends with a decisive flick of the wrist.

As he ran, Chip waved his arms up and down like an enraged warrior attempting to intimidate his opponent with the appearance of insanity.

He sped down the lawn with a traditional schoolyard battle cry, a hand-over-mouth imitation of an Indian chief. Making wide figure eights, he wove down the lawn at a hearty gallop, as though he was trying to damage the greatest surface area of grass. He completed the performance by tumbling onto his stomach just as the lawn hit its steepest grade. He ended the journey at a roll, a feat of physics that caused him to accelerate just as he reached the end of the lawn. He tumbled over the rocky ledge that was, depending on the time of day, between three and six feet from the sandy beach.

The remaining six stood on the lawn, relieved by Chip's disappearance. They stood in silence for several moments, absorbing the echo of his recital and debating their responsibility for whatever strange whim he obeyed next. In some way, they were reluctant to begin the next phase of the evening.

"Where do you guys think he is?" Weesie asked. It was the first time anyone had posed the question, and it struck the group with the force and distaste of an unpleasant smell.

"He's probably hiding out in the attic, having a really good laugh at our expense," said Pete. "You know he can see us from there." He nodded toward the Hayeses' fourth-floor window and waved both arms. "We see you up there, Tom."

"More likely he's passed out somewhere on the lawn," said Jake. "He was loaded back there on the raft."

"Oh God," said Weesie. She was the only one to acknowledge the implicit peril in this statement.

The others shrugged her off. It was their knee-jerk response to pessimism and, in some ways, to everything Weesie said.

"But why would he bolt without saying good-bye?" Annie asked. Once in a while, the girls maintained a minimum level of loyalty, furthering one another's assertions even if they didn't support them outright.

"Did it occur to anybody that he ran away," Tripler asked. But it was more a declaration than a question.

"Why the hell would he run away," snapped Pete.

"Because he's having second thoughts," said Tripler. She punctuated her thesis with an arched eyebrow that functioned like an ellipsis.

"Second thoughts about what? Marrying this?" He gestured at the surrounding property with an expansive flick of the wrist.

Tripler sent her husband a disapproving look, as though he had finally crossed the line between decorum and poor taste, a line that she alone had managed to straddle.

"About what?" Jake asked, taking Tripler's bait.

"About the trade-off," Tripler replied. She manufactured a frown designed to display her reluctance to continue.

"Between what and what?" Pete demanded. Unsubstantiated assertions just like this caused most of the fights in their household, and he was happy for the opportunity to try his wife in the court of public opinion.

"Love and money?" Oscar volunteered. He was, after Tripler, the least guarded—and the most confrontational. But he was a more skilled conversationalist; he shared Tripler's thirst for controversy but not her need to be at its center.

"Between Laura and Lila," Tripler corrected.

"Oh come on, you don't honestly think—" Annie snapped. "What has it been? Ten years?"

"He said it himself," Tripler snapped back. "I'm not making this shit up." She scanned the group proudly as though she had just proposed a solution for world hunger. "That whole thing about not showing up to his own wedding. I mean, come on! What more do you want, people?"

Finally, Weesie lost her battle for composure. She meant to reply firmly but found herself yelling instead. "What you're saying is that the imminent wedding of our best friends, Tom and Lila, has been threatened by the home-wrecking of—"

"Mansion-wrecking," Jake interrupted.

"Whatever," sniffed Weesie. "Of our other best friend, Laura."

Tripler seemed to consider Weesie's rejoinder in earnest. "Well, yeah," she said finally. "That's what I'm saying."

"That's really inappropriate," Weesie snapped. She turned away, disgusted. It was disgraceful for Tripler to let her need for attention taint something as sacred as a wedding.

"Weez, don't let her get to you," Pete said. "I just tune her out. Isn't that right, sweetheart?" Pete punctuated this question with an exaggerated pucker, a request for a kiss that Tripler summarily rejected.

Weesie nodded, noting the unmistakable sting of Tripler and Pete's teasing. Now, she felt even more confused. Despite her anger at Tripler, she was too benign to derive any pleasure from Pete's disloyalty.

"This is outrageous," Annie piped in. "What are we even discussing? They went out in college, for Christ's sake. I barely remember the names of my college boyfriends."

"Honey," said Tripler, mock patronizing, "that says more about your dating history."

"This whole thing is preposterous," Jake interrupted. "And it's poor taste to discuss it here. You girls should know better."

"What's disgraceful," said Tripler, "is the way she carries on when he's around. She's Lila's maid of honor, for Christ's sake."

"Ah," said Pete. "So that's what this is about. You wanted Lila to ask you."

Tripler turned to her husband with profound loathing. To say such a thing in private was criminal, but to say it in front of all of their friends was an unforgivable betrayal.

"What's disgraceful is the way you trash your friends. Talk about vicious," Jake said. Ironically, he was, by all accounts, the most unscrupulous among them.

"You're all full of it," Oscar declared. He had been conspicuously quiet up to this point. "Has anyone considered something really bad?"

"Like what," said Annie.

"I don't know." Oscar shrugged. "That he drowned or something worse." He paused, reluctant to voice the next thought.

"What would be worse?"

"I don't know. Drowning. On purpose."

Annie turned to Weesie suddenly like an outraged customer demanding service. "Oh my God. What if he's dead?"

"Now we're just being dramatic," said Jake.

"Dramatic or realistic?" asked Oscar. "It's irresponsible not to ask the question."

"You always have to stir shit up," Pete snapped. Tensions between the boys were slower to flare than those between the girls but were more heated when they did.

"Someone had to say it," said Oscar. "We're not all as callous as Tripler."

Tripler's eyes widened at the attack—its cruelty and unexpectedness.

The group took this as their cue to disperse, anxious to part before the tiff turned into a brawl.

Laura began to breathe again as she reached the end of the lawn. She stopped just before the grass ended in a ledge, surprised by the distance to the sand. It was a drop of at least six feet, and she had no recollection of descending this height when she had trudged down on her way to the dock. But perhaps this was a function of her distractedness. Of course, she knew the tide was a constant in coastal life, but she had never bothered to think much about it. She only knew, on some vague level, that the tide went in and out, that the schedule of these two things meant it was either high or low, and that one was of great importance to the boats that speckled the horizon.

Standing now, she could only imagine that the ledge was at its highest point—and the tide at its lowest. A sturdy cliff plumbed the ninety-degree drop to the rocky beach. The water lapped every several seconds without managing to touch it. The feat of the cliff's construction was even more impressive considering the force of the tide. It was less a tide and more a gentle pulse that increased and decreased with the wind and weather, a lovely contribution to ambient noise, a decorative facet.

Aesthetics aside, it paled in comparison to real, formidable waves. It would surely have failed to impress those who expected drama and recreation from their ocean, just as Gardner's Bay elicited scoffs from hard-core Hamptonites, and the ripples of the Gulf of Mexico amused true Atlantic surfers. But the height and solidity of the cliff succeeded in impressing Laura. It broadcast the formidable power of the water just beyond the bay, boasting its ability to construct and destruct with unerring consistency. It was as though the tide had been sent as the emissary of the ocean, to convey its power, when appropriate, to wreak devastation.

Undaunted, Laura lowered herself to sit with her feet hanging off the ledge, then jumped the remaining distance from the grass to the sand. She walked into an approaching ripple, emboldened by her recent dip, and stood like this, waiting for the next wave, staring into the darkness. As she waited, she kicked herself for her lack of originality—all she needed was a penny to throw into the bay, then to make a heartfelt wish. But she forgave herself for staring as she confronted the enormity of water. It never ceased to awe and terrify.

Perhaps it reflected poorly on her that her first association with the ocean was death. Surely, this was a clear indication of pathological pessimism. But, she couldn't suppress the sentiment. It was a reflex, like some people's aversion to snakes. Perhaps she could blame her lack of exposure to the water at a very young age. Unlike her friends, she had not grown up frolicking in a bay, tying and untying sailing knots, buttoning well-starched shorts. She had no basis for the common association between water and pleasure. When she swam in the ocean, she felt agitated, exposed. She was braced for contact with jellyfish—was there a more repugnant, slimy creature in the world? And this awareness took all the fun out of swimming, forcing her to keep constant watch on the shore, should she need to make a quick escape. What was the fun of that?

It was not long before she began to indulge yet more morbid thoughts. As she stared at the black water, she imagined Tom floating underneath, his eyes wide with the shock of a sudden gruesome death. In her hideous apparition, a fluorescent jellyfish floated past, blinking with a cadaverous green light. It was outlandish, to be sure, but it wasn't as though she thought he'd been mauled by sharks—were there even sharks in Maine? But there was a lurking possibility in her mind that Tom had come to some harm. And it was pure hubris on her friends' part, she felt, not to entertain this possibility. Tom had been comprehensively smashed when they saw him last, had long surpassed the level of intoxication that would impair his ability to walk or swim in reasonably rough water. And even worse, though he was known to drink with some frequency and intensity, alcohol had always had a strange impact on him, acting on his moods as both a tonic and a poison.

In fact, it was this that scared Laura more than any of the earlier considerations. It was not that he drank more than most, but rather that it affected him more potently, making him intermittently deliriously happy or suicidally depressed. Once, freshman year, after a particularly wild bender, he had hoisted himself through her dormitory window and onto her fire escape, claiming that he would jump if she didn't swear to marry him right then and there. And then, there were the countless soggy nights they'd passed together at house parties and Brooklyn dive bars during which he betrayed slightly more weakness for whiskey than the average guy. It's not that she ever believed he would make good on his threats to use his necktie as a noose, more that she was alarmed by the speed of his transition from reason to recklessness.

Laura did her best to curb her negative thinking. Tom was fine, she decided. He was an intercollegiate champion. She had cheered for him at countless victorious swim meets in school, that is, until Lila supplanted her as his number one fan. She pictured him now, hurtling toward the shore, swimming his unbeatable butterfly like some sort of mythological beast, half-man, half-porpoise. But he would not have swum the butterfly tonight. He would have swum the crawl. And his crawl, though reliable, was his least favorite stroke. Water in his ears, he used to say—a strange complaint for a swimmer—always tripped him up.

But this was nonsense, catastrophic thinking—and she told herself as much. She was certainly prone to letting her imagination run rampant, but she knew better than to give too much weight to improbable notions. She harbored one other yet-more-implausible idea, a theory so absurd and far-fetched she shuddered to acknowledge it. Even so, she allowed it to take shape in its full, grotesque glory. Somewhere, deep within, she hoped and wondered and, yes, in some way, suspected that the brief time she and Tom had spent together tonight—to be fair, it was not true time together, just time in each other's presence—had been as cataclysmic for him as it had been for her and that it had suddenly and completely toppled his worldview, necessitating that he stop in his tracks and change the course of his life forever.

They had not exchanged many words before she walked away from their conversation. And surely, awareness of the group's curiosity had kept them from speaking freely. But it was clear, even in this short time, from the desperate look in his eyes—she could not have hallucinated it—that he was wild with terror and that she had provided a small source of comfort. The coexistence of these two things—terror and comfort—would drive anyone crazy. It was equivalent to being prisoner in a locked cell and spotting a key just beyond the bars. Though it pained her to see Tom in this state, it gave her some satisfaction, not because she wanted Tom to suffer, but because it verified that her own suffering had perhaps been merited. If there was any better definition of true love, she had yet to hear it.

Still, she subjected her theory to a thorough analysis, reviewing every coded moment of their time together—every syllable exchanged, every eyelash fluttered, every repressed desire. And, of course, there was his strange declaration, his contribution to the drinking game. Had he meant it as a warning, or was it just eerily prophetic that less than an hour before vanishing into the bay he had informed the group of his reluctance to attend his own wedding? Laura's spirit improved wildly with every new consideration. Smiling now, she experienced an entirely foreign sensation. This one felt nothing like the familiar constriction in her chest. Now, she felt utterly weightless, as though her brain had distilled into smoke that hovered above her body, instructing it to move and feel but from a comfortable distance.

And rather than shun this bizarre sensation—her hazy recollection of freshman psychology yielded the word "depersonalization"—she focused on it, courted it as a monk courts meditation. Hope, she realized, felt unlike any other emotion. And traveling from fear to hope in the span of thirty seconds felt something like flying. It was so intense—at once so exhilarating and unnerving—that she instinctively sought to curb it. She walked towards the bay and stepped into the water as though to extinguish a fire. The temperature brought her back into her body and ostensibly back to earth just in time for her to brace for a new arrival.

"This must be really hard for you," said Chip. He lay on the beach, a few feet from the ledge, propped up as though preparing to watch a movie.

Laura deepened her gaze at the water. She entertained an idle and unlikely thought: Perhaps a triumph over blinking would somehow amount to triumph over Chip.

"You drive halfway up to the North Pole to watch the love of your life marry the bane of your existence, and this is how they thank you."

Laura closed her eyes, shook her head.

"It's ironic," said Chip, sitting up. "Asking you, of all people, to find the groom and convince him to show up for his wedding."

Finally, Laura blinked. Better to blink than scream.

"Your friends seem pretty calm." He sniffed. "Very nonchalant. Seems like they'd rather turn this into a game than let it put a damper on the evening."

"Honestly, Chip." Laura turned to face him, making a heartfelt appeal for silence.

"I personally don't think he drowned. Not our intercollegiate champion. My bets are on the harbor sharks. They're no match for the tough guys in warmer waters, but those suckers can bite."

At this, he burst into hysterical laughter and fell onto his back. He remained like this, cackling fiendishly, until he became distracted by the sky and stared at it, muted and perplexed. A blur of clouds obscured the stars he had come to expect above his house on a summer night, and their absence struck him as both a surprise and an inconvenience. He had come to think of the stars above the lawn as a part of Northern Gardens' property, and so viewed the obstruction with a proprietor's annoyance, like a farmer watching a swarm of locusts descend upon his crop.

"I'm going to walk down the beach toward the Gettys', see if he overshot the house or got pulled by the tide," said Laura.

"I wouldn't go that way," Chip said. "It gets rocky right after the property line. And then it turns into forest. Trust me. You don't want to get lost there at night."

Laura stared at Chip for a moment, evaluating his sincerity. "If you don't want to come, that's fine."

She paused, daunted by the thought of dense trees in the darkness, then started down the beach anyway, bolstered by the possibility of losing Chip for good. Better to be lost in a haunted forest than spend the rest of the night with him.

"I don't blame you," he called out. "My sister's pretty awful. But he's no better. At least, not anymore. Before, I could see what you saw in him. The wild, unpredictable rebel. The fiery temper, the Irish good looks. But now he's a shadow of his former self. A submissive, humorless, kept man. He might as well hold out his hands for cuffs. And the fact that he knows it makes it so much worse."

Laura stopped against her will, unable to ignore the performance. Some part of her—the lowest, the least admirable part—took pleasure in hearing someone else voice her complaints about Tom.

"Don't worry. I'm not gonna sell you out. I guess I just wish you had higher standards. I always looked up to you, you know."

At this, she started walking again. And walking seemed to help. She had spent precious few moments alone since she had arrived, and the privacy was almost as exhilarating as air against her face.

It was not that she didn't like people. She was comfortable enough with most types. But after being with her friends for extended periods of time, she felt the distinct need to recuperate, just to sit in silence for a little while and revisit her thoughts—to draw a chalk line around herself as though she were a piece of evidence. She wondered if other people felt this way and simply recovered faster, or if she alone suffered from a rare social disorder. Luckily, spending time by herself usually recharged her quickly. With every passing step, she began to feel safer, more protected, so much so that she was totally taken off guard when someone threw the full force of his weight onto her, tackling her to the sand.

Shock and adrenaline combined to disorient her for several moments.

"Tom," she whispered.

"Yes," said a voice.

They lay in a heap, recovering their breath. Being close to him was such a surprise, such a welcome comfort.

"We thought you were lost," she whispered.

"I was," Chip sneered, "until I found you."

His voice finally revealed what his body had not. It was Chip, not Tom, of course. Alarmed, Laura struggled to push him off, but Chip pushed her back to the sand.

"Get the fuck off," Laura shouted. She jammed her elbows into his ribs, loosening his grip.

Gravity conspired with Chip. He pinned her down with a clumsy shove, then pushed with all of his weight.

"Chip, I'm serious," Laura yelled.

Chip said nothing and tightened his grip around the top of her arm. Then, confirming she had no hope of escaping, he buried his face in her hair.

In all the years she'd known him, Laura had never considered Chip a threat. He was often annoying, inappropriate always, but, for the most part, harmless. Now, as she lay trapped under him, she suddenly felt panicked. It seemed feasible that Chip was capable of something depraved, that the twisted heart of his college years had rotted and decayed, that she had no control over him, and he had less of himself. The lights of the house glowed in the distance, but they might as well have been miles away.

She lay like this, one cheek lodged in the sand for what felt like several minutes. She tried to loosen his grip with her nails, but he bore down with new determination. Even drowning, Laura decided, would be preferable to this fate, and the thought sent a rush of rage up her spine, causing her to elbow Chip in the groin and stunning him just long enough to escape.

SEVEN

There were few things Tripler Pane loved more than a good emergency. Even as a child, she thrilled in a crisis, shepherding classmates during school fire drills, appointing herself the additional lifeguard during free swim at summer camp. In college, she was known as a benevolent busybody, a supervisory presence whose leadership skills usually benefited the group. It was Tripler who organized the biannual study review that enabled her friends to pass their finals, Tripler who divvied up the syllabus—often, she alone still had it in her possession—assigning various readings and lecture notes. It was Tripler who organized the late-night study sessions, ordered the pizza, bought the candy and Coke, roused the others to digest a semester's worth of work in the span of one night.

It was Tripler who saw the business opportunity when the quality of these study sessions circulated throughout the student body, and Tripler who conceived of the idea to charge admission to the review. Tripler collected the proceeds and deposited the profits into an account at the New Haven Savings Bank that eventually accrued to pay for a spring break blowout in St. Bart's. Tripler had scheduled and organized every group gathering, with the exception of weddings and funerals, since graduation. Tripler collected money for the crappy ski condos, the joint birthday presents, the New Year's Eve booze. Tripler bought the extra witches' hats—just to have them on hand—for the yearly Halloween bash.

But she had not assumed this post simply because she was the most competent organizer. She did it because she was, she felt, the most competent friend. Her evidence was a staggering list of emotional crises that she had helped her friends to navigate with dignity. It was Tripler who rescued Lila freshman year when she called from a closet in Skull and Bones, having found herself, after five glasses of champagne, the only remaining female in the building. It was Tripler who encouraged Weesie not to drop out of school when she decided, fall of freshman year, that she was not cut out for Yale. It was Tripler who took it upon herself to confiscate Annie's Ritalin when a supply meant to bolster a midterm paper was replenished long past the middle of the term.

It was Tripler who soothed whichever sniveling soul was suffering her latest heartbreak: Weesie, when Jake broke up with her, Jake, when Weesie broke up with him, Annie, when Oscar cheated on her, and Laura, when Tom broke her heart and then reappeared, hours later, to pick up Lila for a date. This auspicious track record contributed to Tripler's suspicion that she knew her friends better than they knew themselves. Unfortunately, this had no correlation to her knowledge of herself.

"It's so obvious where he is," she declared as she traipsed up the lawn toward the house. She turned toward Jake, who was trailing behind, and was greeted by a slap of wind. "If you were Tom," she said, "where would you be?"

Jake paused and looked up at the house, tilting his head back to survey the structure in one glance. "Honestly, if I were Tom, I'd be in Lila's bed right now."

Tripler frowned. She instinctively bristled when compliments were paid to her friends. Compliments were in finite supply, she felt, and their distribution unnerved her.

"Possible," she said. "But unlikely. He's way too scared of Augusta." She paused and made a reluctant confession. "She did look amazing tonight."

Jake nodded wholeheartedly. "She always looks good to me."

Tripler registered a measure of relief. In praising Lila, Jake had simultaneously slighted his own wife. "You always had a thing for her," she teased.

"Me and every other guy on campus."

"But your crush always seemed more tender than most." She pointed toward the third floor of the house, the single lit window that glowed in the center. "That's her window up there, you know. If you want to take a last shot."

Jake sighed. It was Tripler's special talent to turn the most innocent conversation into a controversy. "You've found me out." He sighed, then sped up toward the house.

Northern Gardens looked wildly different at night than it did in the daytime. Whereas sunshine cast a picturesque glow on the house, darkness lengthened its pleasing proportions, causing the house to look foreboding. This quality was even more pronounced from Tripler and Jake's position on the lawn. Looking up at the house, the four-story structure seemed ghoulishly tall, its Victorian flourishes—ornate trim on the eaves, swirling wooden brackets on the porch—overwrought and manipulative, like gumdrops on a gingerbread house. The only lit window in the house—in Lila's bedroom on the third floor—added a strange macabre note, evidence of the quintessential madwoman, locked in the attic.

Still, Tripler was not easily daunted, and climbed the stairs to the porch.

Jake remained still, feet fixed to the lawn, debating his next move. Was it too late to bow out of the search? Would that make him look weak or, worse, callous? He could think of nothing worse than barging into a house full of sleeping guests. One unlucky step on a creaky floorboard—this house was surely a minefield—and he would face Augusta, mouth agape, in a hastily lit hallway. What excuse could he possibly offer for trespassing?

"Why, hello, Mrs. Hayes. Just wanted a last glimpse of your lovely daughter." And then, a polite do-si-do in the hall. He would sooner die. He looked back toward the ocean, then to the Gettys'. A whispered apology and a sprint across the lawn seemed like his best option.

Sensing Jake's unease, Tripler assumed the chipper tone of a camp counselor. "Come on, this is going to be fun," she said. She crossed the porch and opened the back door confidently, as though she were returning to her own house after a pleasant evening out.

"Are you coming?" she whispered.

"What are we going to do?" Jake barked. "Jump into bed with them?"

"No." Tripler sighed. "We'll just crack the door, make sure he's alive, then leave."

Jake said nothing. He continued to stare sullenly at the back door.

Tripler crossed her arms and raised her eyebrows. "Don't be re-tarded," she said.

Jake remained still for another moment. In his own home, he was accustomed to winning arguments like this, so much so that he was almost curious to discover how it might feel to lose one. A rush of wind rattled the door as though cued by Tripler to goad him inside. Lacking the energy for a dispute, he crossed the porch and followed Tripler into the house.

In some ways, Jake Chapman was more vulnerable than most to the influence of his peers. He was, even as he neared thirty, a hopeless mama's boy. Raised in Cambridge, the son of a Boston socialite and an English professor, he had been cursed with the worst of two worlds: an oppressive emphasis on status and a shortage of cash. This confusion of values had resulted in a confusing childhood. While Mrs. Chapman provided invitations to all the best cocktail parties, Professor Chapman ensured that Jake had something to say when he arrived. While Mrs. Chapman shared her memberships with her son—the Country Club in Brookline, the University Club in New York—Jake's father shared Marx and Engels and explained the evils of the elite.

For a time, Professor Chapman won out, steering Jake toward the writing life. A felt fedora and full access to Widener Library made this a plausible fate. Hours were clocked in Cambridge cafes; moleskin journals filled with poems about the violet hour. And soon enough, Cambridge coeds replaced the color of the sky as Jake's favored subject. High school confirmed Jake's promise with an auspicious prize: the Alice K. Stevenson Award for excellence in creative writing. With it, he won a five-hundred-dollar stipend and the respect of every girl in his graduating class.

The next fall at Yale, he capitalized on the trend, camping out at the doors of the blue clapboard house that was home to the *Lit,* Yale's literary magazine. In its cavernous halls, he found new inspiration: a masthead staffed by beautiful brunettes and a clubhouse where he could crash in between classes. These editors, in their strict uniform of black turtlenecks and brown corduroy skirts, seemed to Jake like modern-day muses. They were, in turn, impressed by Jake's quintessential New England charm—he was like a real-life Holden Caulfield! By sophomore year, Jake had seen three short stories published and been tapped as a shoo-in for editor in chief. He vowed to write his first novel by the time he turned twenty-one.

Seven years later, he had yet to write another paragraph. After graduation, he accepted a position at a prestigious New York hedge fund, promising that he would write at night and on the weekends. But as time passed, the goal slowly lost its urgency. He began to view writing as a petty ambition, a frivolous and indulgent whim, creativity itself as the pathology of the very young or very stupid. The shift was painless. Gradually, money grew to inhabit the same part of his brain that art had once occupied. The transition from a literary to a luxurious life was as easy and mindless as slipping from sobriety to a high.

Now, as he entered the Hayeses' living room, he wished for that very transition—from sobriety to intoxication. It was no coincidence that his mood had suffered with the fade of his wine buzz. Frantic now, he scanned the room for emergency relief. Surely, he could not be too far from the Hayeses' well-stocked bar.

To Tripler, the living room offered just the refuge she had craved. It was bathed in a pleasant lavender light—the weather had served as a gentle dimmer for the light of the moon. Two sofas, cream chintz with a botanical print, faced each other like rapt lovers. Their pillows were buoyant and full, as though they had just been fluffed. A cashmere throw curled across the sofa, inviting guests to settle in for a nap. The walls were covered with an elegant damask that looked, in the minimal light, like a velvety film of moss. Tripler relaxed within seconds of entering the room. Sighing dramatically, she threw herself onto a sofa with total disregard for her damp clothes. She sunk in and patted the cushion beside her, inviting Jake to join her.

Jake ignored the summons and circled the sofa leisurely, scanning the room for a bar. He paused at a table covered with framed photographs, distracted from his mission by a Hayes family portrait.

"Wanna know a secret," Tripler asked. She was now reclining on the sofa, one leg dangling over the upholstered arm.

"Sure," said Jake. He knew perfectly well his response was irrelevant. Tripler would share her secret regardless.

"Annie's pregnant," Tripler declared. "I'd say three, no four months."

"Wow. That's great," said Jake. "When did she tell everyone?"

"She didn't," said Tripler. "I figured it out."

"Oh." Jake nodded. He replaced a frame on the table and lifted a new one.

"She had half a glass of wine tonight!" Tripler scoffed. She might as well have outed Annie for committing a violent crime. "The girl can't get through Sunday brunch without a drink. I'm telling you. Preggers. A million to one."

"Hmm," said Jake. He replaced the current frame and picked up another.

"I just find it so precious," Tripler went on. "The whole veil of secrecy. I talk to the girl every day. If she's going to bother me with all the boring shit, the least she could do is share the fun stuff."

Jake nodded. It was the largest gesture he could muster without losing his concentration. He was intent on offering Tripler the same portion of his brain that he devoted to reading books in bed. Without fail, within five pages, he was usually out.

"She looks pretty chunky," Tripler added.

"No, she doesn't," said Jake.

"You guys will know the day I miss my period," she said. "There will be no awkward speculation phase where everyone thinks I've put on a few pounds."

"Don't people usually keep that secret in case something goes wrong?"

"Yeah, but that's bullshit," Tripler said. "It's just another antiquated Wasp custom designed to punish emotions. If something terrible happens to me, it's not my job to spare you from my pain."

It was custom when the friends convened in pairs to indulge in proprietary gossip, to discuss and analyze each other with surgical precision, exhibiting such detachment and cruelty at times that a witness might assume they were enemies as opposed to very dear friends. But this, they felt, was one of the privileges of their long-standing history, as though the time they'd spent together exempted them from basic social amenities like kindness and compassion.

Jake nodded again without looking toward Tripler. Occasionally, she backed her way into a version of sense. It was certainly not common sense, but once in a while, it added up.

Tripler watched as Jake lifted a frame to his face, then, tiring of his neglect, instigated a new conversation. "You guys must be gearing up, too," she said.

"That's none of your business, Trip," said Jake.

"Oh come on, I'm Weesie's best friend."

"Then I'll let her tell you."

"Maybe she has already."

"Highly unlikely," said Jake.

"Why not?"

"Because she doesn't want them for a while."

"Really?"

Jake sighed, kicking himself for the naïve mistake. Tripler had the most amazing knack for teasing information out of people. She should have put this skill to use as a reporter or prosecutor instead of wasting her mind and talent on—what was she, anyway? An actress?

"Weesie never tells me anything anymore." Tripler pouted.

"Don't be ridiculous," Jake said. "Besides, she'll change her mind next week. Decide she wants quadruplets."

Tripler shuddered theatrically.

Jake kicked himself for trading his wife's secrets for Tripler's consolation.

"How is Weesie anyway," she demanded, assuming the overly interested tone of a television talk-show host. "I feel like we've grown apart."

"She's fine," said Jake without looking up. He was transfixed by a photo of Augusta and William taken early in their marriage. In it, they bore an eerie resemblance to Lila and Tom—the same beauty, the same vague boredom.

"Good," said Tripler. "She seems good." She paused. "I mean she seems better."

Finally, Jake took Tripler's bait. "Better? Why? Was something wrong?"

"Oh no, not wrong," Tripler said. She played nonchalance in a way that exaggerated, rather than minimized, concern. "I just know she was having a hard time. With the job and everything."

"Well yeah," Jake said. "And her father, of course."

"Yes," Tripler said. "I'm so sorry. But I'd heard there'd been some improvement."

Jake nodded. But as he did, he swallowed annoyance again. Friendships between women so often compromised the privacy of their husbands. How was he to know what Weesie shared with Tripler about their marriage? It was like sitting in the room with a criminal detective—he had no choice but to spill everything. "And we started counseling, as you surely know."

"Oh, I didn't realize," Tripler gasped.

"Oh," said Jake. "Well, now you know." It was settled: He didn't like Tripler anymore. Now that he thought of it, had he ever?

Sensing Jake's irritation, Tripler strained to change the subject again. She scanned the room imperiously as though she, too, owned a seaside estate and was specially qualified to appraise their parlors. "Augusta did a great job with the renovation."

Jake said nothing, giving up on the pretense of courtesy.

"It kind of makes you think," Tripler said.

Jake responded reluctantly. "About what?"

"Just about this house, you know. About the Hayes family."

Jake focused intently on the photograph in his hands, and it did its part to hold his gaze: Lila, age twelve, in a white tennis skirt. Her legs were like flamingos' legs, all limbs and kneecaps, but her smile betrayed the same certainty and condescension she possessed as an adult.

"You ever think there was something odd about how Tom and Lila started dating?"

"No," said Jake. As he stared at Lila's picture, he could smell the sunscreen on her shoulders.

"It was right after we came here sophomore spring. Remember, we all drove up for that long weekend?"

Jake mustered a nod. His pretense of distraction had become authentic. Perhaps Tripler was right. The thought of landing in Lila's bed right now seemed totally appealing.

"Don't you think that's an odd coincidence?"

"Don't be retarded," said Jake. But he was talking to himself more than her. He had seen many tennis skirts in his day but rarely one that beckoned quite so insistently. As he stared, he imagined the underwear beneath—was it plain, patterned, ruffled? Suddenly, his concern for Tom doubled. Any man with a claim on this body should not have been hard to locate.

Tripler took silence as evidence of interest and continued to build her argument. "He asked her out three days after we got back. Three days," she repeated.

Finally, Jake turned to Tripler. With her legs propped up, her arms stretched above her head, she was a perfect portrait of entitlement. "We were in college," he sneered. "No one cared about real estate yet."

"True, but all of this." She gestured grandly toward the window. "It registered on some level."

"We'd all seen it before." Jake shrugged.

"You and I had," Tripler pressed.

Jake exhaled, disengaging again. He finally understood why Tripler and Weesie fought so much.

"I'm just saying it registered with Tom." She sank deeper into her cushion as though pulled by the force of her conviction.

"You think Tom started dating Lila because he coveted her parents' fortune?"

"You make it sound like an episode of *Dynasty*."

"But that's what you're saying, right?" he pressed.

"All I'm saying is I think it's weird," she snapped.

Now Jake rose to Tom's defense. "Tom's no worse than anyone else in this group. Everyone's got their little act. Laura's a Jew, pretending to be a Wasp. Oscar's gay, pretending to be straight. Weesie's a bore, pretending to be fun. Pete's rich, pretending to be poor. Annie's poor, pretending to be rich. You're intense, pretending to be laid-back. I don't see the difference."

"And what are you?"

"I'm just a miserable bastard, pretending to give a shit."

"Could have fooled me," she said. Why did Jake hate her so much? But she pressed her point. "You grew up with all this. Imagine seeing it for the first time." She paused to select her words carefully. "All I'm saying is I think Lila's lifestyle appealed to Tom just like her perfect tits appeal to you."

"I'm sure those appeal to Tom as well," Jake snapped.

Tripler shrugged and looked away. Though she had won the argument, she registered a painful defeat: another compliment paid to a friend.

EIGHT

Weesie said horribly awkward things even when she felt comfortable. When she was nervous, she could be counted on for abject mortification. She knew it was almost always better just to be quiet. But the habit was so deeply ingrained that it functioned like personality. As she and Pete traipsed across the grass to the Gettys', she made the usual mistake.

"The rehearsal dinner was lovely, don't you think. I thought it was lovely."

"Yeah," Pete agreed. "How about those speeches."

"God," Weesie said. "I can't believe Chip."

Pete sighed and shook his head, summarizing his feelings on the subject.

Weesie racked her brain for a new topic, something that would last a few minutes, at least. "So we've been assigned to the bedrooms," she said.

"Yup," said Pete.

Weesie turned back toward the main house and caught a last glance of Tripler and Jake fading into the darkness.

"You trust him, of course," Pete asked.

"Who? Jake?" Weesie stammered. "Yes, of course."

"Good," said Pete. "That makes me feel better. 'Cause I don't trust Tripler one bit."

Weesie laughed. For some reason, the knowledge that they shared this concern relieved her of it. Comforted, she walked in silence until they reached the front door of the house.

One of the benefits of being partnered with Pete was that he turned on the lights. Jake would not have turned on the lights. Jake would have clutched her arm, terrified of every shadow and sound, including the ones he produced. As a result, it was an utter shock to Weesie when Pete dispatched her to wait in the foyer while he calmly completed a walk-through of the Gettys', checking every dark room for signs of Tom without so much as a flinch.

As she waited, Weesie surveyed the house in detail for the first time: A framed nautical map was covered by a pane of glass with a sliver down its center; in the corner of the floor, wide pine floorboards had been patched with newer, narrower planks. Every detail increased Weesie's sympathy for Augusta. There was no denying the Gettys had let their house go to pot.

"He's not here," Pete said when he returned. He wore a look of satisfied certainty that Weesie had never seen on her husband.

"He's not?" said Weesie. "Are you sure?"

"I checked every room," said Pete.

Weesie said nothing as she digested her disappointment, and entertained a new concern. What on earth would they talk about now?

"Are you worried?" asked Pete.

"No," Weesie lied. "Not at all. Are you?"

Pete pursed his lips and shook his head in a show of masculine bravado.

"Where do you think he is?" Weesie asked.

"That's a very good question," Pete said. "One I need to sit down to consider." He collapsed onto a chair as though settling in to watch a movie.

Weesie's spirits lifted as she followed Pete's example and took a seat on the sofa. The subject of Tom's whereabouts would provide some fodder for conversation.

Fear of not having something to say was, in many ways, the guiding force in Weesie's life, second only to her fear of saying something stupid. Her father, a senator for Virginia, had taken every measure to teach his three daughters the art of sparkling conversation. The dinner table was their training ground, boot camp for political banter, polite small talk, eloquent summaries of current events, and pithy contributions about their feelings. Frequent, exotic family vacations endowed the girls with an impressive arsenal of conversation topics. Washington's Cathedral School provided the polish and the forum for debate.

Of the three girls, Weesie was the only one who had strayed from the political arena. And the choice had cost her, if not the affection of her father, certainly his attention. She dreaded the compulsory one-on-one dinners they shared when he came to New York. For the week leading up to their scheduled meal, she studied the newspaper feverishly, committing editorials to memory as though preparing for an oral exam.

To some degree, she felt this anxiety with everyone she knew, as though she were bombing a very important job interview. This feeling compelled her to act oddly in most social situations. She adopted a bizarre faux-English accent, peppered her language with overly decorative words, and introduced lofty topics that were of little personal interest. At worst, the habit made her sound pretentious, at best, charmingly confused. But over the years, it had become habit, and she reverted to it unless she was in the presence of the handful of people—Jake, Lila, Laura, Tripler, and Annie—with whom she felt comfortable.

"Tom won the Rose Cup four years in a row," Pete announced. "He could have swum that with his eyes closed."

"You think?" asked Weesie.

"I know."

Weesie nodded slowly.

"For all we know, Tripler and Jake have already found him. Knowing Trip, she's got him tied to a chair, doing shots."

Weesie smiled as caution gave way to consolation. She consciously relaxed her arms from their clenched position.

"So where do you think he is?" she asked.

"My bet is this is a prank. He loves dumb shit like this," said Pete. "Always has."

"So you're not worried?" she repeated.

"No," said Pete. "I'm not."

Satisfied, Weesie prepared to relinquish her anxiety. But she summoned another potential concern—it seemed like the responsible thing to do. "He didn't make a toast at the rehearsal dinner. I found that odd. Didn't you?"

"I didn't make a toast at my rehearsal dinner."

"Oh really," said Weesie. "Why not?"

"Tripler's dad had his eye on me the whole time like he was daring me to screw up."

Weesie giggled and tried to conjure a clear image of Pete and Tripler's wedding. Tripler had enforced a strict October theme and dressed the bridesmaids in pumpkin orange—a shade that was only a touch more flattering than Lila's beloved pewter. The centerpieces, Weesie vaguely recalled, were enormous horns of plenty, stuffed with Indian corn, colored gourds, and—was it possible?—Halloween candy. Relaxing slightly, she pressed her point. "Still, he seemed a little off. That thing he said on the raft."

"It would be weird if he was acting normal," said Pete. "The man is getting married tomorrow."

Weesie smiled. She had always admired Pete's dry sense of humor but had never recognized it as generous until now. He had an amazing talent for making the most dour situation seem light and breezy. Jake did not have this talent. "I think my husband still suffers from that."

"Oh no," said Pete. "Don't worry. Your husband was like that before you met. I roomed with him freshman year."

Weesie nodded conclusively—it was inappropriate to indulge a more pointed dig at Jake in his absence. Even so, she wished Pete would keep talking. Laughter was incredibly relaxing, and she appreciated his solidarity. "Did you freak out when you got married?"

"I spent the morning of my wedding in a closet," Pete said. "Of course, Tripler locked me in it."

"But things got better when you said 'I do'?" Weesie pressed, playing along.

Pete shook his head solemnly. "Things never got better."

Weesie giggled. She had never before quantified the value—and the calming force—of a great sense of humor. Compared to Jake, Pete was completely hilarious—or Jake was painfully boring.

By most accounts, Pete was the funniest person in the wedding party. His wicked sense of humor grew out of an instinctive aversion to the emotional realm, an allergic reaction to all things serious and somber. He visibly bristled at the first twang of earnest conversation, tempering it with levity like a chef adding spices to a bland dish. During college, he fine-tuned this aversion to sincerity into a dry, facetious wit and deployed it to detonate gravity before it could kill the mood. The quality of social exchange, he felt, was inherently degraded by sentiment. For him, this was not a belief, but a bodily sensation.

The condition all but sealed his romantic fate. Though many women appreciated his jokes, few shared his distaste for sincerity. In Tripler, Pete found the ideal counterpart, the only woman in the world who shunned emotion more desperately than he. Together, they constructed a protective bubble of sarcasm and disdain. They spent the better part of college snickering among themselves, pointing out the fallacies of the group. Their off-campus apartment functioned as a clubhouse, a refuge where the huddled, hungover masses could find reliably mellow ennui and a massive frittata every Sunday for brunch.

When Pete and Tripler married, two years after graduating, Pete's mother offered a single piece of advice: Sarcasm, she said, was the single greatest threat to a happy marriage. Her own marriage, she claimed, had survived due to a honeymoon vow to abolish it. They had promised never to answer each other in irony or jest, but rather to treat every exchange as sacred and literal. At the time, Pete dismissed his mother's advice as antiquated and simplistic. It certainly explained the sickly-sweet quality of his parents' every exchange. But four years later, he wondered if this had been a foolish mistake. The cumulative effect of so many cutting comments had settled on his marriage like smog, creating a film of anger, a shortage of pleasantries and sex, and lately—he had begun to fear—love itself.

In the last few months, he had found himself fantasizing compulsively about other women, plagued by vivid daydreams about strange girls in filthy positions. But he feared the fantasies revealed more about himself than the state of his marriage. That he and his wife of four years had tired of each other's bodies was understandable; that he was sneaking into the bathroom to jerk off at eleven o'clock in the morning—that was a different issue altogether.

"So you think he's fine," Weesie pressed.

"I think he's alive," Pete clarified. "I never said he was fine."

Weesie sighed and cursed herself for her greediness. It was horribly selfish to pawn off her concern so quickly. Tom had disappeared in the middle of the night in a turbulent bay. He was likely hurt—maybe even dead. How dare she let herself off the hook so easily. "What's that supposed to mean?" she asked.

"I dunno," said Pete. "Just that he's probably somewhere nearby, wringing his hands and pacing."

Weesie sighed, somewhat relieved by the new theory. She voiced her next thought before she could censor herself. "Laura must be freaking out."

"Laura?" asked Pete. "I'd say Lila's got more to worry about right now."

Weesie looked down, willing Pete to infer her meaning without forcing her to voice it out loud. "You realize how close they are," she pressed.

"Tom has tons of female friends," said Pete.

"Who talk and e-mail every day?" Weesie asked. "Probably more than Lila and Tom."

"That's just Tom screwing off at work. He'll waste anyone's time who lets him."

"They went away together last year," she said quietly. "Twice. That I know about."

Pete leaned forward in his chair, engaging finally. "Really? Where did they go?"

Weesie shrugged. "I don't know. That's all she told me."

Each new betrayal filled Weesie with more nauseating shame. But it also produced a feeling of relief, releasing her somehow of the burden of blame for anything that had happened—or might happen—to Tom. She fumbled to change the subject but produced a confession instead. "I sometimes feel like we played a part in it."

"In what?" Pete said.

"In making Laura." Weesie paused. "You know. The way Laura is."

"Oh God," said Pete, leaning back in his chair. "What did you guys do to the poor girl?"

This was not the response Weesie craved. She had anticipated gentle dissent, a cursory vindication. But she continued anyway, eager to be absolved. "It was March of sophomore year, and the deadline for rooming paperwork was coming up. We had decided to live together the next fall. All five of us in one suite. It was going to be tight but everyone was up for it. We were shooting for one of those massive suites in Cavanaugh Hall."

Pete shifted his position, extending his legs to hang over the side of the chair.

"That same week, Tom broke up with Laura and started dating Lila. Laura was a total wreck. Didn't shower for God knows how long. Basically lived in the library. At one point, Lila wanted Tom's varsity jacket, and Laura wouldn't give it back."

"God, I remember that." Pete winced.

"So, the night before the submission deadline, four of us called a meeting. Lila, Annie, Tripler, and me. And we didn't tell Laura. We decided she was too unstable, that living with her could be a drag. So we handed in our paperwork without her name, submitted for a quad. By the time she found out, the deadline had passed. She had no choice but to live alone."

"Wow," said Pete. "That's awful."

"I know," said Weesie. "It is. And I know this sounds weird, but she's never really been the same since."

"You girls are heartless," Pete teased.

"Don't make me feel worse," said Weesie. "But the strangest thing was that Lila felt bad, I guess because she got Tom. So she opted out of the quad, asked Laura to room with her after all. That's when they moved off-campus."

Pete said nothing, appearing to sit in silent condemnation. Weesie shrank into the sofa, digesting her remorse. But in fact, Pete was already focused on something else: a cold, hard object pressed against his ribs from inside his coat pocket. He had been prescient— and stealthy—enough to secure an extra bottle of wine before the group abandoned the raft. Reminded of this, he grinned and produced the bottle, then held up a finger, a signal to wait, while he bolted toward the kitchen.

Weesie waited in her seat while cupboards opened and closed.

"Aha!" Pete yelled.

"What are you looking for?" Weesie shouted.

Another cupboard door slammed shut. "A corkscrew," Pete shouted.

He returned seconds later, carrying two wineglasses and an open bottle. He filled the glasses, handed one to Weesie, and raised his cheerfully.

"To friendship," he said.

"To friendship," she said and, with that, she resolved to drop the subject of Laura.

NINE

During the weeks preceding her sister's wedding, Margaret Hayes had been asked the same question at least one hundred times. A woman in faded tennis attire would peer out from under a large straw hat and raise her voice to a volume she presumed best for communicating with children. "Is it hard sharing the house with your sister?" she would ask while swirling the ice in her glass. "Now that you're used to ruling the roost, it must be quite a shock."

Minnow would shrug and curse her mother for welcoming the intruder into her home, then the intruder would exchange a knowing look with Augusta and down the rest of her drink.

The insult of the query was doubled by the condescending gestures that followed: a furrow of the brow, a wrinkle of the nose, or worst of all, a pat on the head.

"Hard?" Minnow yearned to reply every time. "Hideous would be more accurate."

Instead, she would simply smile and explain that no, it hadn't been difficult. Believe it or not, she would declare, it had been an enormous relief; Lila's demands on everyone else just meant she was left blessedly alone.

At this, the offending party would burst into charmed laughter and declare that Minnow was so grown-up, just looking at her made her feel old.

In fact, the months leading up to the wedding had been nearly unbearable. Lila had invaded Northern Gardens and taken the family prisoner. With Lila in residence, the typically tinkling chime of summer activity revved up to a roar. Lila's demands on the family were par for the course. She had always required a large portion of her parents' attention, but over the years, Minnow had learned how to require just a little bit more. Unfortunately, the planning of the wedding had completely transfixed Augusta, turning her into a robot set to a single mode. She had one mission: to make Lila's wedding as perfect as she remembered her own. Minnow could have set fire to the porch, and Augusta would have looked on, bemused. That is, so long as it could be fixed by August.

In some ways, though, the wedding had proven a boon to Minnow. The commitment forced Augusta to abandon her post as manager of Minnow's summer schedule, releasing Minnow from her usual obligations: golf lessons, sailing lessons, the Mid-summer Mess, a sailing regatta, the July Fourth tennis round-robin, the July Fourth parade, and best of all, the club talent show, in which the Hayes family traditionally performed a mortifying musical skit. All of this amounted to more time for reading on the porch and for dangling her feet off the dock.

Indirectly, the wedding also lessened the burden of Chip, distracting him with various errands and generally driving him out of the house. Tom, too, proved to be a pleasant enough fixture at

Northern Gardens. He drove up on most weekends, not so much to consult on wedding plans as to console Lila. On Race Day at the yacht club, he was an invaluable addition to the team, and on Sundays, he treated the Hayes family to very decent banana pancakes.

Still, regardless of these minor perks, Minnow's greatest consolation was that one person had suffered more than she. The whole endeavor had been hardest on her father. His dependency on his wife increased with every day of her neglect, and his spirits suffered terribly. After accepting defeat to place settings and seating arrangements, he settled into a summer schedule that was even more languid than usual. He abandoned his morning golf game and slept late into the morning, ceased his daily regimen of jogging before afternoon cocktails. When he did emerge from his bedroom, he moved directly to his basement office, a spot he had not inhabited since the early nineties, when he last worked on the musical. The occasional tinkling of the piano wafting up through the kitchen floorboards led the family to believe he had ended his ten-year hiatus and dusted off his composition book.

And yet, every nuisance of Lila's cohabitation paled in comparison to the one true hardship: eight yards of pure white English Victorian lace the texture and consistency of powdered sugar. As a second, third, and final blow: a crinoline of ivory netted tulle, eighty covered satin buttons, a chocolate sash made from raw Indian silk, and a train so majestic it would have humbled an Egyptian queen. The veil stood separate from this ensemble with heartbreaking indifference, resting on its own hanger, a simple mask of tulle that would flow from a crown of white roses. It was cruel enough that a dress so perfect was completely off-limits. But that it would never touch her skin was nothing short of ruthless.

Now, as Minnow lay in bed, she cursed Lila for the insult. It would be one thing if Lila had shared the privilege, had allowed her to caress the fine fabric, to try it on and prance around the house like a cheerful princess. Instead, her sister had treated her like a contagious leper, quarantining the dress as though Minnow might damage it simply by gazing at it. It was almost as though Lila had used the dress to lord her enormous good fortune over her sister, as if to say, "No, you can't be happy too. There is only enough happiness for me." Curled in her rosebud duvet, Minnow attempted to quell her seething anger with a passionate journal entry. Her favored purple pen had not sufficed—red marker was necessary to convey the ignominy of this injustice.

But even this cathartic act did little to relieve her boiling anger. She was haunted by this dress—as truly and terribly obsessed as she had once been by jellyfish. When she was seven, Chip had scarred her permanently by lifting one of the slimy invertebrates from the bay and chasing her with it, waving its slithering translucent flesh as she sprinted to the shore. She did not get back in the ocean until June of the next year.

But the trauma persisted long after that. For years, whenever she was swimming, she jumped at the sight of any ripple, clawing the arm of the closest swimmer or swimming madly for the shore. Even now, seven years later, she remained at the ready for the first swipe of flesh. The false alarms did not relieve her. Just the opposite; the absence of an attack only heightened her fear. By the time she turned ten, she actively wished for a jellyfish to sting her calf. It would be better to know the pain than to continue imagining the torment. It was just the same with the dress. She simply needed to touch it.

Earlier that morning, the dress had arrived with excessive fanfare. At the sound of wheels on gravel, Lila had raced Augusta to the door, each of them nearly tripping the other in her haste to greet the messenger. Lila reached the door first, but Augusta circumvented, seizing the enormous box with the speed and efficiency of an ambulance worker. Lila abandoned the confused messenger, trailing her mother across the kitchen, cursing the designer who had promised its arrival days earlier. They stopped at the end of the kitchen and hastily set down the box, Augusta stabbing it with a steak knife while Lila clawed at it with her bare hands.

Finally, the box gave way, and Lila grabbed for the hanger, thrusting her arm inches from the path of Augusta's serrated knife. A black zippered bag emerged, and Lila tugged at the zipper, as though she were a doctor performing emergency surgery. At last, the dress emerged without a trace of the bloody battle. The sugar-white satin rose from the box like an ascending angel, only to disappear as Lila thrust it back in the box, clutched it, and ran upstairs. The dress was ripped from Minnow's sight even before its box had grazed the floorboards, leaving her to wonder if the whole thing had been an apparition. On instinct, she trailed Lila, following her up the stairs, but Lila quickly shooed her away, promising to ban her from the wedding if she took another step.

Luckily, a studious investigation led Minnow to the dress. Feigning obedience, she took a seat at the foot of the stairs. She listened carefully to the patter of footsteps as Lila progressed through the house and toward her hiding spot. Oddly, Lila did not stop on the second floor to deposit the dress in Augusta's dressing room, nor did she pause on the third floor to hang it in her own closet; she climbed an additional flight to the house's maligned attic, no doubt to secrete the dress in its fragrant cedar closet.

Until now, this closet had never been home to anything

auspicious—overgrown and seasonal attire were occasionally stowed in the back with a surplus of mothballs. But tonight, the closet would host the most refined guest ever to grace Northern Gardens. And it would do so without lock or key—with an utter absence of security. The sound of a closing door and, minutes later, Lila's descending footsteps finally confirmed Minnow's hypothesis—and assuaged her sorrow. Before tomorrow's wedding, she vowed to see and touch the dress.

Now, with six hours until daylight, she realized her moment had come. Tomorrow, the dress would be guarded not only by Lila but her four other bridesmaids. And even the most lenient among them would guard it with her life. Without further delay, Minnow bolstered herself and thrust the covers from her bed, replacing her journal in its hiding place and tiptoeing across her room. For the first time in her life, she would stray from her firm policy never to enter the attic alone.

To date, she had only been in the attic accompanied by her mother, on missions to retrieve wool sweaters the week before Labor Day, and with her sister, to find costumes for the club talent show. These trips had proceeded uneventfully, but she was always grateful for the company. She imagined that a solo voyage would be a wholly different experience, that the first creak of the floor or the faintest moan of wind would compel an immediate retreat. Even the attic's particular scent—cedar, mothballs, and rain—was chilling enough to inspire a sprint down the stairs, breath held until she landed safely in the kitchen, three flights below, terrified and gasping.

Mercifully, as she crept into the attic, desire overwhelmed fear. As she climbed from the second floor to the third, from the third-floor landing up the small, steep staircase, she was graced with an unexpected reserve of courage. She suddenly felt like a much older girl—at least fifteen or sixteen—so that when she finally touched the dress, she immediately set her sight on a higher goal and yanked it off the hanger.

Even under normal circumstances, Augusta could not count on sleep. She slept, at best, six hours a night and even then, her dreams were plagued by an incessant procession of lists. It was as though her subconscious mind was cataloging the unfinished tasks of the previous day. The situation improved and worsened depending on the state of her children's lives. It was worst during the holidays, when she doubled as an air traffic controller for her children's travel plans, and best in the summer, when she retired the family to Northern Gardens for the season.

The house was her panacea. There was something intrinsic to its smell that was utterly transformative. The white gabled Victorian house might as well have been a white clapboard church. Every year, when she arrived in June, car stocked with produce and good olive oil, she felt a version of the same feeling, as though she would suffocate if she couldn't immediately inhale Northern Gardens' particular breeze, as though the car had pulled into the driveway just in time. Even before coming to a full stop, Minnow burst from the car, desperate to stretch her legs or else lose them to pins and needles. As Minnow sprinted toward the water, Augusta followed behind at a walk, equally anxious to hike up her pants and tumble down the lawn.

But she diverged from her daughter's path at the end of the driveway, circling the house, picking up stray branches, noting the hedges that would need the most attention while William unloaded the car. Satisfied with the first phase of her tour, she ventured toward the house, unlocking it ceremoniously and standing still, just inside the threshold, as though she had entered a stranger's home. The next ten minutes were devoted to a tour of the interior. She attempted to gauge the severity of the winter by the state of the windows, the fade of the furniture, the presence of any leaks.

She walked through the whole house just like this, opening and shutting cabinets, rattling shutters, fluffing the occasional pillow. But only part of her mind was attuned to the physical house; every step was in fact a move toward a certain version of herself, a version that she adored and missed during the winter the same way she missed very old friends. With every step, she felt more like that woman and more elated by the reunion. As though on cue, the incessant scroll of lists slowed to a drift. Items like Lila's travel plans and Chip's precarious employment were replaced by things like blueberries and a new lobster pot. A lobster boil would be the perfect way to kick off the summer.

What a lovely summer last summer had been. This summer had been considerably less relaxing. Since early June, the house had been a circus grounds, host to a revolving population of visitors and guests. Between the interviews for florists and caterers, the trips to New York for fittings, the constant stream of phone calls—to this day, she had not installed call waiting on the Northern Gardens phone—it had been nearly impossible to enjoy her morning coffee without some pressing emergency calling her from the porch. And that was only June.

July had brought Lila's arrival and with it, an increase in the house's electrical output. As though on cue, Augusta's lists had returned with a vengeance, crowding her brain with a torrent of uncompleted errands, unreturned calls, and unresolved decisions.

Sometimes, these lists had dared to afflict her even after tasks were completed, presenting themselves as a list of alternative, potentially superior decisions. Cruelly, these lists grew more oppressive when she was trying to sleep, surfacing in dreams when she was lucky enough to have them, and otherwise keeping her up for the better part of the night.

Tonight, she had been possessed by one such phantom list, a list of the various centerpieces she had decided against. Now, as she lay in bed, all of the ideas she had rejected seemed preferable to the one she had picked. A delicate candelabra of glass votives was the front-runner for a while, until the caterer dissuaded her with a horror story about a tablecloth that went up in flames. A summertime cornucopia presented a decent alternative until she considered the risk posed to formal attire by so much purple fruit—grapes and blueberries were particularly unforgiving. A crate crammed with cheerful clementines had appealed to her for a while, but ultimately, it seemed somehow too simple. A large glass vase filled with indigenous sea glass had promised to glisten beautifully in candlelight but threatened to resemble a gumball machine without the proper lighting; a large conch shell could be simple and elegant but would it look too spare on the table? And a pickle jar filled with limes had offered a welcome splash of color but had finally seemed too informal. This was a wedding, not a hoedown, after all.

The one she finally decided upon seemed right at the time. Like Lila, it was sufficiently beautiful and complicated. It had required the following three-step procedure. First, Augusta wandered the grounds of Northern Gardens, collecting fallen branches of a particular size; then, Minnow spent three weeks harvesting sea glass from the beach; finally, the florist mounted the branches on inconspicuous stands and threaded the blue and green crystals through the branches so that they dangled like ornaments on a Christmas tree. The whole effect would be ethereal, turning the tent into a glittering underwater city.

But now, as Augusta lay in bed, she feared the idea was better in theory than in practice. Would the branches that held so much meaning for her look to others like gnarled twigs? Would the sea glass—a massive project for Minnow—even shimmer under so many artificial lights? Suddenly, the whole idea struck Augusta as ill-conceived. A simple vase of white tulips would have been a better choice.

Of course, last-minute second-guessing was the prescribed domain of the mother of the bride. But Augusta's concerns about the centerpieces paled in comparison to her concerns about one other detail of the wedding. That Augusta was conflicted about Tom was certainly no secret. She had made it known to Lila for years and admittedly even to Tom. Lila wrote it off as typical maternal protectiveness—ambivalence that would slowly give way to love. But ambivalence, Augusta decided—if it was that—was much more problematic than aversion. Hatred, at least, lived on the same spectrum as love and was somehow easier to convert. Ambivalence never strengthened or abated; it simply remained—in the subtext of every conversation, the backdrop of every telephone exchange, in the midst of every holiday gathering. Ambivalence was arguably stronger than love. It thrived like a germ until death.

Furious, Augusta turned to her sleeping husband and rattled his shoulder, gently first, then more violently. In general, she didn't mind—sometimes, she even relished his obliviousness, but in moments like these, she hated him for his indifference and his unfettered sleep.

"William," she said.

His eyes still closed, he raised his eyebrows in response.

"William," she repeated. "A terrible mistake has been made."

In some ways, Augusta's voice functioned as an alarm for William even when he was awake. "Yes, darling," he said, opening his eyes.

"The centerpieces," Augusta explained. "I don't know what I was thinking."

"Gussie, come on." William sighed. His eyelids fell against his will.

"William, wake up," she demanded.

"I'm up," he lied. "I'm up." But his eyelids failed him again, falling slowly to close.

Augusta stared at her husband, newly enraged. But she was also somewhat relieved; she now had a legitimate object for her anger. It was easier to be angry at William than a gnarled tree branch. As she stared, it occurred to her that William had much in common with the branch. Both were handsomely weathered when appraised on their own. But both were depressingly mangled when compared to healthy branches. Once again, she was struck by overwhelming dread, as though she had set sail on a cloudless day only to find herself in a storm.

"William," she begged. But it was no use; she had lost him again to sleep.

There was, of course, a time when she had been more optimistic about her husband. When they married, he possessed nine of the ten qualities on her childhood list for a groom. Unfortunately, a child's wish list often fails to imagine the needs of the adult. Still, Augusta supported William's decision when he left his job to pursue his artistic dream. It was a luxury of his circumstance that he could retire at such a young age—and in some ways a status symbol. Of course, she would have preferred if it had been something other than a musical. Why not a novel? Painting, poetry even. But she did her best to hold her head up when friends asked how the work was going. William was terribly excited, she explained. It was sure to be fabulous. But when two, three, then ten years passed without a finished product, Augusta grew more skeptical—and more insistent. For years, she badgered William to share his work. When he finally did, she regretted it.

On a Friday night in July, William invited Augusta to sit by the piano in the parlor while he performed his work in progress from start to finish. *The Last Great Love*, as he called it, was an homage to his deceased parents, adapted from letters they exchanged during World War II when his father captained a minesweeper and his mother waited anxiously at home. The libretto was based on letters that documented, in excruciating detail, the tedium of war, the itinerary of the U.S. Navy, and the romance of a separated husband and wife.

The inherent melodrama of the story was somehow doubled by William's treatment. Musical highlights included songs such as "Mein Minesweeper," "Rosie, I'm Riveted," "Uncle Sam, I'm Your Man," and the incomparably horrifying "Nuremberg Trials and Errors." When William finished his performance, Augusta was in tears. Mercifully, he assumed she had been moved by the story. But pity is, of course, a dangerous blow to any marriage.

For the first time, Augusta understood her role in her husband's paralysis. She had allowed him to choose between life's two most important aspirations—art and money—and the choice had proven fatal. He had come unmoored, as useless as a compass at the North Pole. But even more disturbing than the spectacle of her husband's incompetence was its eerie resemblance to the predicament her own children faced. She shuddered to think that their own privilege might condemn them to equally directionless lives.

Chip had certainly exhibited many of the same weaknesses. Lacking a pressing need—and therefore, the drive—to make money, he had identified art as an outlet, if only insofar as he expressed it as a thirst for disorder. To be sure, Chip's problems were not so simple as to be solved by a painting class, but at least the freedom of creative pursuits had offered some liberation. Minnow was much like her mother, creative but ultimately practical. Lila had always been immune to the lure of most abstract things and so had landed squarely and unapologetically in the realm of materialism. Her choice of husband, Augusta had always felt, represented a sort of a concession. Tom, however, seemed to be headed in the same direction as William—only he lacked the financial resources to support the lifestyle. Or rather, he had until he met Lila.

It was this, finally, that kept Augusta awake as it neared midnight: the knowledge that her impeccable daughter would imminently pledge herself to someone imperfect. More to the point, she feared Tom harbored a hidden agenda, that he intended to burden Lila—and her family—with a lifetime of patronage. Lila would surely have disowned her mother had she ever voiced this opinion. But if Tom counted on this—and of course, he did—well, this was nothing short of despicable.

"William," Augusta whispered. "Please wake up."

William sat up, mouth agape.

"Please tell me they'll be beautiful," she begged.

"What will, darling?"

"The centerpieces," she said.

"They'll be beautiful," he promised. "Perfectly beautiful."

TEN

There was not a single member of Pete's high-school class who was not shocked and slightly appalled when Pete received his acceptance letter to Yale, and early admission to boot. They attributed the break to his impressive athletic record and, of course, his impressive last name. The Allerton family was an early leader in the tobacco trade and had profited almost as much from Philip Morris as Philip Morris himself. Shortly after admissions letters went out, Pete's high-school student center was vandalized with an outraged slogan: PETE + THE ALLERTON ATHLETIC CENTER = EARLY ADMISSION.

It was not that Pete was dumb. No one was admitted to Yale below a certain level of intelligence (although the sports recruits did their part to bring down the average). But Pete's college counselor had been wise in her pitch for Pete. She told Yale's director of admissions that Pete had "raw potential," invoking a term used to describe students with higher test scores than grades. It was, in fact, a

brilliant spin on Pete's high-school performance. The other interpretation was, of course, that Pete had blown off his work, squan-
dering the high IQ that his test scores revealed. In other words, he
was the very kind of student Yale sought to sift from the pile.

Luckily, he rose to the occasion when he arrived in New Haven,
meeting his requirements due to the collective effort of his friends.
But after graduation, lacking this crutch, he had struggled significantly. Most recently, he had considered mounting an application to
film school, having heard of one too many classmates selling a pilot
for a mint. Ultimately, he bailed on the application because of the
essay requirements. But he did purchase the expensive screenwrit-
ing software, read the first several chapters of the manual, and write
thirty pages of a script about a clique of college friends who reunite
at a funeral.

"Let's go through every one of our friends and say what we really think of them," Weesie declared. She had progressed through
various positions over the last hour, from the sofa, to a fraying upholstered chair, back to the sofa where Pete now sat, to a reclining
position with her feet in Pete's lap. This was the most comfortable
position so far, and also the one that best obscured her view of the
house's spooky dark hallway.

"You're drunk," said Pete.

"Well, yeah," said Weesie. "We've been drinking since five
o'clock. What time is it now?"

Pete shrugged. "Hell if I know."

"Of course, you don't wear a watch."

Pete smiled. It was a point of pride that he didn't wear a watch.
In college, it had seemed a more quaint rebellion. Now, it seemed
subversive, a true rejection of societal rules.

"Jake wears a watch," Weesie declared.

"I think he wears two," said Pete.

"I bought him a really nice one for Christmas," Weesie said, then she deflated. "It's such a boring gift."

"The worst," Pete agreed. "Tripler gave me one for my last birthday." He assumed a robotic monotone. "The gift you give when you want your spouse to show up on time."

"Ha," said Weesie. She let loose with a sharp jab to Pete's thigh.

"I'm just kidding," Pete added. "It's beautiful. She had it engraved with our anniversary."

"Aw, that's so sweet," Weesie said. "I should have done that."

"Not sweet. Practical," Pete said. "I had forgotten it one too many times."

Weesie attempted to administer another jab to the leg, but this time, Pete anticipated the motion and grabbed her foot by the ankle.

It occurred to Pete that holding Weesie's ankle was inappropriately intimate, but he dismissed the notion quickly and held it firmly in his grasp.

Weesie made a halfhearted attempt to disengage from Pete's grasp but, relishing the charge it sent through her body, quickly gave up. She batted one arm across the floor, searching for the wine bottle.

Weesie did not start drinking seriously until after she graduated from college. At school, she had earned the adorable, if slightly embarrassing, reputation of being the member of the group most likely to end the night sober. It was not for lack of trying. She tried to party voraciously. But instinctively, she didn't enjoy it. To watch common sense, balance, even walls evaporate as a night progressed struck her as decidedly un-fun. Luckily, fate conspired with Weesie's preferences. As a freshman, she was pretty enough to walk into any dorm room without a drink in her hand.

That her mother's diet of vodka gimlets and peppermint candies formed the basis for her aversion to alcohol did not occur to Weesie until she married Jake. At this point, it became clear that Jake shared her mother's proclivity and, more importantly, that Weesie needed to acquire it in order for the marriage to survive. Even so, she had not developed an especially high tolerance. She was still as charmingly vulnerable to alcohol—red wine especially—as she had been during those first few months of her marriage, when she had ended most nights sitting on her bathroom floor, counting the tiles on the wall, wondering how she'd ended up with someone so much like her mother.

"Here; I'll go first. Annie Wallace," Weesie said. She elevated her diction as though she were presenting a diploma. "Lovable but neurotic. Totally obsessed with her looks. Not sure about her fiancé. Not as smart as she thinks."

"Ouch," said Pete.

"Sorry," said Weesie. "I told you I was drunk." Without getting up, she fumbled for the wine bottle resting on the floor. She lifted it to her mouth sideways, like a canteen.

"It's empty," said Pete.

"No," Weesie whined. "What are we going to do now?"

"Oscar Clark," Pete announced, and it functioned, for the moment, as a distraction.

"The smartest one among us," Weesie said. "And the most annoying."

Pete nodded his agreement.

"So far in the closet," Weesie added, "it's a wonder the boy can breathe."

"You think so?" asked Pete.

"Know," Weesie said.

"Interesting," Pete said.

"What the hell is 'wireless content' anyway? If he says that again, I'm going to smack him."

"It's huge, you idiot," Pete said.

"Whatever," Weesie went on. "Can someone please tell him the dot-com bubble burst?"

"He works for Google, dumb-ass."

"Oh God," Weesie said. "Really?" She sat upright and turned to Pete. "You would tell me if I were insufferable, wouldn't you?" She fell back onto the sofa before Pete could respond. "Someone should tell Oscar."

Pete poked the arch of Weesie's foot, and she recoiled, giggling. He had never realized how hilarious she was until now. Tripler often contended that Weesie was the funniest girl in the group, but Pete had rejected the sentiment as a kind of consolation prize; it was better to be Lila, the prettiest, or Laura, the smartest. In all his time knowing Weesie, he had never seen evidence of this vaunted sense of humor. But now he realized the observation was justified, understated even.

"Your turn," Weesie demanded.

Pete said nothing. He had never before spent this much time alone with Weesie, and he was surprised, not only by her rowdiness but also by the smell of her skin. It was a guilty realization, of course, but one that he quickly dismissed. How to feel this way with his wife, he decided, was the lesson he could take away from this night.

"Laura. Brilliant, tortured, hates Lila, completely obsessed with Tom," he said.

Weesie smiled and saluted. "Well stated."

"Lila. Perfect, beautiful, gorgeous, tortures her friends for sport." He paused, debating his next disclosure. "Not very good in bed."

"No!" Weesie squealed.

"Afraid so," said Pete.

"When did this happen?"

"Freshman year." He paused. "And then one other time that nobody knows about."

"What! When?" Weesie demanded.

"We were still in college," Pete said.

"But you were dating Tripler when you were still in college!"

Pete nodded. "Scandalous, I know." He moved on before Weesie could launch a more extensive interrogation. "Tom. Heartthrob. Genius. Charmer. Missing, as we know. Not in love with Lila. And yes, I think that's why."

"Aha!" said Weesie. "I knew it." She sat upright and turned to face Pete. "So where do you think he is?"

"Somewhere, freaking out."

Weesie stared at Pete for a moment, nodding and smiling. "I knew it," she said. "I totally knew it. That makes me feel better."

So much better that she quickly lost interest in Tom and moved on to the remaining victims.

"We skipped ourselves and our spouses," Weesie said.

"Seems fair enough," Pete said.

"Come on. It'll be fun," she said. "I'll do Tripler, and you do Jake. So we both have something on each other."

Pete grinned and shook his head, pretending to refuse. Without thinking, he slid his hand from Weesie's ankle to her calf.

"Tripler," Weesie began carefully. "Hilarious. Driven. Terrified."

Pete swallowed a treacherous feeling.

"I just worry sometimes that she's going to snap."

"I think she already did," said Pete.

Weesie nodded solemnly.

Pete frowned as he digested the enormity of the betrayal.

"Your turn," Weesie said. She reached again for the bottle, but tipped it to the ground.

"Jake," he began. "Talented. Sensitive. One of Yale's finest. But if the poor guy doesn't write something soon, I'm afraid he's going to go postal."

Weesie covered her mouth with her hand, as though the gesture could obscure her agreement.

"They'd actually be really good together," Pete said.

"Oh my God, you're totally right," Weesie shouted.

"Maybe we should set them up," Pete said.

"I think Tripler's already on it," said Weesie.

"Good point," said Pete. "But I bet we're having more fun."

It occurred to Weesie that the conversation had reached the threshold of propriety. But she waited too long to respond—or decided against it—and by the time she did, she was too drunk to tell the difference.

ELEVEN

Tripler stood suddenly from the sofa and beelined for the bar. The ideal ratio of vodka to vermouth eluded her at the moment, so she erred on the side of too much vodka. It was a policy she followed as a rule: masking self-doubt with self-assurance. Drinks in hand, she returned to the coffee table and set them down with a ceremonious clink. She produced a small white plastic bag and scanned the coffee table for an adequate surface. She rejected the coaster, a book on Colonial architecture, and the glass pane of the table before settling on a framed photograph of Lila.

"You've got to be kidding," Jake said. Cocaine was never a part of the group's repertoire in college. It was a staple of the classes that matriculated a few years later but considered by this group to be as passé as bell-bottom jeans.

"Come on," Tripler said. "This is your last chance to do blow off of Lila's thighs."

Jake closed his eyes, the only response to this kind of provocation.

When he opened them, Tripler was hunched over the table, playing the role of the beautiful mess. The performance was perfectly calibrated—repellent yet irresistible. Before she had inhaled the first line, Jake was sitting by her side.

Despite her efforts to present herself as a confident, together person, Tripler felt, at the age of twenty-nine, as lost as she had at nineteen. No matter what she was wearing, she felt like a mannequin, shoddily pulled together, desperate to be reinvented in the coming season. It didn't matter that she had finally kicked a ten-year eating disorder. Unfortunately, her particular disorder was the one that didn't amount to weight loss. Instead, it had caused her weight to fluctuate over the same fifteen pounds and consumed much of the day with the search for a secluded bathroom. Choosing acting as a vocation certainly played into the disease. But oddly, the crushing rejections of auditions were not problematic in themselves. In some way, the dismissive directors and apathetic producers offered a kind of consolation, echoing a voice as familiar and nostalgic as milk and cookies.

An only child, Tripler had been subject to all of her mother's attention and none of her approval. That her mother frowned on her vocation was predictable, but that she disparaged every other choice Tripler made—her weight, her wardrobe, the color of her hair—was almost too much to bear. Mrs. Pane was not even satisfied with Yale, having hoped for Harvard. The constancy of her disapproval permeated Tripler's every thought, causing her behavior to oscillate, much like her weight, between obedience and rebellion. It was as though her mother had infected her with a germ at conception, haunting Tripler with the suspicion that she was defective. Nothing she had done in her twenty-nine years had done much to convince her otherwise.

Her girlfriends heaved a collective sigh when, just over a year ago, Tripler asked, by way of mass e-mail, if anyone knew of a good shrink. All four had replied within the hour. And it seemed to be a divine intervention. In the last year, Tripler had kicked bulimia, lost twenty pounds, and gotten her first part in an indie movie, a three-day stint that confirmed her belief that movie sets were her natural habitat. Unfortunately, this progress was offset by a handful of new bad habits. The state of her marriage—and her affair with cocaine—had been unsettling of late. She had looked forward to Tom and Lila's wedding with childlike anticipation—as though it were her own wedding—hopeful that time with her best friends from college would give way to the feelings *she had* in college—the giddy excitement, the hopeful anxiety, the oblivious confidence. She had not felt any of those things for so many years.

"Hey," said Tripler. She swatted at Jake as he leaned in for a second sniff. But she was too slow to respond. Jake had already inhaled the pile.

The basement seemed like the right part of the house to tackle first. It was accessed from the kitchen, so the path was likely deserted. Even so, the chill of clay tiles on their feet took them by surprise.

"Shit," Tripler snapped, looking down at the floor. "Of course, she did terra-cotta."

Jake was actually relieved by the cold. The feeling of tile against his bare feet reaffirmed his connection with the ground.

"Are you sure this shit isn't laced," he demanded. "I've done cocaine, and this is not how it felt."

"Don't be retarded," Tripler said.

She took the lead and opened the door to the basement, marching fearlessly ahead while Jake followed behind.

The planks of the stairs were wider and darker than the floorboards in the rest of the house, revealing the shifts of the house's foundation far more honestly than the polished floors of the public areas. This realization gave Tripler an odd sense of satisfaction. It was pure thrift, the sneakiest of economics, that would compel a homeowner to skim-coat the dining room walls but shortchange the hidden spaces.

A muffled but indisputable thud stopped them in their path.

"What the fuck was that?" Jake whispered.

Tripler froze, cocked her head to the ceiling, then continued down the stairs. "It's a spooky old haunted house," she quipped. "What do you expect?"

A single bare lightbulb hung from the ceiling, surrounded by spiderwebs. Tripler fumbled for a moment, then tugged at the string, spreading light throughout the room. She moved past an old refrigerator into a smaller adjoining room. The furnace and fuse box rattled with every step she took.

Jake trailed slightly behind, ears pricked for suspicious sounds. He was already quite overwhelmed by the high. Everything in the room seemed to spin as though he were the axis of a carousel. He clenched and unclenched his hands, suddenly convinced they were going numb. Gulping his drink helped the cause, sending tingles of sensation to his extremities. Against his will, he forced himself to scout the adjoining room. Inside, he found a bare, makeshift office that was bathed in an inch of dust. A plaid sleeper sofa languished on a worn Persian rug. Two metal music stands stood across from the sofa, their height and distance causing them to look like eager guests. Calming slightly, he crossed the room to examine the music stands. They held consecutive pages with a five-line staff, a musical work whose title was scrawled at the top of the page: *The Last Great Love.*

A flickering light interrupted Jake's investigation. He followed the signal back to the main room to find Tripler standing under the bulb, tugging its string impatiently.

"He's not here," she announced.

"Yeah, I noticed," Jake said.

"He's obviously with Lila," Tripler said. She tugged violently at the string, casting them back into darkness.

Cocaine, though not a hallucinatory drug, had a strange effect on the search. Even Tripler found the task of tiptoeing through the unlit house a trial. As she walked, objects appeared in sharp relief, as though it were noon on a winter day, not sometime after midnight. Her balance was dulled to the same extent that her perception was sharpened. And the combination of these two things made it very hard to walk.

She had intended her supply to last through the weekend but quickly gave in to the drug's logic, concluding that one excessive night was better than several moderate ones. As they crossed through the kitchen, she treated herself to a quick replenishment. There was something irresistible about doing lines off Augusta's countertops.

"How's your job going anyway," she demanded. She poured and divided a sizable pile into two unequal portions, then handily inhaled the larger pile and offered Jake the smaller one with a gracious nod.

"I got fired last week," said Jake. "But I haven't told Weesie yet, so please don't say anything." Jake attempted to mimic Tripler's technique, but he lost concentration in mid-snort and sacrificed the rest to a cough.

"You haven't told Weesie yet?"

"Nope. And I'm not planning to for a while."

"Where does she think you are all day?"

"I don't know. I don't care."

"Oh God, Jake. That's awful," said Tripler. She ran her finger over the counter. "I'm sure she would understand."

"You think? But would you understand?" Jake paused. "If I was totally pulling your leg?"

"Fuck off," she snapped. "Excuse me for giving a shit about my friends."

"I'm just joking," Jake said.

"Hilarious," said Tripler. "Next time, I won't even ask."

"I'm sorry," said Jake. "Don't be mad. How about you? How have you been?"

"Lately?" asked Tripler

"I don't know," said Jake. "How have you been since college?"

Tripler opened her mouth to reply with typical bravado. But the drug revised her response, and the truth came out instead. "Not so great," she confessed.

"How are you and Pete?" Jake tried.

"Great," she lied. "Really good."

"That's good," said Jake. "Us too."

Tripler looked down and stared at the counter, as though she were trying to count the grains in the stone. She remained like this for a moment, stifling a wave of sadness. But before she could name the emotion she was fighting against, she burst into tears. "We're terrible," she admitted. "Really bad." A cascade of sniffles obscured her speech.

"Oh Trip," said Jake. He leaned across the counter and placed his hand on her shoulder.

"Everyone seems so happy," she sniffled.

"No," said Jake. "No one's happy."

"Really?" she asked. She stopped sniffling for a moment, as though comforted by this thought.

"Really," Jake said.

"Well, you people should try acting. You're better at it than me."

Jake tilted his head thoughtfully in mock consideration. "Hmm, maybe I should," he said. "The writing thing hasn't panned out."

Tripler offered a grateful smile. "At least you know you have talent. I haven't done anything worthwhile since I was eighteen years old."

"What'd you do then?" Jake asked.

"I got into Yale," she said. She shook her head, fighting another swell of despair. "I was headed for greatness then."

"You still are," Jake said.

Tripler closed her eyes as a teardrop slid down her cheek. "I can't even take credit for that." She winced. "I cheated on my SATs."

On reflex, Jake's mouth fell open, and he sat, gaping for a moment. Then he realized the severity of his expression and consciously closed his mouth.

Tripler sat, head bowed and eyes closed, reveling in the release of the confession, then, without warning, she burst into tears again as though trying to best her previous performance. "We're such horrible clichés," she said. "Everything we are. Everything we say."

Jake smiled compassionately, shook his head.

"Now's where you say, 'Don't be silly, you *are* a great actress. And then I say, 'Your novel is going to change the world.'"

"And then I say, 'Weren't we supposed to *save* the world?'"

"And then I say, 'The world's all gone to shit. What does it matter anyway?'"

"And then we kiss in a desperate displacement of our need to connect."

Tripler paused, confused by the new tenor of their conversation. Were they still speaking theoretically? Or had they agreed on a secret code? And because she had reached the summit of her high and the low point of her self-respect, she was at a loss to tell the difference. So she took Jake at his word, leaned over the counter, and kissed him on the lips.

Jake kissed back for several seconds before pushing her away.

"What," she said. "What's the big deal?"

"Weesie, for one. And Pete."

"God," said Tripler. "Don't be such an altar boy. I'm totally wasted."

Luckily, this explanation succeeded in relieving both her guilt and mortification. Unfazed, she dismissed Jake with a disapproving shrug and inhaled the remainder of her supply.

The trek up the stairs was far more treacherous than the basement search. It essentially required sneaking past an entire household—eight rooms filled to capacity with sleeping family members and guests. Therefore, the best approach, Tripler and Jake decided, was to move at maximum speed, to sprint on their tiptoes from the living room to the third floor of the house.

They completed the climb to the second landing easily, their footsteps muffled by a runner bolted to the stairs. The second flight was far more precarious as the runner gave way to wooden planks. Jake paused for a moment as he approached the third landing, cautioned by a partially open door and the glow of a bedside lamp. Tripler motioned for him to proceed with an exasperated look.

Moving slowly, she walked to Lila's door with exaggerated stealth. She craned her neck around the door, already wearing a triumphant smile. But she was totally stilled by the scene inside: Lila sat on her windowsill, staring out at the lawn. Tom was nowhere to be found.

Surprise cost Tripler her composure. Instinctively, she recoiled. As she leapt toward the stairs, she inadvertently rattled Lila's door.

"Hello?" said Lila.

Tripler froze. Jake gestured toward the attic.

"Mother?" called Lila.

Tripler darted up the stairs with Jake trailing behind. As they fled, they abandoned propriety, bolting up two steps at a time with all the subtlety of wild boars.

When they opened the door to the attic, they were greeted by a chilling image: a figure dwarfed by a wedding dress several sizes too large, as though it had emerged from the grave, shrunken and brittle, to reclaim the forgotten apparel. The surroundings did little to soften the image. The spectral figure was lit by the moon so that light sifted in from the window through her hair, casting a ghoulish shadow on the nearest wall. At the sight of the eerie silhouette, Tripler nearly fainted. Jake, however, was quick to respond. He turned on his heels, sprinted down the stairs, and disappeared into the darkness.

TWELVE

Tripler slipped out the door to the attic and stood still as Jake peeled off across the lawn. But she rued the decision within seconds. God knew how many people he had roused as he fled. She should have run while there was still time.

"Hello," said Lila. "Who's out there?"

Tripler tried to mute her panting by breathing through her nose.

"Laura, Tripler? You guys are late." A door swung open on the third landing.

"It's just me," Tripler called, then she improvised, "Are the others here yet?"

"No," Lila snapped. "They're not."

Tripler started down the stairs, walking very slowly. When she reached the third floor, she entered Lila's room and loitered awkwardly near the door, hanging her head like a teenager busted for missing her curfew.

Lila's room was an impeccable, if slightly studied, model of femininity. A white lace bra dangled from an upholstered chair. An antique mirrored vanity offered up a trove of silver dishes, each one crammed with alluring rings and bangles. Tiny flowers seemed to bloom in every corner, dotting the sofa and the curtains. This room, even more than the rest of the house, had the quality of caricature, presenting a vignette of purity that all but called for deconstruction. As Tripler waited for her scolding, she wondered idly how many boys had seen the room before her.

"Where the fuck is everyone?" Lila barked. She stood in the doorway in pink pajamas, a petite variation on an angry general.

Tripler stood in silence, staring at Lila's attire. Her pajamas were scattered with puffy white clouds, and her hair was pulled back in a loose braid, both of which combined with Lila's acid tone to be comically incongruous. "I'm sure they're on their way," she lied.

"They better be," Lila said. "You guys promised you'd be here at midnight. You're almost an hour late."

"I know," Tripler lied. Drugs and alcohol had conspired to blur her memory of their scheduled visit. "Jake smuggled wine from the club," she said, selling out her friend without hesitation. "They've all had so much to drink, I'd be surprised if they're still conscious."

Lila stared at Tripler, unmoved.

Tripler looked to the window, focused on the rosebuds.

"It's unbelievably rude," Lila hissed.

"You said you wanted us to have fun," Tripler tried.

Lila widened her eyes, enraged.

Tripler immediately regretted the joke. All Lila craved was contrition. "I'm sorry," she said, recanting. "We totally let you down."

"Yeah, you did," Lila said.

"We're assholes," Tripler added, remembering that the key to pleasing Lila was to degrade yourself in her presence.

Lila raised her eyebrows and nodded slightly.

"Can you ever forgive us?" Tripler asked. To her surprise, it was actually less degrading to prostrate herself to Lila in private.

"It's fine," Lila said. She shrugged her shoulders in an exaggerated show of detachment, then crossed the room and seated herself on her bed, letting Tripler stand for several seconds before gesturing toward an ottoman. The disparity in height between the bed and the ottoman required that Tripler look up at Lila like a handmaiden at a princess.

"So, how are you feeling?" Tripler said, forcing a transition. "You must be shitting your pants right now. Luckily, you've never looked better."

Lila smiled, taking the bait. "Actually, I'm not." This was Lila's preferred mode of conversation: two people jointly dissecting a theory about Lila. "Am I supposed to be nervous?" she asked.

"No," Tripler said. She kicked herself for walking into another trap. Lila's second favorite mode of communication was debunking a popular theory. She took any opportunity to trash a favored film, support a hated political figure, or otherwise promote the notion that she was a wild iconoclast.

"Were *you* nervous the night before your wedding?" Lila asked. The question was designed as both a query and an accusation. She might as well have cited a statistic that those who felt nervous on their wedding night were most likely to watch their marriages end in shambles.

Luckily, Tripler was familiar with the routine. "Actually, I was," she said.

"What were you nervous about?" Lila asked.

"God, I don't know. Everything? Having lame sex for the rest of my life. Having nothing to say over breakfast."

"Hmm," Lila said.

For a moment, Tripler wondered if her defense had been too compelling. It was the night before Lila's wedding, after all, and her job was to boost her enthusiasm, not make an argument against marriage. But she quickly realized she had walked into another trap.

"Wow, that sucks," Lila said. "I guess I'm just really lucky."

Without fail, Lila managed to turn acts of kindness into acts of humiliation. "So, what can I do for you? Your bridesmaids are at your service, after all." It was the first wise thing Tripler had said since entering the room. And the hypocrisy of the statement struck her. Surely, it was also a bridesmaid's responsibility to make sure the groom didn't go missing.

"Nothing," Lila said. She finally dispensed with the animosity she had harbored since discovering her guest.

"You really should sleep," Tripler said. "You'll need all your energy for smiling."

Lila sighed amiably.

"And don't forget, you have to have sex tomorrow night. By the time you're finally alone, you're going to be exhausted. But you have to force yourself—"

"Oh, I don't need to worry about that," Lila said, cutting her off. "That's never been a problem for us."

Tripler inhaled, resisting the urge to engage Lila in a new debate. "Either way, you need some rest."

"I'll try," said Lila, and she finally reclined, extending her legs and sinking into her bed.

Tripler stood and crossed the room. She paused at the door, her hand on the switch. "I'm sorry about the others," she said.

"Oh, it's fine," said Lila. "Just when you see them, could you tell them they're not in my wedding anymore?"

"I'll do that," Tripler said. She smiled with the patronizing wisdom of a beleaguered den mother. She made it only two steps down the hall before Lila called out again.

"Was Tom with you guys?" Lila asked. Here, the pretense of nonchalance finally revealed a crack.

Tripler stepped back into Lila's room. "He was for a while." She paused. "Then, he disappeared."

"Disappeared to where?" Lila snapped.

Now, it was Tripler's turn to feign nonchalance. "I assumed he snuck in to see you," she said. "But I guess he just went back to his room to dream about nuptial bliss."

"Oh," said Lila.

Tripler switched off the light before Lila could press any further. She was suddenly overcome with guilt. She had absolutely no clue where Tom was at the moment and, worse, since he had disappeared, she had not given the subject much thought. In moments like this, it was hard to know the true ingredients of remorse: actual regret for one's actions or fear of being found out. Wanting little to do with either, Tripler rushed down the stairs—and continued walking until she got to the Gettys'.

Annie was not the kind of woman who was easily spooked by the dark. In fact, it was she who usually spurred a group to launch into ghost stories. As a child, she had devoted whole weekends to horror-movie marathons. So she agreed without hesitating when Oscar suggested that they leave Northern Gardens and canvass the surrounding island. Tom was unscathed, Oscar had concluded. He was likely walking off his anxiety, or sitting at one of his favorite haunts. The island was small enough, Oscar wagered, that they would surely find him if they followed the main road.

But within an hour, Annie regretted her decision to follow Oscar. The utter absence of noise had quickly become unnerving. The main road, which was paved as you approached Northern Gardens, gave way to dirt as you walked inland. The endless expanse of graveyard had not helped, nor had the sparse, seemingly abandoned houses that dotted the road. Forget Tom. There was nary a sign of life at any of these landmarks. The houses seemed likely to have been just as dark during the daylight hours. Finally, they reached the swimming quarry at the north side of the island. Crickets and the haunting call of loons broke the silence.

"I'm not going over there," Annie said.

"Why not?" said Oscar.

"There're probably ghosts. Or buried skeletons from when this place was a quarry."

"You're more likely to find dinosaur bones," said Oscar. "Maine was the dumping ground of the biggest land bridge of the Mesozoic Era."

"How do you still remember this stuff?" Annie asked.

"Unlike some people I know," said Oscar, "I actually did my reading in college." He punctuated the insult by abandoning Annie and striding decisively toward the quarry.

"Very funny," said Annie. She followed Oscar for a few steps before deciding it was preferable to be left alone. But she quickly regretted the decision: The hoot of an owl and the snap of a twig sent her running after him.

"That's very courageous," Oscar teased.

Annie scoffed, then took his hand. "They still don't even know how they disappeared," she said. "You'd think with all these great minds on the case, they'd have figured it out by now."

"How who disappeared?" Oscar asked.

"The dinosaurs." Annie sniffed.

"They know what it wasn't," Oscar maintained.

"That's certainty for you," said Annie.

"They know it wasn't one great big bang."

"I thought that one was for sure. What's the latest theory?"

"Things changed gradually. Weather patterns, ocean levels, food supplies, the shape of continents."

"So basically, they just starved to death."

"Basically," Oscar conceded.

"See that's what I hate about scientists," said Annie. "They have to make everything so complicated."

Oscar stared at Annie for a moment, torn between setting her straight and saving the breath. Realizing it was a losing battle, he tried to change the subject. "So where do you think he is?" he asked.

"The dinosaur?" Annie asked.

"Tom," said Oscar.

"Hell if I know," said Annie. "You're the one with all the theories."

Oscar nodded, accepting the critique. It was true. He was stumped on this one. "What we have here is a classic conundrum in physics."

The comment was met with a groan, a reception earned by years of didactic pontification.

"That's what you get for marrying a science major," said Oscar.

"I haven't married you yet," said Annie.

But Oscar, like most objects in motion, was not so easily stopped. "The Problem of Three Bodies states that bodies interact due to the gravitational forces between them. With two bodies, their motion can be analyzed and predicted. With three, it is much more complicated. The behavior can be chaotic."

"It doesn't take a summa in quantum mechanics to know that a threesome can be complicated," said Annie.

"It's the basis of chaos theory," Oscar said. "Why the earth, the moon, and the sun remain in a fixed orbit."

"Who's the moon, and who's the earth," Annie demanded.

"Lila is the earth," said Oscar.

"And Laura's the moon?" asked Annie.

"Yes, why not," said Oscar. "She's mysterious, nocturnal, exotic. That long dark hair, those dark eyes."

"Why don't you just say she's so Jewish," Annie snapped, "instead of dancing around the subject?"

Oscar ignored the dig and continued to build his argument. "It's a question that's baffled physicists for centuries."

Annie interrupted again with a chilling impersonation. "Though, I daresay my work at Yale did shed some light on the subject."

Oscar paused to register his indignation, then continued with his sermon. "It's analogous to asking a woman if she loves you when she's still unsure. The act of asking may induce some certainty that wasn't there before you asked."

"Lucky you asked me when you did," Annie quipped.

"Well, not exactly," said Oscar. "The collapse of wave function suggests I may have forced a response that was random."

As they spoke, a new sound graced the quarry, but this time it had a calming effect: rain, first in tentative drops, then with accelerating force, landing on the water in the quarry with the tenderness of a mother's whisper.

"Do you love me, Annie?" Oscar asked.

"Of course," said Annie. "Don't be dumb."

"But what does that mean?" Oscar paused. "Would you be sad if I died?"

"Oscar. Yes," Annie said.

"How sad?" Oscar pressed.

"Heartbroken," Annie said.

"People recover from heartbreak."

"Devastated," Annie tried.

"Devastated?"

"Completely and totally destroyed."

Oscar paused to consider the claim, as though evaluating a piece of produce. "I love you, too," he said finally.

They stood for a moment, listening to the rain, breathing in the scent of leaves.

"Can we go back now?" Annie asked.

Without a word, Oscar took her hand, and they set back on the drenched dirt road, running toward the house.

THIRTEEN

J ake entered the Gettys', breathless and damp, just after one in the morning. His sprint from the Hayeses' to the Gettys' was equal parts frightening and exhilarating—frightening because shadows seemed to lurch from the trees, exhilarating because he had made a narrow escape from Lila. His sudden entrance to the house was equally confusing for Weesie and Pete, who were, at the time, entwined and half-dressed and, at the sound of the opening door, forced to disentangle and rebutton. When they heard Jake enter, they recoiled from each other as though they had touched a hot stove. The rushed fastening of straps and zippers made them feel particularly debauched and pathetic, like characters in a seventies sitcom.

But the mood calmed considerably after this awkward jolt. Thankfully, Jake was too agitated to notice Weesie and Pete's odd behavior. And soon enough, the storm offered its own interruption as wind rose from a rush to a whistle, and rainfall settled on the island. For the moment, they forgot their secrets and took solace in the warmth of the house.

Though none of the three had had any luck finding Tom, they rushed to find comforting excuses. Chances were good, they decided, that Tom had been found by one of the other search parties. Why else would they linger so long outside in this unpleasant weather? The only question was whether Oscar and Annie or Chip and Laura would claim the hunter's prize. So they waited, huddled under blankets and pillows, poised to greet Tom when he returned. They resumed the game they had begun on the raft, sufficiently drunk to find otherwise boring confessions impossibly hilarious.

"I'm going first," Weesie announced.

"Honey, you're too drunk to play," said Jake.

"Am not," said Weesie.

"Are too," said Jake. "There's no way for us to know when you're telling the truth."

"You'll know because you're my husband," she said.

"Besides, it's always so obvious," said Pete. "You can tell from the gestures and the eyes."

Jake eyed Pete, annoyed at his public allegiance with his wife.

"Can I go or not," Weesie interrupted.

"Fine," said Jake. "Just don't cheat."

Startled by the word, she turned quickly to face Jake. But he had only been referring to the game, she realized. Humbled, she proceeded calmly. "When I was seven, I fell off a horse."

"That explains so much about your childhood," Jake quipped.

Weesie rewarded the slight with indifference. "I failed physics sophomore year. And I love my mother."

Pete and Jake remained silent as they considered Weesie's assertions.

"Foul," said Pete. "Jake has an unfair advantage. He knows everything about you."

"Actually, I'm stumped," Jake confessed.

"You are?" Weesie shouted. "You're my husband. You're supposed to know these things."

"Do *you* know what my grades were sophomore year?" Jake quipped.

"Actually, I do," she said.

"Then you have a better memory."

"No," she said. "I just listen better."

Jake paused for a moment, contrite. "You're absolutely right," he said, then he lunged from his seat to kiss her cheek.

Weesie shoved him off. The touch of his lips, so soon after kissing Pete, made her feel guilty and nauseated.

"I'm sorry, Weez," Jake said. "Don't be mad. I didn't even know you took physics."

"I didn't," she snapped. "That was the lie."

"But you do hate your mother."

"I do not," she sneered. "We just argue a lot." She tugged her blanket to her waist, as though chilled by Jake's ignorance.

Jake placed his arm on her shoulder tenderly, but Weesie flinched at his touch, causing Jake to recoil with equal animosity.

"Jake, you're up," Pete said.

"I don't want to play anymore," said Weesie.

Jake ignored her and narrowed his eyes, racking his brain for the best retaliation. "I did a gram of coke tonight. My marriage is in serious trouble." He turned to Pete and addressed him directly. "And your wife tried to get in my pants."

Jake's assertions were followed by several moments of tense silence.

"You fucking asshole," Pete said finally. "You always have to take it there."

"Just playing the game," Jake chirped. "It was your bright idea."

They stared each other down in a parody of virility.

Finally, Pete retreated. The claim was too far-fetched—it was clearly a provocation.

"The cocaine is the lie," Weesie interrupted. "He's way too much of a pussy."

Pete continued to stare at Jake, as though he was assessing an incriminating clue. "No, the lie is that it was a gram. He'd be on the floor right now."

"I'll leave that to your imagination." Jake smiled. "Since our marriage has never been better."

Weesie looked from one man to the other. "Okay, let's stop. This is lame."

"I've got mine," Pete said, ignoring her. "Are you ready?"

"Yup," said Jake.

"I got arrested when I was fifteen," he began. "I've only kissed five girls in my life. And, I slept with your wife." Pete smiled deviously. "Earlier tonight."

Weesie turned suddenly to face Pete, her eyes wide and indignant. Then, doing her best to compose herself, she turned to her husband and shook her head frantically. He was watching her closely, studying her gestures, taking Pete's strategy to heart.

"What the fuck is he talking about?" Jake barked.

"It's a game," Weesie said. "Chill out."

"Which is the lie?" Jake demanded.

"Obviously, the last one," said Weesie. She turned from Jake to glare at Pete.

"I think it's the second one," Jake announced. "He's way too much of a slut."

Jake looked from Weesie to Pete, suddenly helpless in his confusion. But he was deprived a thorough investigation by the sound of the opening door. Oscar and Annie stood in the foyer with Tripler trailing behind. All three were drenched from head to toe. Their eyes were wide and alarmed.

"Any luck?" Oscar demanded.

"No," said Weesie. "You guys haven't seen him either?"

They shook their heads solemnly.

"We searched the entire island," said Annie.

"He's definitely not here?" asked Oscar.

"Definitely not," said Weesie.

A moment passed as the group made a series of silent calculations. Their collective failure to find Tom meant all hope rested in Chip and Laura.

"That's fucked," said Jake. Anger was his default reaction to helplessness.

"Tell me about it," said Annie. "Oscar made me walk the entire island, and I'm four months pregnant."

A token effort was made to express surprise and congratulations. But much to Annie's annoyance, the subject was quickly tabled in favor of more pressing issues.

"I have a really bad feeling," said Tripler.

"Now you say so," said Weesie.

"What if it wasn't an accident?" said Tripler.

"Either way," said Annie. "Lila's going to kill us when she finds out."

"Come on. Let's not get hysterical," said Pete. "I'm sure Chip and Laura have found him by now."

"If they're even still together," said Oscar.

"What's that supposed to mean?" Annie snapped.

"I'm just saying." Oscar paused. "Laura might be part of the problem."

Several moments passed as the group struggled to comprehend Oscar's logic.

"Come on, you guys," Tripler said finally. "Let's not get *Lord of the Flies* on each other."

"Shut up, Tripler," said Weesie.

"Yeah, shut up," said Annie.

"Both of you, just fuck off," Tripler snapped. Then, under her breath, she sniped, "Besides, we already knew you were pregnant."

Tripler's comment triggered the inevitable explosion of dissention.

Jake silenced the group with an unpopular suggestion. "I think we should tell Lila now."

"No way," said Tripler. "She'll freak."

"At this point, that would be an appropriate response," said Jake.

"I agree," said Oscar. "We're walking the very fine line between witness and accomplice."

"We need to call the police," said Weesie. "Let them do a proper search."

"But we looked under the sofa," Pete quipped.

"Shut up, Pete," said Tripler.

Weesie eyed Tripler with new irritation. "We tried it your way, and it didn't work. We need to do something drastic."

"I say we wait until dawn," said Tripler. "Give Tom a few more hours to show up. If he's not here by six, then we call the police. There's no point in getting Lila worked up if we can avoid it."

"No," said Weesie. "That's too long to wait. We need to do something now." More waiting, she felt, was dangerous. It amounted to both continued denial and a cover-up.

But despite Weesie's opposition, Tripler enjoyed a groundswell of support. The three new arrivals joined the three on the sofa, resolving to thrust bad thoughts from their minds and wait out the darkness together.

FOURTEEN

It was admittedly illogical to miss someone before he was gone. But so much about Tom and Laura's romance defied convention. Usually, missing was preceded by holding, and holding by having. For Laura and Tom, the having phase was short-lived, and the holding was long over. Ever since, they had made up for lost time, seeing each other whenever they could, and, until Tom and Lila got engaged, speaking on the phone all the time and e-mailing even more frequently. The quality and intensity of their correspondence made it feel like the center of both of their lives.

E-mail was the perfect canvas for their relationship, providing the space for honesty and the cover for secrets. The addictive nature of the technology conspired to turn their friendship into a prolonged courtship. At times, their messages were breezy and nonchalant, filled with trivial information—I hate my job, the weather sucks, I really want to see this movie. At others, their e-mails were thoughtful and self-reflective, as though they were collaborating on a novel in which they were the main characters. Throughout, the computer screen provided a cloak, allowing them to correspond when they otherwise could not.

That certain moral boundaries had been crossed over the years was not lost on Laura. But ten years of grievances against Lila helped her justify the transgression. Still, as the wedding approached, Laura became increasingly fixated. She was like an athlete with perfect recall of a losing championship game. Every moment of time she had spent with Tom played out with startling clarity as though it were a netted serve, or a missed drop shot. She had been condemned, as penance, to watch the highlights of their romance.

The first time Laura saw Tom freshman year, he was heading toward her on Old Campus. She lingered even knowing how late she was for Nineteenth-Century English, a bold move considering the size of the classroom and her professor's policy of humiliating latecomers.

"Do you know where Linsley Chittenden is?" he had asked.

Yes, she was headed there now, she replied.

When they discovered that he was in the same class, he said, "Will you show me where it is so we can ditch it together?"

And he kept his promise. Together, they spent the better part of freshman year skipping classes, strolling around campus, listening to music, and otherwise wasting their parents' money. It was as though they were racing to exchange every conclusion they'd drawn about the world in their eighteen years before the end of the semester. Most of their fervent discussions took place in Tom's cluttered dorm room, where they huddled on the bottom of a camp-sized bunk, pretending to read or sleep, or indulging their feverish attraction. The year was only occasionally tainted by schoolwork, but they tackled it as a team, pulling all-nighters together and pooling their resources for whichever one was cursed with the more daunting assignment.

The end of sophomore year marked the end of this perfect era. But after the initial shock of their breakup and Lila's sudden intrusion, Laura gradually recovered—and benefited from the time to herself. She devoted the next two years to more useful pursuits than first love, such as memorizing the jukebox selection at Rudy's, devising the ultimate hangover cure, and on the rare occasion, attending her lectures. Throughout college, a strange tension remained between her and Tom, as though they had been interrupted in the middle of a pressing conversation. Still, the arrangement was comfortable, convenient even. Even as Laura moved on to other boys, Tom was never far from sight. And there was some comfort in knowing he was with Lila. At least, she knew he had not fallen in love.

Two years passed with an utter shortage of new memories. But they picked up again after graduation, when Lila moved to Boston to go to law school, and Tom moved to New York to start his M.F.A, and assess his dismal job prospects. He made these calculations as a tenant in Jake's Brooklyn Heights apartment, two train stops from Laura's in Carroll Gardens. Once again, the pace of their relationship—and their memories—picked up. It was as though they had resumed the old conversation. They talked breathlessly, for hours on end, at the expense of all other commitments.

Countless mornings were spent exchanging excerpts from life and work, drinking coffee from paper cups by the dolphin statue in Cobble Hill Park. Countless afternoons were spent in Laura's apartment, flipping aimlessly through old magazines or talking over the muted TV, before sprinting madly to the last show at the movie theater on Court and Butler. Together, they survived New York's emergencies and heartbreaks. On September 11, they raced to Laura's roof at word of the first tower's collapse and remained there, standing shoulder to shoulder until the next morning. During the transit strike, they met in Union Square after work and traipsed across the Brooklyn Bridge together. During the blackout, they recovered Tom's bike and Laura's roller skates from storage and wheeled to the city, mesmerized by its darkness.

But despite the time they had clocked together, they had only transgressed a few times: when Laura's grandmother died, when Tom finished his master's, and the night before they stopped speaking altogether. The first time, it seemed a forgivable faux pas, a frailty of the moment. Tom drove Laura to the funeral in Baltimore, and they spent the night lying on a made motel bed, Laura staring out the window while Tom traced the perimeter of her dress. When Tom handed in his master's thesis, Laura met him on the steps of the university library with a bottle of tequila. They woke up the next morning on her living-room floor, oblivious to every detail of the night including their transportation back to Brooklyn. And once, when Jake went out of town for the weekend, they borrowed his car, drove until they were exhausted, checked into the nearest motel, and remained there until Sunday evening. But even that trip was fairly innocent. They were happy just to be together, and talking was almost as fun as kissing.

Then the last night—had she only known at the time it was to be their last night, she would have treated it, treated him, so differently. She would have studied each moment, photographed every image, anything to make it last longer. She would have treated him so much better—she had only kissed and let herself be kissed. Had she known, she would have spoiled him more, lavished his body with every known pleasure.

Thinking back, she should have known right away from his strange behavior. He had walked her home from the Warren Street Tavern and invited himself upstairs. This was typical enough. But when they got upstairs, they never made it inside the apartment. They spent the next several hours standing in their coats in her darkened doorway, touching each other over their clothes like a pair of nervous teenagers. It was not until three or four in the morning that they finally fell into her apartment, pulled not so much by the force of their bodies but the weight of so much longing. Technically, nothing sordid took place on any of these occasions. But even Laura would concede that betrayal lived in a separate realm than sex, a realm that was far more innocent, and far more erotic.

And then he disappeared. Phone and e-mail contact ceased without word or explanation. The next morning, Laura awoke with the feeling of an intense hangover, her vision, thinking, and judgment blurring as though she had combined an entire bar's selection of alcohol. Her bed, her bathroom, the street below—all were still and empty. Instinctively, she clutched her heart. Until today, that was the last time she had seen him.

For the first few days, she forced herself to maintain a positive attitude. He was busy with an all-consuming deadline, or he'd fallen into his yearly funk. But as days passed without a response, she became increasingly distraught, obsessing over her silent phone as though she were waiting for the results of a medical test. At any given moment—she could be sitting on the subway, answering the phone at work—she was, in fact, reconsidering the merit of something she'd said to Tom, replaying the last minutes of their time together like a criminal detective, as though locating the offending sentence might lead her back to him.

At first, she assumed he would write back—he was conducting a test of sorts. Perhaps he needed time to recover from his guilt. Or perhaps he had realized that he couldn't be with Lila and was gearing up for the task of breaking up with her. Calmed by these theories, she adopted an indifferent stance to her empty inbox. She forced herself to take greater intervals between thinking of him, went several days without turning on her computer. Perhaps the pain would lessen over time, as cravings did when she quit smoking after two-week stints in college. But the opposite was true; she missed him more with every moment of withdrawal.

As days turned to weeks, she started to fear Tom had survived his own withdrawal period, that perhaps she had missed some crucial period during which to change his mind. This realization proved far more oppressive than the sorrow she had felt to date. She became bereft, inconsolable. The notion that she had served as an accomplice to her own neglect was too much to bear. It was as though she had locked herself in a closet only to wake up in a coffin.

Three weeks into Tom's silence, she made one attempt to get in touch. She left one emphatic message, then acknowledged the futility—and the indignity—of trying and stopped. Slowly, she began the process of grieving for him in earnest. And surprisingly, it was an enormous relief. Despite the purity of her love for Tom, their relationship had brought equal amounts of pleasure and pain. It was freeing to consider life without him. When the phone finally rang, she had nearly succeeded in forgetting the sound of his voice. But the call was a devastating setback. It was Lila calling to announce the engagement.

Assigning degrees of blame to betrayal is a difficult project, much like deciding which of two murderers has the more wicked heart. With murder, there are tangible distinctions. First degree is intentional; second degree, irresponsible; third degree, accidental. But with crimes of the heart, the distinctions are more subtle. Who is to say when a secret turns into a sin? With a daydream, a kiss, a confession? Who is to say which transgression is worse: sexual or emotional, coveting or carressing?

Fortunately, Laura was in no position to assign blame to anyone. For years now, she had actively loved her best friend's boyfriend— accepting the title "maid of honor" was grossly hypocritical. Even as she acknowledged this, she indulged a more wretched thought: If Tom were not found alive tonight, part of her would be relieved. It was almost better that no one have him. But as soon as she'd given shape to the thought, she condemned her own depravity. She longed for the safety of her bedroom—the abundance of pillows, her dim bedside lamp, her view of the East River. What would happen if she caught the first ferry in the morning and simply skipped the wedding?

Amused by the thought, Laura fixed her eyes on a massive slant-ing oak. Its leaves rustled audibly as though they were trying to drown out the sound of the wind. And its branches swayed gently. Was the wind picking up or subsiding? As she stared, a strange facet of the trunk caught her attention: It diverged as it rose from the ground so that it resembled two trees emerging from the same root system.

A sudden shift in the base of the trunk stopped her in her place. As she stood, she considered her limited options: turn and sprint for the Hayeses', or distrust her perception and keep walking. Be-fore she could act on either alternative, one side of the trunk shifted again, this time folding over itself like a crumpled handkerchief. Her body knew before her mind gained full comprehension.

"Tom," she said.

He looked up from the grass, his eyes large and nervous.

"Tom," she repeated.

He seemed to nod—it was too dark to tell.

For a moment, it occurred to Laura that Tom intended to keep his silence. Enraged, she opened her mouth to yell to the group that he'd been found. But she lost the urge as she gained a full glimpse of his face: His hair was wet and matted; his eyes betrayed his broken spirit.

"Laura," he whispered.

"Tom?" She took another step toward the tree. His shoulders were shaking. "What are you doing here? Everyone thinks you're dead."

"That would be preferable," he said.

She was suddenly overwhelmed by the urge to touch his face. But she quickly checked the sentiment. Remembering her pride, she waited for an apology, an excuse—any explanation. When none came, the anguish of the last year flooded her memory, and she resolved that forgiveness, however tempting, was simply too pathetic. "I better round up the troops," she said. "Tell them to stop looking."

Tom looked back with utter terror. "Please don't," he said. "Not yet."

Her relief was followed by a series of disheartening realizations. Tom was alive; therefore, he had not changed his mind; therefore, he would marry Lila tomorrow.

"I have to go," she said.

"No, please don't," he said.

She paused for a moment but finally rejected the possibility of staying. She turned and set off toward the Gettys', renewed in her determination.

"Wait," he called.

Laura stalled, turned around.

"I'm sorry," he called. "I had no choice."

This was far from the plea she had scripted for him. In fact, it was deeply unsatisfying, bordering on insulting.

"I had to move on," he said. "I couldn't be confused anymore."

Laura considered this for a moment. His volume and diffident tone made it clear that it was a defense. But the defense, valid or not, was miles from the apology she craved—and deserved. "Everyone's really worried," she said. "We need to tell them to stop looking."

"Yeah, that would be good," Tom scoffed. "If *we* showed up together."

His flip tone took her off guard—and his mockery. She had two choices: degrade herself or walk away. She started toward the Gettys', this time with purpose.

Tom let her walk several paces.

The wind picked up from a dull rasp to a high-pitched hiss.

"Don't go," he called. Then softening, he tried the affirmative. "Please stay."

For Laura, the difference was crucial. It stopped her in her path. Tom loved her most the moment that she turned away. She knew this, and even still, she could not keep walking.

"No one knows where I am," he said.

Laura stood still as she deciphered his logic. The state of being lost, he seemed to imply, granted him a kind of freedom. And the task of searching for him, in turn, granted her invisibility and an alibi. She thought of a story she'd heard after September 11: A woman discovered her husband's affair minutes after the towers went down. She had called his cell phone to make sure that he was alive and he, oblivious to the tragedy, had betrayed himself right away, explaining that all was well, that he was at work, safe and sound.

But Laura preferred not to think of Tom in the same category of morality. In the same moment, it occurred to her that Tom had designed the whole ruse—the raft, the swim, the "drowning"—to create the time and space for them to be alone together.

Once again, she walked back to him—for and in spite of herself.

FIFTEEN

Tom's breathing sped up as Laura approached. The reality of her was so different from the version he had invented to replace her. The intensity of her eyes, the curve of her legs, the fall of her dress struck him all at once, and he felt as he had as a teenager after listening to very loud music. What an ass he had been—and an idiot—to treat her so badly. How on earth had he gone one day without seeing this beautiful woman?

In some ways, she had never seemed very far away. Those first few weeks, a thought did not pass that was not consumed by her. She inhabited his brain, hovering above his consciousness like a cloud. Every musing observation was halved by—haunted by her face. In the first confused moments of morning, he said her name involuntarily, repeating it out loud as he lay in bed, as water soaked his hair in the shower.

Forgetting would be impossible, he realized, so he applied a new strategy. If he could not expunge her from his memory, then he would attack the memory at its root. He launched a steady campaign to reimagine her, hacking away at her image with spiteful thoughts. With new resolve, he itemized and exaggerated her worst qualities. Her lips, though lovely, were too thin; her eyes, though intense, too closely spaced; her legs, though sensual, too bulky; her breasts, unimpressive. Her recklessness, though appealing at times, was ultimately a liability.

Just like this, he replaced Laura with a phantom version of herself. Mercifully, the new version was easier to dismiss. In his mind, Laura morphed into a wholly distinct creature, a hologram of her worst qualities, a composite of his worst fears about women. She embodied at once his mother's temper, his first love's cruelty, his second love's histrionics, his first-grade teacher's disinterest, and the guilty pornographic notion of sex common to all Catholic boys.

And though the project did not in itself cure the obsession, it succeeded at least in turning its object from a coveted to a threatening thing. When she wrote, Tom only grew more irate, his image of her more unflattering. Her prostration was a burden, her weakness, totally repellent. The idea that he should be blamed for this was utterly infuriating. Guilt and pity did their part to squelch any remaining affection.

But just as soon as he'd succeeded in expunging her from his heart, he yearned for her again, even more intensely. He fought the urge to call her, to reread old e-mails, to camp out just beyond her apartment door and accost her, ashamed and contrite. He got off the subway at her stop and wandered by her stoop, circled the block, hopeful that she might happen to walk out. Somehow, a chance encounter would be easier to forgive. Hating her and coveting her were equally painful.

But gradually, her absence proved to be a relief. Living

between two loves—and two lives—had been its own brand of torture, fracturing his heart slowly like a window with a hairpin crack. At all times, he was torn between Lila and Laura, Boston and New York; he was an angel and a devil, a sweetheart and a cheater, and the paradox, despite its ephemeral perks, was too much to bear. It was preferable to associate pain with Laura than to remember the full spectrum of feeling she inspired. That he had once felt a giddy thrill in her company—well, that was just too bad. In its place, he had gained peace of mind. It felt like a fair trade.

"So, is this all you hoped it would be?" she asked. She sat with her back against the tree as though it were a cozy armchair.

"What? Seeing you?"

"No, stupid. Your wedding."

"Oh," Tom said. He sighed and extended his legs, resting his head on his arms.

"You looked a little freaked during the rehearsal."

"Have you ever felt Augusta's grip?"

"Well, at least you have the rest of the family," Laura quipped. "Chip is a reassuring presence."

"He outdid himself tonight," said Tom.

"That was nothing," said Laura. "You can look forward to performances like that for years to come."

"That'll be enough," said Tom.

"No, really. I think you two will grow very close. And if you don't, you'll always have William."

Tom dismissed the dig with a smile.

"What?" Laura said. She widened her eyes. "I'm just trying to picture your future."

Annoyed, Tom lifted his head from the ground and rotated his body, then replaced his head on Laura's lap as though a pillow had been placed there for him.

"Hey," said Laura. "Your hair's all wet." She lifted his head and placed it on the grass.

"I've been sitting here in the rain," he snapped. Then, more softly, "Waiting for you."

But Laura didn't take the bait. "Please," she said. "From the looks of it, you weren't waiting. You were escaping."

"You act like I'm here by default," Tom barked. "I chose this. This is what I wanted."

Laura bristled at his directness. It was jarring to jump from sarcasm to sincerity without warning. Of course, she knew he chose Lila over her. She didn't need to be reminded.

"I don't question that you chose it," said Laura. "What I don't understand is why."

Tom sat up suddenly and turned to face her, his eyes wild and defiant. "You think you've got a special gift for knowing what's in my heart. Did it ever occur to you that I need a woman like Lila?"

Laura flinched, this time more visibly, said nothing for several seconds. "What kind of woman is that?"

"Someone happy."

"Meaning simple."

"Someone ambitious."

"Meaning busy."

"Someone confident."

"Meaning rich."

"Someone who doesn't need to tear people down in order to build herself up."

Laura paused and fought the urge to stand. But she knew she had no grounds for offense. She was undeniably critical—at best, a bad friend, at worst, a hypocrite. But she was more insulted by Tom's first comment. When he said "happy," he meant someone less emotional, someone more stable. And this attack to the core of her temperament made her feel raw and exposed. "So someone very different from you?" she sniped. Lashing out when she felt weak was a reflex.

"I guess you could say that," said Tom. He turned and lay down in the grass again.

"I never bought the idea that opposites attract," said Laura. "Different usually means boring."

"Boring is better than maddening," Tom said. "Maddening gets old really fast."

"It works for some people," Laura said carefully.

"But it nearly kills them," said Tom.

It dawned on her that she was losing the argument. "Then I suppose I'd rather be dead," she said.

Laura sighed. When had this conversation become a court battle and she, her own defender? It was so like Tom to turn a question of love into a theoretical discussion. He would always win in this realm; his mind was simply more logical. "Besides, I don't think I have some special gift for knowing what's in your heart. I think we both do."

Tom looked up, now truly attentive, as though he wanted to be persuaded.

"For each other," Laura said.

Laura kicked herself. All these words were so trite, so horribly clichéd. But the right ones were even worse. What could she say? That even now, on the eve of his wedding, she yearned to feel his skin, to taste his lips, that every day without him had been unbearable, like a day without water?

"If it makes any difference, it was an accident," said Tom.

"What was an accident?" said Laura.

"Sophomore year. When Lila and I started dating. It just sort of happened."

She sat for a moment, digesting the claim—it was absurd on so many levels. "Do you honestly think I'm still hung up on what happened when we were nineteen?" she scoffed. She reached down to the ground and absentmindedly unearthed a large clump of grass.

"No," said Tom. "I'm just saying . . ."

"But how exactly do you end up in someone's dorm room by accident?" She separated the clump and began hurling single blades at the ground.

"I came back for you," Tom explained. "To tell you I'd made a mistake."

"Oh please," said Laura.

"I did," said Tom.

"And then what? You changed your mind again?" Exhausting her supply of grass, she removed another chunk from the ground.

"I guess it doesn't make a difference," Tom said.

"No," said Laura. "It doesn't." She dispensed with the clump in a single hurl.

They sat for a moment in silence.

"Did the same thing happen when you proposed? You dial the wrong number?"

"I hate how you do this," Tom snapped. "I share something personal, then you use it as a weapon."

"What you do is hardly better," she said. "Rewriting history like a politician."

For a moment, they remained united in mutual irritation. But as always, the distance between them gave way to a need to be closer.

"I'm sorry," he said.

"I'm sorry," she said.

"No, you're not." He smiled.

"You should be," she said. "A single digit, and everything would have been different."

They laughed, bonded more closely now by their shared regret. The feeling weakened Laura at her core, and she suddenly felt as though every muscle in her body had gone slack. Giving in, she extended her legs and lay down at Tom's side. As they lay, they stared up at the sky, as though trying to locate the stars beyond the mass of clouds.

"I remember when I moved to Brooklyn," he said. "I was very confused by the view. I'd expected the sunset to be farther away, blocked by all those skyscrapers. For some reason, I thought it would set behind Manhattan's skyline. But it was just as close."

"The skyline?" Laura asked.

"No, the sun," Tom said. "Just as close as it was in Manchester. As close as it was in New Haven."

"You wanted evidence of change."

"No," he said. "I wanted evidence of distance."

Laura smiled and nodded.

She settled into a more comfortable position and indulged in a moment of nostalgia. "Remember that paper sophomore year? The one that inspired your thesis."

"The Hopeless Romantics," Tom said, smiling. "Chronicles of a Failed Movement."

"Only you could start a fifty-page paper the night before . . . "

"And still get an A minus," Tom said slyly.

"Only because I wrote it," Laura said.

"Hardly!" said Tom, mock offended. Then, he smiled. "Okay, maybe half of it."

They sat in silence for a moment, enjoying the memory of that night—the anxiety, the exhaustion, the importance.

"I do feel sorry for them," Laura said.

"Who?"

"All those distraught poets."

"How could you feel sorry for a poet," said Tom. "Is there anything more useless and indulgent?"

"Oh no," Laura said. She turned to face Tom, insistent on eye contact. "They were radicals, revolutionaries. More influential than Newton and Darwin. Without them, there would be no point-of-view, no ecstasy, no heartbreak, no novels."

"The Romantics cannot be credited with the birth of emotion," Tom said.

"No, but maybe, without their work, we wouldn't know how to express it."

"That doesn't mean we wouldn't feel it," Tom said.

"Who knows," Laura marveled. "Maybe we wouldn't experience those sensations if they hadn't defined them."

Tom paused, mesmerized, considering Laura's assertion. There was no one—nothing else in the world—that had this unbelievable effect on him: thrilling electrification. But just as soon as he acknowledged this gift, he sought to destroy it.

"People dreamed before Freud," he said. "Maps existed before Copernicus."

"But no one knew to interpret," she said. "And the maps were ridiculous."

Tom shook his head, refusing to acknowledge Laura's argument. "They were nothing more than the lucky witnesses of a crumbling religion."

"No," Laura said, whispering. "*They* were the reason religion crumbled. They were inventing a new one." How had she found herself, once again, arguing with the same intensity as a lawyer defending a man set for execution?

"They were just confused kids," Tom said conclusively. "A bunch of freaks and depressives." He turned away, signaling his loss of interest. "Love and hysteria are easily mistaken."

"You *would* look at it like that," Laura said. In the past, an idea like this would have marked the launch of a sparkling new conversation. But now, it sputtered to its death, estranging them further.

"Oh, Laura, I'm weak," he said, turning to her. His eyes conveyed his plea for forgiveness.

"No you're not," she said, still looking up. It was too much to look in his eyes.

"Am I making a horrible mistake? Tell me. I need to know what you think."

"You already know what I think," she said. "You want to know if I think you'll regret it."

"Stop torturing me," Tom said.

Laura smiled. The irony of this statement was almost comical. But he was sincere and his tone had changed. She noticed the movement of tears before the sound. His shoulders shook slightly, and his body contracted as though he had been punched in the stomach.

"You broke my heart," she whispered.

"You are my heart. I love you," he said. "I really love you."

Laura smiled. "I love you too."

Tom shook his head, wild with confusion. "But why? I'm a total asshole."

Laura laughed, choosing not to dissuade him of this fact. But she answered the question. "You inspire me," she said.

Tom stared back, incredulous. "I'm so sorry." He shook his head. "I ruined everything."

Laura paused, unsure how to respond. What could you say after that? How could two people be so close and yet so distant?

Luckily, a new rain shower conspired to bring them together. At the first timid drop, they instinctively huddled. They spent the next several hours clutching each other, running their hands over each other's bodies as though it was their last night on earth, a last precious chance to memorize the shape, to know the fleeting warmth, smell, and taste of another human body. For Laura, it felt like a respite from blindness, a glimpse of color after years in the dark. For Tom, it was an emergency rescue, a hand offered through the silver spray before waves took him under.

Technically, on the spectrum of very bad things, they did nothing truly wicked. But of course, that spectrum has no measure for the greatest of all carnal sins, the kind that occurs before skin touches skin, before wondering turns to yearning, yearning to having, having to holding for dear life, when two people cling to each other so desperately that even when they lie, inches apart, neither is fully satisfied until the light between them turns to darkness.

SIXTEEN

Chip awoke with a start to the shock of falling rain. God knew how long he had been lying on the beach. He vaguely remembered falling to the ground and mistaking the sand for a desert. The sensation of a hangover—the mind-numbing dehydration, the vertigo, the bludgeoning headache—was familiar enough. But now, in addition to the usual distortions, he was faced with a summer shower. For a moment, he wondered if he had drowned. But memory returned in a series of flashes. He remembered the raft, the race back to shore, and Laura—had he tackled her to the ground?—and began to reconstruct the last few hours.

Like most addicts, Chip was extremely skilled at reducing the effects of a hangover. He knew how to manipulate his intake—the type of alcohol he drank, the chasers he used, the post-party ritual—to ease what would be a devastating crash to less seasoned partiers. In its stead, he had perfected the slow comedown, a process that lasted several days and required various herbal concoctions. It was best achieved with excessive sleep, constant television watching, the occasional late-afternoon jog, and a complicated assortment of macrobiotic teas, whose salutary purpose was lost on him entirely. Alternatively, the whole process could be circumvented with continued drug use.

Choosing the latter, Chip made his first attempt to stand. Eight vodka sodas, a bottle of wine, and the buffet of pills he had added to hors d'oeuvres was not an extreme tally for one night, and yet he now wondered if he had finally ingested a toxic amount.

Dehydration was an urgent problem. His brain felt as though it had withered from his skull like dried earth in a flowerpot. With new desperation, he looked out at the bay and wondered why ocean water had to be off-limits. The problem of dehydration at sea had always struck him as the cruelest torture. Being surrounded by the very substance that could save your life and yet finding it totally useless—it was, to Chip, even more than freak accidents, good cause to doubt God's existence. Every time Chip heard a tale of shipwreck, he felt certain the solution had been overlooked. Surely, there was some small pocket of the ocean whose water was not contaminated by salt. Perhaps, if he cupped his hands tightly and took only a very small sip, he would happen on one such pocket of purity and save himself.

He had searched for this very thing—a pocket of purity—for his entire life and yet, even in this seeming paradise, had found only corruption. He amused himself as he stumbled up the lawn by making a list of those people in his life who were guilty on this count. He ordered his list from most to least rotten-to-the-core and so began with his mother.

Augusta Hayes, in Chip's humble opinion, was a deluded woman. The same could be said of his father, of course, but William at least evidenced some discomfort with the disparity between his beliefs and reality. Augusta, on the other hand, seemed to thrive on the contradiction. She performed an impression of warmth and yet felt very few emotions; she projected an air of nonchalance and yet was compulsive in all her activities; she claimed to love her children at all costs and yet recoiled from neediness. That she could be blamed for all his problems and unhappiness was a conclusion he'd drawn years ago. Ironically, he'd done so under the guidance of a therapist whom she'd funded.

Together, Chip and Dr. Shineman had distilled his childhood to a single moment. He was seven years old and had slipped as he emerged from the bathtub, landing first on his bottom, then on his back, and knocking his head in the process. Oddly, it was not the bruise that had traumatized him but rather his mother's response.

"You're okay," she had said when she found him wailing. She bestowed a ceremonial forehead kiss. Then, she patted his bottom and dispatched him to go. "You're okay, Chippie," she had said again. "You're absolutely fine."

And the result was, Chip and Dr. Shineman agreed, to deny Chip the opportunity to experience the pain, a form of emotional censorship that had not only scarred his childhood but stunted the formation of his adult personality.

More disturbingly, Chip went on to infer, it was an ailment of the entire Wasp culture: The refusal to express and process pain amounted to a cumulative repression so enormous it rivaled the force behind a volcano. It was no surprise therefore that Chip's adolescence had seen a series of painful and powerful explosions and, more fitting still, that a Jew was the only person in whom he could confide these feelings.

William was not beyond reproach, but he was somehow less

culpable than his wife. Where Augusta was corrupt, he was crippled; where she was pathological, he was passive. His surrenders amounted to a crime that was more disappointing but ultimately lesser. As the weaker parent—and the father, no less—he inspired more pity than rage. When he married Augusta, he resigned himself to a life of idle chatter, and that crime was far greater—and far more tragic—considering he had once had something to say.

Proceeding from most to least corrupt, Lila fell next on the list. Her failings were almost too obvious to review. Lila, like her mother, was vain, controlling, and emotionally frigid. Yet she feigned a saccharine demeanor. She was doggedly ambitious and yet took issue with evidence of aspiration in others. She was only truly interested in those people who provoked her competition. She had chosen Laura as her best friend because she was her most formidable rival. She had chosen Tom as her husband for the same reason Augusta had chosen William, because their goals dovetailed and his "artistry"—the only thing she lacked—amplified her status.

Tom was closely tied with Lila. Why more people didn't see him for what he was—a shameless social climber, a gold digger, really— was truly a mystery. Tom was bound to abandon his artistic goals just as William had. And worse, he had found—and seized—in Lila, the financial means to this end. If this fact were not evident from the lack of chemistry between Lila and Tom, it was immediately clear from the spark that existed between Tom and Laura. When Tom was in Laura's vicinity, his entire frequency changed. That they were in love was clear to anyone but a total buffoon. It was, in fact, a testament to Lila that she recognized this fact and yet managed to ignore it. Changing his mind, Chip revised his list: Tom was more corrupt than Lila.

And then there was Laura, who was not so much corrupt as corrupted. Her jealousy of Lila was petty, certainly, and her covetousness unappealing. But there was something endearing in her conflict, something redeeming about her goals. And when she was in a good mood, albeit rare, she was wild and hilarious. She was a riveting conversationalist. And she was so much more beautiful than the waxy, freckled girls with whom he'd grown up, the Westfields, the Biddles, the Grants. Tragically, Laura would always view him as Lila's repulsive little sibling. And, of course, she was painfully in love with Tom, a fact that was unlikely to be changed even by his marriage to another woman.

Chip's unscrupulous taxonomy was interrupted by the weather. After showering sporadically for the last several hours, the sky finally made good on its threats with a hearty downpour. It began as a drizzle that dusted the lawn but gained speed quickly until its unison rhythm could be heard across all of Dark Harbor. It seemed to start on the roof of the house, then move into the rustling trees, ending its journey on the bay, where it picked up momentum.

Luckily, Chip was halfway to the house by the time it was really pouring. He knew it was halfway because, as a child, he had attempted to measure the distance from the porch to the water. Placing one foot in front of the other, he had counted the steps to the beach, committing the halfway mark to memory with the aid of a large elm tree. That this tree had witnessed all the same storms as Chip was immeasurably comforting.

But as he passed the tree, he was stilled by a strange rustling near the trunk. Then, a shocking silhouette appeared: two forms merging into one, as though the earth had opened up in a quake, swallowed two human bodies and then spit them back out. His first instinct was to blame the pills, but somehow he knew to trust his perception. He had stumbled onto his suspicions, proof of his intuition. And, to his shock, he felt an absence of rage—on behalf of himself or his sister. He felt relief for Laura followed by pity. Today's wedding was as inevitable as the weather.

SEVENTEEN

Daylight returned just before six with plucky determination, ending the pesky spell of night and renewing the promises of summer. The clouds of the previous afternoon had replaced themselves with a blue sky, as though to chide anyone who had doubted Augusta's persuasive powers. Two months after the solstice, the sun had lost its reddish hue, but the light it offered was still warmer than the blue shades of winter, and succeeded in comforting the sleeping friends as they stirred from their huddle on the sofa.

The windswept lawn lay in stark contrast to Northern Gardens' manicured sheen. The storm had deepened the color of the grass from mint to emerald green and littered the formerly immaculate lawn with a collage of strewn branches. A pole from the main wedding tent had come unearthed. Luckily, it had not pulled down the tent but had tilted slowly and hit the ground like a wounded soldier, disengaging from the tent without ripping the canvas. Lacking the support of the pole, the tent had collapsed slightly.

For Tom and Laura, the night extended long beyond the darkness. As they slept, the world receded somewhat, as though the sky had discreetly turned its head to grant them a private moment. For four short hours, they remained oblivious to the sounds of the world. Even the rain registered as little more than ambient noise. They remained this way even after the first glints of sunlight. Laura was finally jolted from sleep by an alarmist bird and woke to find sun in her eyes and a matted patch of grass where Tom had been.

She grasped at her dress instinctively—it was horribly rumpled and damp—and attempted to tell the difference between what had occurred and what she had dreamed. But opening her eyes only made it harder to tell the difference, so she closed them and lay back down, willing her memory to grace her. Gradually, images from the night revealed themselves, but they were strangely remote for the recent past, like words written in the sand.

Suddenly, she felt exposed, desperate for cover. To be seen in the dress she had worn last night would be horribly incriminating. How would she explain her disarray? She would be less conspicuous running naked across the grass, wearing a scarlet letter. A chorus of birds joined the one that had sounded the alarm. The noise cemented her decision. She needed to get back to the Gettys'. Hopefully, the night's heavy consumption would prevent her friends from waking up when she made her entrance.

As she walked, she rubbed her hands against her arms in a pitiful attempt to generate heat. A rabbit scampered behind a tree just ahead, a reminder of the countless creatures with whom she and Tom had shared the lawn. But any delight she might have derived from the sighting was quickly replaced by dread. Did Tom's latest evacuation mean he had decided to remain hidden, or had he simply gone back to his room, renewed in his resolve to get married? The confusion was maddening. And each alternative demanded a different response. Still, she felt certain of one thing: Tom was in love with her. And this knowledge was immeasurably comforting, perhaps even more so than his presence.

She picked up her pace and fixed her gaze on the distant house. But within a few steps, she stopped again, detecting an approaching figure. She stood still for a moment, debating a quick escape, but thought better of it. Turning around would betray her guilt; running away would only draw more attention. At first, it appeared as a single body, advancing across the lawn. But as she watched, it revealed discrete forms, six of them, marching on the grass, silhouetted by the water.

Thinking fast, she devised a credible alibi: She had slept on the chaise on the porch after arguing with Chip. He had finally pushed her to the breaking point, and she had gone looking for new company. Fearful of waking Lila, she had taken a seat on the porch and had remained there, waiting for someone to emerge for what felt like hours. She only just woke up minutes ago, freezing and bug-bitten.

But just as soon as she'd settled on a narrative, she considered an alternative approach. Other than Tom himself, she was the only one who definitively knew Tom had made it to shore. She could use this knowledge—and her friends' ignorance—to her advantage. As the distance between them closed, she settled on a strategy: She would not deceive them outright, but she would not enlighten them either. It was not her responsibility to cure her friends of their delusions.

Predictably, Tripler spoke first. "Have you seen him?" she demanded.

Laura looked down. Despite her planned tactic, it was still difficult to lie to her face.

"Us either," said Weesie.

"We're fucked," Pete declared. It was an attempt, albeit ineloquent, to acknowledge their mutual blame, to indict every member of the group for the crimes they'd committed over the course of the night, over the course of their friendship: complacence, apathy, duplicity, mistrust, and disloyalty, just as a start.

"We're telling Lila now," Tripler said, reasserting her leadership.

"But wait," Laura said, forgetting herself, her alibi, her tactic.

"Wait for what?" Tripler snapped. "Until we know he's dead?"

"God, Tripler," Laura said.

"What," Tripler snapped.

Weesie interrupted, resuming her role as mediator. "Better sooner than later. While there's still time to do something."

The others nodded, acknowledging the new shorthand. These abbreviations—the vague pronouns and sweeping generalizations—were somehow more digestible than saying what everyone was thinking.

"Where were you anyway?" Tripler demanded.

Laura struggled to meet her gaze. The decision she faced, to lie or tell the truth, was a choice between strength and weakness. But she was suddenly confused again. Which choice amounted to strength: sharing the truth or hoarding it?

"I was alone," she said finally.

Tripler's eyes rounded with indignation. "Oh my God. You know where he is."

Laura stared back without flinching. "Go fuck yourself, Tripler."

"Come on, guys," said Weesie.

"What?" Tripler said. "Everyone knows she'd rather see him dead than watch him marry Lila."

This was a test, Laura knew, and there was only one way to pass it.

"Where did you sleep?" asked Tripler.

"Where did *you* sleep?" Laura replied.

They stared at each other for several moments, stalemated in mutual hatred.

Finally, Weesie broke the silence, taking Tripler's place at the front of the line. "We're going. Are you coming or not?"

Tripler stared at Laura for another moment, then she turned and complied, as though she'd finally tired of waiting for an answer.

Laura watched as her friends set off toward the house. Their togetherness was eerie, militaristic, and she cringed as she thought of how many times she had followed behind, in step. But this time, her conscience compelled her to join them: If Tom had indeed gone back to Lila, it would be better to know sooner than later. If he hadn't—and intended to miss the wedding—it was important to call off the search before authorities were alerted. To stay behind was cowardly, she decided, a crime of omission, so she sprinted to catch up with her friends, weaving in and out of the sunlight as though she were dodging bullets.

ila awoke in a confusion of emotions—elation, terror, relief. It felt something like waking on Christmas morning as a child and wondering, for a split second, if yet another day had been added to the month of December. But now, confusion was followed by a sinking sensation, a feeling of toxic familiarity. Even your fifteenth

Christmas yielded unexpected delights; a wedding, for Lila, lacked this element of surprise.

She did her best to focus on the most promising parts of the day. It would be amusing, at least, to live out the conventions. The promenade down the aisle, the cutting of the cake, the first dance with Tom—each moment would be a satisfying culmination of a childhood fantasy. But a mortifying emergency compounded the problems of the day: After one short night away from Tom, she could not picture his face. She knew his features by heart, of course—brown hair, green eyes, pink lips. But when she strained to conjure him, her mind went suddenly blank. And she feared this was a chilling—and telling—reflection of her feelings.

One thing succeeded in soothing her where everything else failed. A feeling of calm returned as she pictured herself in her dress. Perhaps it was vain to imagine herself in the eyes of her guests, but she forgave herself the indulgence. A modern wedding would always lack a certain sexual charge. In the absence of virginity, the wedding dress offered a vestigial mystique, presenting the ultimate challenge to the bride: to look at once as pure as a girl and as sensual as a woman. The paradox was itself the source of the dress's power. Renewed, Lila lifted herself from her bed and headed for the attic.

The house was blessedly quiet when she emerged from her room. Padding up the stairs, she entertained another guilty thought: She was more excited for Tom to see her in her dress than she was to see Tom. Few people were honest with themselves, she decided, about the difference between these two things, willfully confusing the glee of reunion with the vanity of exhibition. Of course, she yearned to see Tom. Spending the night apart had only strengthened the urge. But when she pictured the day ahead, she imagined it from someone else's perspective. She saw herself in the eyes of

Tom and her guests, her body displayed at its best, every feature on her face reflecting the warmth of her audience.

Her first glimpse of the dress did not fail her memory. It hung neatly where she had left it in the cedar closet. Starched and stuffed for its shipment to Maine, the dress looked strangely alive. The bodice, stuffed with a mass of tissue paper, looked as though it had just taken a hearty deep breath. Each of the buttons remained tightly secured. The skirt flowed effortlessly from the bodice, skimming the floor like a dollop of cream. The train fell to the hemline before swooping up to the hanger. The veil hung on a separate hanger, a shadow in white tulle.

Even as she caressed the dress, Lila failed to notice the damage. Minnow had gone a ways toward replicating its pre-torn state. Lila stood, running her hands over the bodice for several moments before she noticed. Just like this, she was able to picture Tom or, rather, to picture herself with Tom: They would look so beautiful today; they would have such a beautiful life. This realization was so comforting it nearly obscured the horror of her next one: The dress was ripped at the seam between the bodice and the skirt, so that half of the skirt billowed out from the corset, forming a gaping hole. In an instant, Lila's peaceful musings were replaced by homicidal thoughts. She immediately deduced the perpetrator and started down the stairs at a run.

"Margaret!" she shrieked.

Augusta was the first to react. She lunged from her bed as though braced for a clock's alarm.

Minnow, too, responded quickly. She had slept very little throughout the night. At the sound of Lila's voice, she darted out of bed and sprinted up the stairs, propelled by remorse and curiosity.

Luckily, Augusta arrived first, sparing Minnow the vicious attack she would have suffered had she found Lila alone.

"I hate her," Lila was screaming, as Minnow rushed up the stairs.

Overhearing, Minnow froze in her place. Lila heard the footsteps and turned toward the noise, then charged the door, screaming threats, arms flailing.

Augusta reacted, restraining Lila before she reached the door. She managed to detain her just long enough to give Minnow a healthy lead.

"I hate you, too," Minnow cried as she sprinted down the stairs. "I'm glad it's ruined."

The new provocation renewed Lila's wrath and, in turn, her ferocity. With a frantic grunt, she got free of her mother's grasp and bolted down the stairs, catching the tail of her sister's nightgown as she rounded the third-floor landing. But gravity conspired with Minnow's cause, propelling her down the next two flights with a small advantage. After a clumsy tour of the kitchen and living room, the chase culminated on the porch, with Minnow disappearing into the protective throng of the wedding party.

Lila collapsed operatically onto an empty chaise. She threw herself facedown on the chair and wept like a lovesick teenager. Her friends stood on the porch, assembled awkwardly, watching her cry, saying nothing. Fearing the worst, they checked each other's eyes. Had she already learned of Tom's disappearance? But the patter of bare feet on wood soon relieved them of this concern. Minnow sped across the grass, hooting and gloating. It seemed the cause of tears had been a family dispute.

Instinctively, Tripler stepped toward her friend. Lila's hysteria was, in some way, serendipitous, an opportune moment to share more bad news. "Li," she said. "There's something we have to tell you."

The others exchanged a series of glances, a critique of Tripler's timing.

"What," Lila sniffled. "What else can go wrong? Don't tell me it's going to rain."

"No," Tripler said. She nodded cheerfully at the sky, as if to imply that she alone had arranged for the weather.

"What is it?" asked Lila.

Tripler looked to Weesie helplessly as it dawned on her that she had appointed herself the messenger.

Lila scanned her friends with new concern. Why did they look so guilty? Perhaps they had broken some valuable heirloom at the Gettys' or harbored the knowledge that a certain guest had cancelled at the last minute.

As they stood in silence, each member of the group considered his guilt in Tom's disappearance. Whatever his crimes—negligence, disloyalty, betrayal—each one fought the urge to confess the sins he'd committed over the last twelve hours.

Laura surveyed the group and waited for anxiety to seize her. She had expected to feel something—self-loathing or something darker, satisfaction even. But instead, she felt an utter absence of emotion toward Lila. And when she thought of Tom, she felt a heady thrill. He had not run from her arms straight into Lila's. Apparently, he had not yet resolved to attend his own wedding.

"Tom's missing," Pete said finally. He blurted it out like a confession, and Lila heard the guilt in his voice.

"No, he's not," Lila snapped. "Chip saw him last night."

Laura froze. What had Chip seen last night and what had he told his sister?

"Chip was trashed," Jake said. "You saw him at the dinner."

"No," said Lila. "He's not missing. We planned to spend the night apart." Her tone was irritable, as though she had been asked to explain a menial task to a servant.

"We were with him last night," Tripler explained. "And then." She paused. "We lost him." It was a rare occurrence for Tripler to make a correction in which she took no pleasure.

"What?" snapped Lila.

Tripler lowered her head.

The others nodded in confirmation.

"He probably just went on a walk," said Lila. "He does that. When he's nervous."

Annie turned to the others hopefully, as though Lila had arrived at a superior theory none of them had considered.

The others shifted, looked away. Somehow, it felt unethical to allow Lila to be too optimistic. But no one among them had the nerve to explain, so they tacitly agreed to collaborate on the confession.

"We all went swimming," Weesie began. "After dinner. Down by the dock. We got onto that raft. We were pretty messed up. It was stupid."

Lila glared at Weesie with profound loathing as she rambled. It was one thing to stammer inarticulately about politics, but another for her to bumble on like this about her future husband.

Sensing Lila's anger, Tripler interrupted with an excess of factual information. "After the rehearsal dinner," she explained, "we all went down to the water."

"Pete smuggled booze," Jake volunteered.

"Asshole," snapped Pete. "We did it together."

"Guys," said Tripler.

Lila looked from one to the other and sighed in a silent appeal for clarity.

"Someone got the idea about the raft," Tripler went on.

"That would be you," said Annie.

Tripler turned to Annie, shocked by her disloyalty.

"It started with Weesie," said Jake. "She wanted to go skinny-dipping."

"Hey!" said Weesie.

"Guys," yelled Tripler. "She doesn't need to hear this." She silenced the group with an instructive sneer, then turned back to face Lila, comfortable once again in the role of fearless leader. "We sat there for a while on the raft, drinking, singing, being silly. Then, all the sudden, we looked up at the house and realized the raft had come unmoored. The tide was carrying us out."

"How far?" asked Lila.

"Hard to tell," said Jake.

"A couple hundred feet," said Pete.

"So we broke into pairs and started back," said Tripler.

"The water was pretty rough by then," Annie interrupted.

"And when we got to the shore." Tripler paused. "Tom was missing."

Lila stared at the ground while she digested the new information. When she finally spoke, her voice was thick, her eyes, narrow with hatred. "What are you talking about?" she snapped.

Tripler turned to Weesie, then Annie, desperate for corroboration. "We're so sorry," she said.

"You're sorry?" said Lila. "You knew he was trashed, and you let him swim anyway?"

"Lila, he's a championship swimmer," said Weesie.

"Don't tell me what he is," said Lila. But her tone was strangely businesslike, as though she was annoyed with her friends, not for endangering Tom's safety but for spoiling her party.

"Besides, we were *all* shit-faced," Pete said. "None of us should have been in the water."

But Lila was only more incensed by Pete's flimsy excuse. "So where do you think he is?" she hissed.

"We have no idea," Weesie admitted.

"But we don't think he drowned," Annie volunteered.

"Wow, that's comforting, Annie," said Tripler.

"What *do* you think?" Lila demanded.

"We just think . . ." Weesie turned to Tripler for support.

"We just think he's missing," said Tripler.

Lila flinched, as though she'd swallowed pure lemon juice. "You people disgust me."

Oscar jumped in, anxious to rein in the conversation. "We need to call the police," he said. "Before it gets any later."

"No," Lila said. Her eyes were wild, her mouth feral and parted. "If this is some kind of joke," she said, "I swear to God. I'll never forgive you."

The group stood in awkward silence as a ray of sunlight inched up the porch step.

"Oscar's right," Pete said. He took a step toward the door.

On reflex, Weesie grabbed his elbow.

Tripler bristled at the familiarity of the gesture, digesting her suspicion. But suspicion turned quickly to certainty. When she looked at Weesie, her face was flushed, her eyes fluttering and guilty.

"Where are you going?" Lila demanded. "What are you doing?" she repeated. Once again, she collapsed into tears as her friends looked on, guilty and helpless.

The sound of Lila's weeping served as an alarm of sorts for Laura, but not because it triggered compassion or pity. Instead, it served to reinforce the two sides of her dilemma: To stand by and allow Lila to grieve was undeniably callous; but to comfort her, while hiding her own betrayal, was equally duplicitous. Oddly, Laura felt the most pressing obligation to her other friends. Regardless of their shortcomings, their collective corruption, it seemed horribly unscrupulous to remain silent in the face of their discomfort.

Bracing herself, she stepped toward Lila and took a seat at the end of her chaise. She placed her hand on Lila's back. "It's going to be fine," she whispered.

Without warning, Lila whipped around and swatted her hand away. "Don't touch me," she said.

Laura looked down, ashamed. Lila's response was, after all, prescient.

"Why would he do this?" Lila sniffled.

"It's going to be fine," Laura repeated.

"What if it's not," Lila said.

"It will be," Laura said. She replaced her hand on Lila's back.

"How do you know?" Lila snapped.

Laura considered for a moment. She could easily go on just like this, deflecting, generalizing, omitting. But if Tom had decided to skip his own wedding, then why prolong the confession? She took a deep breath and gathered her strength. "Because I saw him," she said.

"When," Lila demanded.

"After," said Laura. She fidgeted with a loose piece of wicker on the chair.

"After what?"

"After we got back to shore," said Laura.

"But where?" Lila whimpered, equal parts pathetic and forceful. "Where was he headed?"

Laura paused as she realized Lila's misunderstanding. There was still time to retread, to say nothing. But some part of her, some horribly human part relished the triumph. "He wasn't headed anywhere," she said.

Lila stared, eyes narrowed in confusion.

"He was standing still," Laura went on. Then, she clarified. "I was with him."

Lila continued to stare in silence as she gained comprehension. Her features contorted from uncertainty to disgust, as though she'd ingested poison.

But the two friends were spared an exhaustive discussion of the betrayal.

"Holy shit," Jake was saying.

"I told you," said Pete. He shook his head and blinked as though he were trying to verify a mirage.

Laura and Lila followed their gaze out toward the water to find Tom walking up the lawn, his hair backlit like a matinee idol. The sun was such that everyone in the group had to squint to behold his arrival.

He greeted the crowd with a dapper wave like a magician emerging from a box.

"I hate you," Lila whispered, though it was hard to tell whether she had addressed Laura or Tom. Then she wiped her tears, assumed a gracious smile, and sprinted across the grass to meet him.

Laura watched the next several moments play out in slow motion.

Lila ran until she reached Tom, throwing herself into his arms.

Tom received her enthusiastically, like a quarterback catching a football.

They pulled away to stare at each other and stood like this, completely enthralled, as though they were reuniting after several years apart as opposed to several hours. They remained oblivious to their audience for a full minute, then they pulled apart and headed back to the porch, arms woven around each other.

"I told you he went for a walk," Lila announced.

The group responded with a hearty laugh, an expression of their overwhelming guilt and the relief of blame absolved.

"Oh no," said Weesie. "It's bad luck for you guys to see each other before the wedding."

"Shut up, Weez," said Tripler.

"Yeah, shut up," Annie agreed.

And with that, the subject of Tom's disappearance was permanently dropped.

EIGHTEEN

Northern Gardens was invaded an hour later without warning or fanfare. An army of caterers, florists, and servers descended on the estate, assuming their respective posts like dancers in a ballet. Their arrival was a merciful relief for the wedding party. Upon Tom's return, they had unanimously heeded Lila's tacit command to deny the incident. In the hour since, even the best conversationalists had been challenged to make small talk, socializing on the porch despite fatigue and emotional upheaval. Luckily, the arrival of the wedding staff provided a natural intermission, allowing the group to excuse themselves to refresh before the festivities. Lila and Tom retired to their rooms, content to disregard the bad luck of their pre-wedding kiss.

Laura spent the better part of the hour recovering from shock— or rather, several. First, the shock of seeing Tom, finding him alone by the tree; then, the shock of holding Tom, living out something that had been so long forbidden; then the shock of seeing Tom embrace

Lila, still sticky from her own kisses. As far as Laura could tell, Tom intended to careen back into a life he had only hours ago professed to hate. But by the time she had managed to close her mouth, to peel her eyes off the grotesque spectacle, the sun was high and the strange enchantments of the night seemed like a hallucination.

Augusta's arrival on the porch cemented the fact of the wedding day. Lila's wedding dress would prove no match, she declared, to her sewing basket. With typical determination, she stationed herself on the chair traditionally reserved for morning coffee and remained there for half an hour, dress strewn across her lap like a wounded soldier. She completed the repair of the dress just like this, pins and needles tucked between her teeth, intermittently issuing commands to workers on the lawn, gesturing floral arrangements toward their rightful places, tent poles to firmer ground.

The wedding party returned to the Gettys' in a fraught and concerted silence. Despite the gift of their hangovers—dimmed recollection and slightly blurred vision—they walked across the lawn, not as friends or couples, but as individuals, content that the consequences they had imagined had become as irrelevant as yesterday's weather. Fatigue and relief conspired to blur their gripes and suspicions for the moment. Unfortunately, relief—and the humility it reaps—tends to fade quickly.

As they neared the front door, Weesie caught up with Jake and gave his arm a proprietary tug.

Jake shrugged her off. The crash from the drug had made his skin so sensitive that the gentlest nudge felt like a brutal assault.

Walking behind, Tripler watched the exchange and detected the guilty sentiment. But her anger was diverted by her husband. Pete sprinted up from behind and surprised her, wrapping his arms around her neck and smothering it with kisses.

"I missed you," he whispered.

Tripler pushed him off, conscious of the manipulation. He had done something wrong—this much was obvious—but she couldn't tell what and how much.

"I missed you," he repeated, strengthening his grasp.

And Tripler, hungry for the attention, resolved to suppress—or at least, table—her mistrust.

Only Annie and Oscar enjoyed the moral impunity to address the group.

"Group pact?" Oscar suggested.

His suggestion was met with token ridicule.

"To forget everything that was said and done last night," he went on.

"And not said and not done," added Annie.

"Why? What did you do?" Pete taunted.

"No worse than you," Oscar snapped.

"Good idea, sweetie," said Annie. "I was horrible."

"Yes you were," Oscar agreed. He coupled the reprimand with an incongruous look of adoration.

Annie glared, feigning righteous anger, then gave up the ruse and jumped onto his back.

"Group pact?" Oscar demanded, raising his voice theatrically.

"Group pact," Tripler agreed without conviction.

"Group pact," said Jake.

And one by one, the others assented.

Laura took her time walking back to the house as her friends drifted ahead. It was not a conscious decision, but rather a choice that her legs made for her. They simply lacked the strength to move. Or was it her brain that lacked the will to move them? What a sad, constricting feeling it was to live out a convention. She was the jilted lover, the other woman. The only thing more degrading was knowing that her friends now shared this knowledge and silently pitied her for it. She might as well have worn black to the wedding, announcing her treachery.

What a fool she had been. No. Worse than a fool—a hypocrite. But a hypocrite enjoyed the satisfaction of betrayal. She was not even that lucky. As she walked, she grew increasingly disgusted with herself. The world seemed to push in on her from either side, and she felt as though she might be flattened at its center. A cloud passed, and the sun redoubled its efforts to light the sky. The gentle hum of birds and bugs rose to an electric buzz.

"Laura," someone shouted. "Hey, wait up."

Before she could think to pick up her pace, she turned to find Chip trotting beside her like an impatient dog.

"That was quite a little speech," he said. "Very honorable."

She set her gaze on the Gettys', prayed he would lose interest.

"I personally would have cut it shorter. You know what they say. Less is always more."

Laura channeled her energy into her feet, willing them to move.

"For example, when I told Lila I'd seen Tom," he went on, "I didn't tell her I'd seen you, too. I felt it confused the issue."

Laura paused for a split second, but quickly checked herself for her credulity.

"She is my sister, of course," Chip went on, "and I thought she deserved to know he was alive. But that's all I thought she deserved."

Laura stalled again, a reflexive attempt to verify Chip's claim. She knew better than to take him at his word, but there seemed to be truth under his glib tone. Could it possibly be a genuine note of compassion?

"You did?" she whispered.

Chip nodded.

"You didn't tell her," she confirmed.

Chip shook his head.

"So I did that for nothing?"

"Come now." Chip paused, and in the pause, he betrayed the contents of his heart. "You did that for integrity," he said. "And that is the difference between you and everyone else here."

Chip smiled at Laura with sincere admiration, then turned and headed back across the lawn toward the bustling estate.

The Reverend Hipp arrived at eleven o'clock, an hour before scheduled. He was, of course, officiating the ceremony, so technically he was not the first wedding guest. But he was, after all, a close family friend and would be attending the reception, so he was greeted with all the thrill and momentousness of the first arrival. Augusta met him in the driveway then ushered him to the porch. She had asked the caterer to set up a tray of fruit and lemonade in anticipation of just such a deviation from the day's schedule. Standing on the porch, she seemed to vibrate with the voltage of so much excitement. She remained with the reverend for a few, efficient minutes, inquiring about his time at the rehearsal dinner and summarizing last-minute revisions to the ceremony logistics.

She had realized, for example, at four in the morning, that Betsy should be the first flower girl to process. Even though she was younger than her cousin, Sarah, she was the more poised of the two and more likely to set a good example to the subsequent fleet. God forbid the first flower girl failed to throw her white rose petals as charged or parade at an adequate pace, causing an unattractive bottleneck on the wedding aisle. This was hardly the image she wanted for the first impression of the day. No, she must inform Betsy herself, as opposed to her mother, Kate, for Kate was sure to protest in defense of her elder daughter's capabilities.

In addition, Augusta had forecast a major organizational error. The wedding party's formation at the altar was sure to look fine to the attending guests, but would likely appear hideously two-dimensional in photographs. The only solution was to tell the bridesmaids and groomsmen not to form a straight line, as planned, but rather to fan out and stagger, one slightly ahead of the other, so that the whole formation created a subtle "v" like a flock of migrating gulls. She needed to find one of the bridesmaids—any would do—to convey the message to the group.

As she stood, Augusta indulged in a quick survey of the lawn. The repaired wedding tent stood gracefully at the center, its white canvas seemingly starched and bleached by the rain of the night before. A trio of uniformed service staff hovered at the edges of the tent. A pair passed through, delivering heaping crates of wine-glasses. Blue ribbons billowed playfully from the poles like a stage curtain the night of a premiere. When the breeze rustled the tent, the ocean revealed itself, its silver and navy sheen offsetting the white of the canvas. Exhaling, Augusta congratulated herself—the color scheme was a triumph, a blessed union. She only hoped the bride and groom would entwine so harmoniously.

At the Gettys', uncomfortable silence was quickly usurped by the blow-dryer's buzz as the girls reconvened in their porcelain war room to begin the grooming process. It was still a bit early to start getting dressed, but they were too wired to go back to sleep. As a result, the typically jovial ritual was joyless. Even Tripler was quiet as she ran the water for the shower and waited for the temperature to rise.

Laura's arrival was met with an awkward shift in the ambient noise. Just as she entered, Tripler gave up on the prospect of a hot shower—she would simply bathe in the cold—and Annie switched off the blow-dryer, causing all noise in the room to drop out but the rhythmic swoosh of Weesie's toothbrush.

Laura paused in the doorway, then proceeded toward the sink, turning on the water and leaning over the basin to wash her face. As she cupped her hands and let them fill, she struggled to reaffirm her existence. The cold water only helped to a degree. She could make out one or two fingertips.

"How's Ben?" Tripler asked.

Laura rose to stand upright and met Tripler's gaze in the mirror. She opened her mouth, poised for a sharp defense. But Tripler's expression gave her pause. Her brow was furrowed in an uncharacteristic show of compassion, and her eyes were raw and swollen.

"He's fine," Laura said.

"You must miss him," said Tripler.

"No, not really," she confessed. She paused and searched Tripler's eyes, then losing her trust, she added, "A night apart is never a bad thing."

"True enough," said Tripler. "Would you agree with that, Weesie?"

"Agree with what," Weesie mumbled, her words garbled by a mouthful of toothpaste.

"A night apart from your husband is a good thing."

Weesie brushed her teeth with new vigor before answering with an emphatic spit. Ignoring the question, she leaned into the mirror, bared her teeth, and gave them a careful inspection. "You would know better than me," she said. "It was your idea. Remember?"

The four girls stood in silence for several seconds until Annie assumed Weesie's traditional role and attempted to diffuse the tension.

"I hope the food is yummy," she said. "I hate when the food's not yummy."

Weesie and Tripler stared at Annie as though she'd uttered the thought in a foreign language.

"The worst is that chocolate-and-raspberry shit," Annie continued. "Someone should ban those two flavors. They don't taste good together."

Laura looked from Weesie to Tripler, rapt with curiosity. What a relief to see controversy surround someone other than her. But Tripler refused Weesie's challenge, and Weesie lacked the courage to press it further. Remembering the running water, Laura leaned back over the sink and cupped her hands under the faucet.

One floor above, Pete stood in the hall, waiting outside a locked door. Sun sifted through a shaded window, saturating the entire landing with specks of floating dust. By the heat and color of the light—it had warmed from the silver of dawn to the yellow of morning—Pete guessed it was close to ten o' clock.

"Oscar, hurry up," he said. He rattled the door with renewed urgency. He waited for a response then banged the door with his fists. "What the fuck, man," he yelled.

"Chill out," said Jake.

Pete turned to find Jake approaching from the stairs.

"Let him be," Jake said. "From the looks of things, Annie's been giving him the gate."

Pete stood, staring at Jake for a moment like a deer assessing a hunter's shot. Finally, he exhaled a mild, reluctant laugh.

Jake took another step toward the door.

The two stood in thwarted silence while steam seeped from the closed bathroom door.

"You can go first," Pete said.

"That's fine," said Jake. "You were here."

"I already showered," Pete said. "I just want to brush my teeth."

Jake nodded slowly as though Pete had revealed incriminating information. His tone had already betrayed a tremendous amount of guilt.

Another moment of silence passed as both boys stared at the floor.

"I'm sorry," said Pete.

"Me too," said Jake.

Pete turned to the door as though it might offer its own apology. The muffled rush of the shower added a strange element of suspense.

"Wait," said Jake. "Why are you sorry?"

"Come on," Pete said. "Don't be lame."

"No," said Jake. "I want to know. For saying it or doing it?"

Pete was spared further interrogation as the sound of running water gave way to a cascade of drops, and Oscar emerged, towel wrapped around his waist.

"You boys showering together?" he teased.

"You wish," said Pete.

"You sure?" Oscar pressed. "You two look awfully cozy."

"Nah," said Jake. He pushed past Oscar. "Pete's all good. He already got some from my wife."

By noon, the calm of the morning had given way to controlled frenzy. Parking had been diverted to a discreet part of the property, but a select group of vehicles had been granted access to the gravel driveway leading to the house. They might as well have been stagecoaches, hitched to horses, awaiting a royal cadre. Activity on the lawn signaled the guests' imminent arrival. The servers had all changed to a neat uniform of black morning coats, and they stood in their assigned positions like soldiers defending a fort. A few select guests—all members of the Hayes and McDevon families—stood in tentative clumps on the lawn or advanced slowly toward the assembled chairs. Seen from above, the pastels of their dress made them look like eggs in an Easter basket.

Augusta had chosen a dress in a radiant red over numerous more conservative pieces she'd considered. But finally, navy and baby blue, even gold or an elegant silver did little to compete with the magnificence of this dress. A thick-woven brocade and the designer's signature buttons gave the suit a regal quality. The skirt, which flared slightly below the knee, was traditional while still au courant. It was a style she could imagine her own daughter wearing. The color was certainly not one she had pulled from the wedding's palette. But why should she match the flowers and table settings? She was not a part of this wedding; she was its orchestrator. It was fitting that she stood apart from its elements just as a conductor stood apart from his musicians.

Satisfied with her appearance, Augusta emerged from her room and descended to the lawn for a final sweep of the grounds. She glided down the stairs and through the house like a winged creature, patting pillows, smoothing creases, pivoting picture frames without compromising her pace. It was only habit. She knew that the house already looked its best.

Outside, she traversed the porch in four strides, then nearly jumped the steps to reach the lawn. Still moving, she surveyed the beautiful precision of her marching orders. Her delight doubled as she entered the tent. The green tablecloths were the ideal choice, playfully echoing the grass outside. The tables lay in wait for the guests, china set, napkins folded, silver glinting with anticipation. The beauty of the flowers was matched by the thrill of their fragrance. She had been absolutely right to combine peonies, gardenias, and lilies of the valley. The peonies offered the arrangements desirable heft and the scale they needed to appear full at a short distance. The lilies provided a wonderful winning surprise for the more intimate viewing. And the gardenias—well, their scent was simply intoxicating. She had to fight the urge to swoon.

As she approached the back of the tent, she was cheered by one final realization: Her centerpieces were a triumph. How could she have doubted the choice? Even without the illumination of candlelight, they transformed the tent into a shimmering underwater kingdom.

Exiting the tent, she approached the final object of scrutiny: the venue for the ceremony. White chairs had been assembled just as she'd asked, in straight, perfectly spaced rows. The backs of the chairs had been laced with fern and more lilies of the valley—a last-minute change when the ivy revealed an unappealing brown wax residue. A simple white-lattice arch had been miraculously transformed with flowers and ribbons, unifying the elements of the landscape. The wedding party would complete the tableau with their dress and bouquets.

Turning back toward the house, Augusta paused for the first time, taking in the enormity—and completion—of her endeavor. She inhaled deeply. There was both satisfaction and sadness in her achievement. There was Minnow, of course. But she would never again plan the wedding of her first daughter. For the first time since learning of Lila's engagement, she was overcome with grief.

She was quickly rescued by a thrilling revelation. Of all her accomplishments, she had yet to add her greatest one to the list. Her meticulous planning and rabid prayers had been rewarded with extravagant weather. The day was more resplendent than she imagined a day in heaven itself. The air was soft and warm, and the breeze still bore the faintest trace of rain—or was it the promise? It didn't matter. The wedding was hours away. Not even God could prevent its temperate resolution.

The girls arrived at the Hayes's and advanced to their scheduled meeting, gathering at the door to Lila's bedroom like nervous children awaiting a punishment. With Tripler subdued, Weesie enjoyed a lapse from the typical hierarchy. She eyed the others, mocking their timidity, and knocked on the door herself.

Even before she'd rapped a third time, the door flew open. Lila stood in a white bustier and high-heeled white satin shoes.

"This fucking bustier," she hissed. "I swear to God. I forgot it had seven thousand hooks."

The girls stood at the threshold, paralyzed for a moment. In white lingerie and heels, Lila looked strangely promiscuous and virginal at once, and her friends stalled, embarrassed by the confusion of imagery.

"Someone get over here now," she shrilled.

The girls remained still for another moment, as though temporarily detached from their senses. En masse, the wisdom of the bridesmaids' dresses revealed itself. The silver fabric, though not especially flattering to any girl in particular, had a pleasing effect when viewed en masse, making the bridesmaids look like a shiny string of pearls.

Finally, Annie heeded the call and rushed to Lila's aid, taking a seat on her bed and tackling the hooks.

Tripler, Weesie, and Laura continued to stand tentatively by the door. If they had ever found Lila intimidating, she was ten times more so now.

A strange and mystical thing happened to a bride the day of her wedding. She ascended somewhat, an inch closer to God, suddenly transforming from girl to a woman, a woman to a sexual being. And though this was hard to decipher in the frenzy of excitement and white satin, it was clear to everyone as they entered Lila's room that something irreversible had occurred.

"What are you guys doing?!" she demanded. "Is my makeup that bad?"

"No, it's perfect," said Weesie.

"You think?" Lila demanded. "I think he overdid the eye shadow. Do I look like a drag queen?"

The girls appraised Lila's eyes as charged and dutifully shook their heads. They remembered their assigned roles for the day: Their sole purpose was to nod and shake their heads at the appointed moments. And to adhere to Augusta's schedule.

"I promised Augusta we'd have you downstairs in twenty," said Annie. "She wants you in the sitting room, straightening the train."

"Oh God," Lila moaned. "I can't believe she's going to force that retarded ritual."

"It's sweet," said Weesie.

"It's sickening," said Lila.

"It's tradition," Tripler offered. She took a seat on Lila's bed next to Annie, relieving her of her duties.

"Oh my God!" Lila gasped. She widened her eyes in horror.

"What?" gasped Annie.

Lila blinked and inhaled. "You guys look so beautiful," she said. "You're my best friends. I love you."

At this, the girls indulged in a perfunctory swoon, joining hands and giving in to adrenaline's effect.

The silence was broken by a knock on the door and a sudden drop in the room's noise level. The door opened to reveal a sheepish Minnow, who stood brushed and ready in a periwinkle dress with a slight hint of silver in its thread. She held the mended dress in her arms as she had once held a recovering doll after surgery to replace a severed arm. She looked up at Lila, eyes wide with remorse, then burst into tears and ran across the room into Lila's open arms.

Tripler reacted quickly and lunged from her seat to collect the falling dress. Within seconds, she had secured the precious cargo and readied it for Lila's arrival. Eyeing the daunting cascade of buttons, she parted the dress at its back so that it looked like the cavernous maw of a great white whale. She smiled as she waited for

Lila and Minnow to come apart, poised for Lila to enter the beast's belly.

Finally, the sisters came apart. Eyes were dried and grudges forgotten. Lila stepped toward and into the dress, covering her hair and closing her eyes as it was hoisted to her chest. The girls assumed new positions. Annie took her place crouching on the floor, Weesie took a seat on the bed, Tripler stood at Lila's back, and they worked in silent concentration to fasten the satin buttons.

Lacking a task of her own, Laura stood in the middle of the room, folding and unfolding her arms as though she could hide herself by hiding her dress. "What can I do to help?" she asked. As she said it, she felt even more useless than she had a moment before.

"Oh," said Lila. She twisted her neck to face Laura and stared for a minute in silence, as though assessing the fit of Laura's dress.

Laura stared back, refusing to be intimidated. Surrounded by her bridesmaids, Lila looked like the coach of a small athletic team. "Actually, there is something," she said finally. "The bouquets are in the fridge in the basement. Could you possibly get them?"

Laura nodded, checked to see if anyone else needed some last-minute errand run, then turned and headed toward the door, elated for an excuse to exit.

Alone again, Laura's thoughts began to decelerate. She took a seat on the basement stairs, relieved to have a moment in private. Coherent insights crystallized at a constant, discernible rate, as opposed to the whirl of sounds and images that had plagued her for the last several hours. Her first thought was a factual one, a reminder to herself: Tom was going to marry Lila. Lila was going to marry Tom. And this long-awaited event would move from the near future to the past tense in just over an hour.

But why should the nearness of this event change her feelings about the outcome? She had known for months that Tom and Lila would marry, that this day would eventually come, and even though the thought had filled her with jealousy—rage even—she had done little to prevent it. She had simply never believed, she now realized, that it would actually come to pass. But now, as she accepted the possibility—no, the inevitability—of this imminent and ostensibly irreversible act, she was suddenly overcome with panic. Tom was about to marry Lila. Lila was about to marry Tom. With two simple words, Tom would set his and her own life on the wrong—the mediocre and miserable—path, and there was nothing words or will could do about it.

Remembering her task, Laura opened the refrigerator to find the requested bouquets. The flowers lay on the metal shelves, their petals dewed with condensation. Each one was tied with a bow of grosgrain ribbon and fastened mercilessly with green pins. Four smaller ones were composed of bursting peonies, laced by lilies of the valley, and nestled among gauzy ferns that fell to the same length as the ribbon. Lila's, the largest among them, was a tight huddle of the same, only with more flowers and on a larger scale. The lilies cascaded just beyond the ribbon like a fountain of poured champagne.

Ignoring the threat of stain to her dress, Laura gathered the smaller ones in her arms, then, cradling these, reached for Lila's arrangement at the back of the fridge. As she grasped it, she was suddenly filled with all-consuming rage. Her throat seized up and her head went hot and the room looked suddenly darker. She rose to stand quickly and hurried up the stairs. If Tom lacked the courage to tell Lila the truth, she would simply do it herself.

She heard her friends even before she'd reached the main

stairs. They were already assembled in the sitting room on the
parlor floor. The bridesmaids hovered around Lila like hornets
around a rose. A photographer lurked behind curtains and furniture, failing at her attempt to be unobtrusive. Lila stood near
the window, gazing out at the lawn. Her train extended behind
her to span the full length of the room, ending at the opposite
end, where it had been draped over a chair. The ritual—designed
to straighten the bride's train in the moments before the
procession—required complete immobilization. Trapped, Lila
looked to Laura like a rare exotic insect trailed by a sticky white
sheen. It was, for all intents and purposes, the perfect time to
talk.

"Lila," said Laura.

"Thank God you're back. We were starting to think you'd run
off with those." She twisted her neck and gestured at her bridesmaids to collect their bouquets.

Laura opened her arms and allowed her friends to retrieve the
flowers.

Lila turned back to the window, fixing her gaze on an object in
the distance. Laura followed Lila's gaze to find its subject before a
click of the photographer's camera revealed it was just a pose.

"I owe you an apology," Laura said.

Lila deepened her gaze, said nothing.

"If I were a stronger person, I would have told you this a lot
sooner."

Lila turned suddenly to face Laura. "It's too late," she said.
"Don't bother."

But Laura continued. It wasn't too late. "What I did to you, no
friend should ever do to another. Of course, you did it once to me.
But who's counting?"

Lila's eyes flashed wide and bright, lit by true hatred. But her dress and her position restrained her somewhat, and she refused to give Laura the satisfaction of seeing a disturbance.

"I found Tom last night," Laura said. "When he was missing."

"Great," said Lila. "Good for you. Would you like some sort of ribbon?"

"No," said Laura. "I just thought you should know. He wasn't lost. He was hiding."

Lila closed her eyes as though obscuring Laura might make her disappear. "He came back of his own accord, Laura. I'm sorry if that upsets you."

"It doesn't upset me," Laura said.

"He's a groom. I would be concerned if he *didn't* get nervous the night before his wedding."

Laura paused, rethinking her impulse to confess, to sabotage. But she had come too far to turn back. She took a deep breath and relinquished control. "What if he had been with another woman the night before his wedding? What if he had loved this other woman for every minute since they had met, if all these years, even while he professed to love you, he was actually loving someone else. What if he had proposed to you because you pushed him into it? What if he never loved you at all? Would that concern you?"

Lila said nothing for several seconds. She simply stared out the window without emotion. When she finally spoke, she did so without moving any muscles in her face. "Unfortunately for you," she said, "you'll never know."

The photographer emerged at just this moment and snapped a picture of the two friends.

Lila smiled with chilling indifference, then turned to face her bridesmaids. "For Christ's sake, can I move yet?"

But before the girls could protest, Augusta arrived to dismiss her daughter from her post. She ushered the whole group toward the back door. The chairs were filling. The boys were assembled. It was nearly time to process.

NINETEEN

The chatter of two hundred fifty guests was a totally surprising sound. It was probably similar, Laura imagined, to a flock of descending locusts. As she emerged from the house, she felt totally displaced, physically disoriented. Her arms felt weightless and her vision warped, as though she had tried on a friend's pair of prescription glasses.

The groomsmen stood outside the back door in a shaded patch of the lawn, jostling each other like restless horses in a stable. They greeted the bridesmaids with all the excitement of students at their college graduation. In many ways, they felt much as they had that day six years ago when they had joined hands and hurtled their caps into the sky, as though the right amount of force would convince gravity to suspend the rules.

Then, without warning, Laura was being pushed into a line. Chip appeared out of nowhere and he was smiling and offering his elbow, pulling her toward escalating music, matching the beat with his stride. The melody wafted in then out of her consciousness. Then a sea of white chairs, an ocean of eyes, a kaleidoscope of color. In halting steps, she made her way up the aisle, pulled by Chip's commanding arm. At the last row of chairs, she stalled for a moment, forgetting yesterday's instructions, then she stumbled forward—thanks to Chip's nudge—and took her place next to Weesie in a staggered—or was it a straight—line.

Then there was Tom, standing right in the center of this ghastly vision. In a morning coat and tails, he looked like a child, costumed for a game of dress-up.

A chorus of gasps drew Laura's attention back to the seated guests. A new melody began, and a manic hush replaced the whispers. The rustle of clothing and turning heads announced Lila's entrance.

Walking briskly, on her father's arm, Lila began her procession. Her pace was a heartbeat faster than the beat of the music. Her eyes were bright as she surveyed the chairs, scanning the rows for familiar, important faces. Her hair was upswept in an elegant twist but for the few delicate tendrils falling to her shoulders. Her lips were moist as though she'd just emerged from a kiss. The satin of her dress shimmered in the sunlight, while the lace seemed to hold its shadows. As she glided along the grass, she was undeniably flawless.

From the fit of her dress, guests could never have guessed its recent disarray. The satin was smooth as vanilla ice cream, revealing neither seams nor a hint of damage. The fabric itself might as well have been stitched from the cloth of a cumulus cloud. But perhaps this was a bad omen, for the moment Lila completed her march up the aisle, something cold and wet landed on her bare shoulders. Luckily, she was too nervous to notice.

A few feet away, Tripler eyed Weesie. "Did you feel that?" she whispered.

"What?" mouthed Weesie.

Weesie paused and waited for confirmation. "No," she said. "I didn't."

Next to Weesie, Laura was jarred from her trance by another raindrop. She looked up to find the sky had changed. It had darkened in a matter of minutes to a decidedly dark shade of gray.

Lila smiled as her father lifted her veil. She received his good-luck kiss without hesitation. Then she took her position next to Tom and squeezed his hand to steady herself.

The string quartet sounded their last note. The guests held their breath on cue.

The Reverend Hipp scanned the guests, then began his sermon. "When I first met Tom McDevon, it was on a day much like today, a day so glorious it provided final, irrefutable proof that God exists." He paused. "Or at least that Augusta had had a word with him."

The guests paused, checking each other for permission before exhaling with polite laughter.

"Augusta had invited me over for iced tea, and we were catching up on her porch. Tom arrived, after a long drive from New York and that endless ferry ride. And, let me tell you." He shook his head in wonder. "The look on his face when he saw Lila was unlike any look—and I've seen many in my day—any look I'd ever seen."

Laura scanned the crowd as she listened, studying the guests' reactions. Looking at Lila or Tom was out of the question. Watching the audience was a good compromise, like watching a scary movie through the spaces in between your fingers.

"I've known Lila forever," the Reverend Hipp continued. "Since she was one of several towheads stumbling around the courts at the club. It will come as no surprise that she was an adorable child long before she was a beautiful woman. And yet, I have never seen her look more radiant, more delighted, more certain of her place in the world than she did that day as she greeted Tom in the driveway of this house. These two are not only graced with an abundance of God's earthly gifts, they have been graced with the ultimate reward: everlasting love."

Laura kept her eyes on the guests, anxious for their interpretation. Their beatific smiles confirmed her worst fear; they agreed with the minister. All at once, her hope disappeared. She had been foolish, delusional. She was the single body in a crowd of two hundred fifty who had yet to acknowledge reality.

"Love," the Reverend Hipp continued, "is like the ocean. Vast, seemingly endless." He paused to allow the guests a token chuckle. "Rocky, at times. Peaceful, at others. Daunting for all its unexplored depths. But a constant source of wonder and amazement."

It was settled, Laura decided. Tom would live and die surrounded by—sated by—clichés.

"Marriage," the minister went on, "is like a raft. Imperfect but sound so long as the builders fortify the structure and, once afloat, pledge to strive for balance."

The guests rewarded the Reverend Hipp's awkward simile with a saccharine sigh.

Finally, Laura looked away, accepting defeat. She fought the urge to scream, to run, to dive into the bay. She had known it for years but ignored it even still. She had outgrown these people—this world.

"Now," said the Reverend Hipp, "if you'll turn with me to page three hundred and fifty-seven, I would like to read from First Corinthians, chapter thirteen, verse four."

A rustle of pages was followed by a collective exhalation. The ceremony was nearing its close.

"Love is patient; love is kind and envies no one," said the minister. "Love is never boastful, nor conceited, nor rude; never selfish, not quick to take offense. There is nothing love cannot face; there is no limit to its faith, its hope, and endurance. In a word, there are three things that last forever: faith, hope, and love; but the greatest of them all is love." He paused with decorous formality. "Tom and Lila have written their own vows as an expression of their love and creativity."

Finally, Laura forced herself to watch the proceedings. The reverend closed his Bible and turned to the couple, gazing with import.

Lila closed her eyes, a decelerated blink used to stave off tears.

Tom inhaled as though he were preparing to rappel down the side of a building.

"Tom," said Lila, "the day we met was the happiest day of my life. Ever since I've known you, I knew you were the one. Even when you didn't know it. Every day you amaze me in some new incredible and amazing way. I promise to love and honor you each and every day of our life."

Laura stomached despair as Lila concluded her vow. This was what Tom had chosen over her, this mediocrity, this utter lack of inspiration.

"Lila," said Tom, "I look at you. And I'm speechless. I literally have nothing to say."

Tom paused for a second—two, three—staring at the ground, as though he was attempting to count the blades of grass in a particular clump.

Laura focused. She recognized the dull stare. It was the same blinded feeling she had experienced while delivering Lila's toast the night before.

"Words fail the depth and complexity of my feelings for you," he went on. "I need canons of literature, unwritten poetry, an entirely new language."

Laura's heart sank. He had saved himself.

"But the thing is." Here, he paused again. "Without words, I have nothing to offer. Words are my only riches," he said. "Words," he said, then he trailed off again. He looked back at the ground but, finding the grass a hopeless ally, turned to survey the bewildered guests, his eyes wide and mouth parted like a runner at the end of a race.

Without further warning, rain tumbled from the darkened sky, the drops accelerating rapidly into a rush that sounded like a shouted whisper. A ghastly yellow lightning bolt bisected the bay, sending horrified guests dashing from their chairs, running toward the wedding tent.

Lila thought only of her dress. She grabbed what she could of its endless train and sprinted across the lawn.

Weesie and Annie hustled behind, doing their best to hoist the train from the ground.

Tripler followed at a more leisurely pace. She hated her dress and so felt no compulsion to protect it. And the rain felt warm and sweet on her skin, a welcome refreshment.

Oscar, Pete, and Jake moved as a single contingent. Before long, they forgot the problem at hand and gave in to the temptation of a three-man race, thrilled to have found a new forum for competition.

Augusta surveyed the scene from her chair during the first desperate moments. As she watched, she felt she knew what it was to be the captain of a sinking ship. First, there was the acknowledgment of disaster, then the assessment of its scope, followed by the realization—and finally, the acceptance—of helplessness. As her guests dispersed, she remained very still, standing in front of her chair. On instinct, she opened her palms to the sky as though to discern whether it was truly raining. Then, accepting that a calm response could not intimidate the rain into submission, she clutched her dress and followed her guests' migration. The ship was sinking, but who would be served by her going down with it?

Within thirty seconds, all but a few of the guests had evacuated the lawn, leaving the grass, flowers, and chairs defenseless to the rain but for the wasted, if steadfast, protection of two remaining bodies.

Laura stood, her face streaked with rain, oblivious to the downpour.

Tom faced Laura, shaking his head, his clothes as soaked as his soul.

"I can't do this," he said.

"Then don't," she said.

"I feel like I'm drowning," he said.

The rattle of raindrops on nearby chairs created a drumroll of sorts. Laura thought of the china on the tables under the tent, the champagne flutes huddled on servers' trays. Two hundred fifty glasses filled to their brims even before hors d'oeuvres had been passed.

"Love is like an ocean," Laura said. Her smile conveyed all her disdain and disappointment, all of her sadness and hope.

Tom returned her smile, but his was full and bright.

And Laura felt, in that moment, as breathless and elated as a swimmer gasping for the shore.